Single white male, early forties, six feet, four inches and two hundred pounds of solid muscle.

Dark hair, brown eyes, have all my own teeth. Friends say I'm a good-lookin' son of a gun, but you'll have to judge that for yourself.

"I'd say your friends are right, pal," Dani muttered, glancing at the photo before reading on.

Don't like to hang around bars, and am on the shy side. Like to snuggle in front of a roaring fire on a cold winter night. Run a large family ranch in northern Wyoming. Lots of animals and room for kids to run free. Want kids of my own, but if you've already got some, that's fine by me. Want something permanent, and I know my dream woman is out there somewhere. Come on and write to me now, honey.

Dani groaned and flopped back onto her pillows. "Be still, my heart. I think I'm in love."

Dear Reader,

Welcome to Silhouette **Special Edition** . . . welcome to romance. Each month, Silhouette **Special Edition** publishes six novels with you in mind—stories of love and life, tales that you can identify with—romance with that little "something special" added in.

June has some wonderful stories in bloom for you. Don't miss *Silent Sam's Salvation*—the continuation of Myrna Temte's exciting *Cowboy Country* series. Sam Dawson might not possess the gift of gab, but Dani Smith quickly discovers that still waters run deep—and that she wants to dive right in! Don't miss this tender tale.

Rounding out this month are more stories by some of your favorite authors: Tracy Sinclair, Christine Flynn, Trisha Alexander (with her second book for Silhouette **Special Edition**—remember *Cinderella Girl,* SE #640?), Lucy Gordon and Emilie Richards.

In each Silhouette **Special Edition** novel, we're dedicated to bringing you the romances that you dream about—stories that will delight as well as bring a tear to the eye. And that's what Silhouette **Special Edition** is all about—special books by special authors for special readers!

I hope you enjoy this book and all of the stories to come!

Sincerely,

Tara Gavin
Senior Editor
Silhouette Books

MYRNA TEMTE
Silent Sam's Salvation

Silhouette Special Edition

Published by Silhouette Books New York

America's Publisher of Contemporary Romance

To Goldie V. Gum and Ethel I. Gowen, my own dear Grandma Ds

Acknowledgments

My thanks to the following people for help with research: Melody Harding of the Bar Cross Ranch, Robin Lozier and Chera Temte of the Box "R" Ranch, and Alice Dame, Cora, Wyoming; Sharon Ziegler, Pinedale, Wyoming; Debra White, Laramie, Wyoming; and Linda Van der Gaag, Spokane, Washington.

And an extraspecial thank-you to Charlie L. James and Cupcake, St. Ignatius, Montana, publishers of *Sweetheart* magazine, who gave me the idea for *Cupid's Arrow*.

SILHOUETTE BOOKS
300 East 42nd St., New York, N.Y. 10017

SILENT SAM'S SALVATION

ISBN: 0-373-09745-X

First Silhouette Books printing June 1992

Printed in the U.S.A.

Books by Myrna Temte

Silhouette Special Edition

Wendy Wyoming #483
Powder River Reunion #572
The Last Good Man Alive #643
*For Pete's Sake #739
*Silent Sam's Salvation #745

*Cowboy Country Series

MYRNA TEMTE

grew up in Montana and attended college in Wyoming, where she met and married her husband. Marriage didn't necessarily mean settling down for the Temtes—they have lived in six different states, including Washington, where they currently reside. Moving so much is difficult, the author says, but it is also wonderful stimulation for a writer.

Though always a "readaholic," Ms. Temte never dreamed of becoming an author. But while spending time at home to care for her first child, she began to seek an outlet from the never-ending duties of housekeeping and child rearing. She started reading romance novels and soon became hooked, both as a reader and a writer.

Now Myrna Temte appreciates the best of all possible worlds—a loving family and a challenging career that lets her set her own hours and turn her imagination loose.

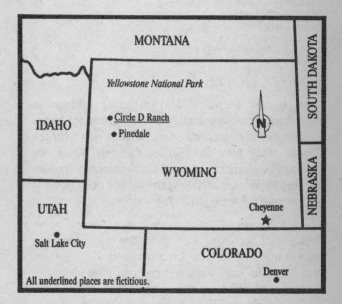

MONTANA

SOUTH DAKOTA

Yellowstone National Park

• <u>Circle D Ranch</u>
• Pinedale

IDAHO

WYOMING

NEBRASKA

UTAH

Cheyenne
★

• Salt Lake City

COLORADO

Denver
•

All underlined places are fictitious.

Chapter One

Amelia Dawson clamped her hands over her bony hips and glared in righteous indignation at her grandsons, Sam and Hank. "I don't have to take this anymore, and I'm not agoin' to!"

"Calm down now, Grandma D," Sam coaxed in the soothing tone he used on high-strung mares.

"Don't you tell me to calm down, Samuel James Dawson," the old woman raged, shaking an arthritic finger under his nose. "You may be too big to spank, but by God, you'll show proper respect for your elders. That's what's wrong with both of you boys."

Sam exchanged a furtive glance with Hank, and bit the inside of his cheek to keep from laughing. He was forty-one and stood six foot four in his bare feet; Hank was thirty-nine and only an inch shorter. Having their tiny, eighty-six-year-old grandmother calling them boys and talking about spanking was a little hard to take.

"I apologize, Grandma D," Hank said, flashing the legendary smile that had charmed more than one cantankerous female out of a temper tantrum. "I swear I'll never yell at you again."

Unfortunately, that smile didn't faze Grandma D. She sniffed and folded her arms across the front of her neon-green sweatshirt. "Damn right, you won't. I'm not givin' you the chance. I'm goin' to live with your sister, and I'm takin' Tina with me."

Sam cursed under his breath. "Grandma, you can't do that. We need you. For God's sake, Hank can't even walk on his own yet."

Pursing her lips, Grandma D shot a look of regret at Hank's crutches. He leaned toward her, a pitiful, hangdog expression on his face. She must have caught a gleam of amusement in his eyes however. Her own suspicious eyes narrowed to slits behind her big, red-framed glasses, and she pulled herself up to her full five-foot-two-inch height.

"What you need," she said tartly, "is a wife. It's high time one of you did his duty and produced a son to carry on the Dawson name. But as long as you've got somebody here to wait on you hand and foot, it don't seem to me like either one of you is gonna do anything about findin' a woman who'll have you."

"C'mon now, Grandma. Don't start that again," Sam said, heaving an impatient sigh.

"All right, I won't. But you two can either learn how to take care of yourselves or starve. Your sister's havin' a rough time right now, and she'll appreciate my help more than both of you put together. I'm leavin' just as soon as I get a suitcase packed for me and Tina."

"You can't just take my daughter anywhere you want," Hank protested.

"The hell I can't!" The old lady snorted in disgust. "You think I'd leave a seven-year-old child here with you jugheads? Why, she'd never have a clean stitch to wear or decent food to eat. When you can give her a real home, I'll bring her back.''

With that, Grandma D turned and marched up the stairs to the bedrooms. Sam glared at his brother. Hank glared right back at him.

''I hope to hell you're happy,'' Sam said. ''First you run off three nurses and four housekeepers with that damned temper of yours. Did you have to run Grandma D off, too?''

''Oh, sure. Blame it all on me,'' Hank grumbled.

''What did you yell at her about?''

''She got some fool notion to clean my room. You know how she is, Sam. Nag, nag, nag about every little thing. I just couldn't take it anymore.''

''Well, now you've got us both in one helluva mess. That stubborn little woman meant what she said. She won't be back until I find another housekeeper, and the word is out about you. There's not a woman within two hundred miles willing to work for us.''

''So what are we gonna do?''

''You're gonna have to learn to cook and clean and do laundry, Hank,'' Sam said.

''Me! No way in hell, brother. That's women's work.''

''Somebody's gotta run the ranch, Hank. Since you can't ride or rope or even drive a pickup yet, I'm the one who's gonna have to do it. This whole thing's your fault, anyway.''

''That's right, I'm useless. Why don'tcha rub it in some more, Sam?'' Hank muttered.

Sam massaged the back of his neck with one hand and scowled at his brother. ''Look, I'm not tryin' to rub anything in. You've only got a few more months of physical therapy. If you'd just try to get along with folks—''

''Hell, Sam! That's easy for you to say. Those exercises hurt like the devil. Everything's hurt like the devil for damn near a year. I'd like to see you try to stay all nice and sweet if you were laid up this long.''

Struggling to hold on to his patience, Sam leaned down and looked his brother right in the eye. "I understand that, Hank, and I know it's been hard on you. But you can't go around actin' like a rabid dog with his tail caught in a wringer. The rest of us have feelings too, ya know?"

"Well, maybe I'll just call Becky," Hank threatened, bracing his palms against the handgrips of his crutches to raise himself closer to Sam's eye level.

"You do, and I'll break your face," Sam warned. "Our baby sister's given up enough of her life lookin' after us. Shoot, we almost turned her into an old maid. And you know damn well she's still havin' mornin' sickness."

"Beck's tough. She won't mind takin' care of me."

"Yeah? Well, her husband might have somethin' to say about that. Let her alone, Hank. We're on our own now, and that's the way it's gonna be."

Hank glared at him for a long moment, then subsided and struggled over to the recliner, his shoulders slumped with resignation. "Aw, all right."

Grandma D appeared at the top of the stairs. "Sam, come get this suitcase for me, will you?"

"Be right there, Grandma."

With a sharp ache in his chest, Sam studied his brother and wished he hadn't been so hard on him. Hank had been to Hades and back in the past year, and it must be pure torture for a man who'd once been a rodeo champion to suddenly lose his mobility. Sam figured it was natural for Hank to feel angry and resentful over what had happened to him, but he couldn't go on lashing out at everyone who crossed his path.

Sam honestly didn't blame Grandma D for leaving. In fact, it would probably be best if Tina didn't see much of her father until he was back on his feet. But damn, Sam didn't relish becoming the only target for Hank's bitterness. And he sure as hell didn't relish the thought of eating Hank's miserable cooking, either.

Muttering a curse, Sam trudged upstairs to Grandma D's room. He supposed he'd have to fight her in order to drive her over to Becky's place, too. She insisted she could still drive as well as anyone, but it had been obvious to the rest of the family for some time that her eyesight wasn't what it oughtta be.

While he reached for the suitcase, Grandma D collected her pocketbook and draped a sweater over her arm. Then she picked up a magazine and after taking one final look around the room that had been her haven for the past twenty years, she straightened her thin shoulders and walked through the doorway.

Sam followed her down the stairs and into the living room, smiling slightly when he caught sight of her hot pink Nikes. Grandma D had announced on her eighty-fifth birthday that from then on she was going for comfort instead of fashion, but she wasn't gonna put up with any drab, "old lady" colors. That was one vow she'd certainly kept.

Hank lay back in the fully extended recliner, his eyes shut tight, his mouth a thin, disgruntled line across his face. With the fingers of his left hand he kneaded the thigh muscles of the leg he had shattered ten months earlier.

"I don't want any hard feelings, Hank," Grandma D said quietly, standing beside his chair. "I'll make sure you get to see Tina every week. I hate to admit it, but I'm just gettin' too old to handle all of this."

"It don't matter, Grandma," he replied in a sullen tone. "Every other woman I've ever known has deserted me when I needed her. I don't know why I expected you to be any different."

The elderly woman drew back with a hurt gasp.

"That's enough, Hank," Sam warned, laying a comforting hand on his grandmother's shoulder.

Her eyes blazing, Grandma D shrugged it off and dumped the magazine she carried into Hank's lap. "When you're done feelin' sorry for yourself, take a look at that. It might be a place to start lookin' for a woman desperate or stupid enough to put up with the likes of you."

Hank picked up the magazine, perused the cover, then threw back his head and let out a harsh bark of laughter. "*Cupid's Arrow?* What the hell is this? A lonely-hearts rag?"

"That's exactly what it is," Grandma D confirmed. "It's for farm and ranch people. Cousin Mamie got it when she went to visit that friend of hers in Montana last month. There's letters from people all over the western states and lotsa other places, too. Most of 'em sound real nice."

"Come on, Grandma," Sam said, anxious to get her away before Hank blurted out something that would damage their relationship for good. "I'll drive you and Tina over to Becky's place."

"Hank?" the old lady said, her voice quavering slightly. "You know, I love ya."

Hank gave her a crooked grin. "Yeah, Grandma, I know. You go on and have a good visit with Becky and Pete."

Shaking her head, Grandma D turned away, headed out to the kitchen and called Tina in from her swing set in the backyard.

"You need anything before we go?" Sam asked his brother.

"Nah. I'll see ya later. Tell Beck hi for me."

Sam gave him a brisk nod, then carried his grandmother's suitcase out to the pickup. Tina insisted on bringing her cat and its latest batch of kittens along. Sam spent ten minutes in the barn helping her catch all the little varmints, wishing he had time to go out and change the irrigation head gates before they left.

Finally he drove off under a blazing July sun, hoping he was doing the right thing by taking Grandma D and Tina to stay with his sister. Grandma would be a big help to Becky, and Tina still missed her aunt. Maybe a break would do everyone good. If only Hank could be a little more patient during the next couple of months. . . .

Hank watched Sam and Grandma D drive past the living room window, then leaned back in the recliner and sighed. Damn. He'd really done it this time, but it would be a mighty cold day in hell before he'd let Sam or anyone else turn him into a housekeeper.

He glanced at Grandma D's magazine. A thoughtful smile slowly spread across his mouth. The old girl might have a point. Maybe it *was* time one of the Dawson brothers got married.

Dani Smith banged down the receiver and bit the inside of her lower lip hard enough to draw blood. It was the only way she knew to prevent herself from throwing a screaming fit that would wake up both of her children. After spending eight hours at her regular bookkeeping job and another five hours on her feet as a barmaid at Johnny's Tavern, the very last thing she'd needed was another lecture from her mother.

"'You're just not giving those children enough attention,'" Dani mimicked her mother's whiny tone. "'You should be with them at night. Come home and let us help you.'"

The phone rang again. Dani glared at it balefully. She considered not answering it. Unfortunately, if she did that, her mother would drag Pop over here, convinced that something terrible had happened to Dani or Colin or Kim. Never mind the fact that it was eleven-thirty at night, or that they'd just finished talking a minute ago. Sighing, Dani grabbed the receiver.

"Mom, it's late, I'm tired and I don't want to talk about this anymore. Now will you please go to bed and leave me alone?"

"Whoa, sounds like the old lady's really getting to you," her older sister's voice replied.

Dani laughed, more grateful than Micky would ever know, to hear the sound of a friendly voice. "No kidding. How are you, Micky? How are Greg and the kids? How's Montana?"

"Which question do you want answered first?"

"I don't care. Just talk to me like a sane, rational adult."

"Let me guess. Mom and Pop want poor, widowed Dani to move home so they can help you take care of your poor, neglected children."

"Bingo. You must be psychic," Dani answered.

"Nah. I just remember what Mom was like before Greg took me away from all that, may God bless his soul each and every day. What set her off this time?"

"Colin got caught shoplifting last week."

"Oh, jeez," Micky muttered. "Is he still hanging out with those creepy kids from down the block?"

Dani sighed, letting the bone-deep weariness and discouragement come through in her voice as she massaged one aching foot. "Yeah. Maybe Mom's right, you know? Maybe I *am* raising a juvenile delinquent."

"Come on, Dani. That doesn't sound like you. Colin's just testing you, like every other kid his age."

"Well, he's doing a good job of it. I don't know what to do with him anymore. He's already taller than I am."

"It doesn't take much to be taller than you are, Dani."

"Don't start with the short jokes, okay?" Dani blinked back tears and held one hand over the speaker so Micky wouldn't hear her sniffle. "I'm scared, sis. If he's shoplifting at fourteen, what's he going to be doing when he's seventeen? Grand theft auto?"

"He's not that dumb, Dani. What about Kim? How's she doing?"

"Her schoolwork's great, as usual. But she gets quieter every day. Let's face it, I'm not exactly up for the Mother of the Year Award."

"But do you really want to move back home?" Micky asked quietly.

"I'd rather scrub toilets at the bus depot with my bare hands," Dani wailed, "but I'm running out of options. Mom's right about one thing. I *do* need to spend more time with the kids. Unfortunately, they have these nasty habits of eating and outgrowing their clothes, and the only way I can afford to indulge them, is to work two jobs."

"You need to get out of Chicago," Micky replied. "It's not as expensive to live in Montana, so pack up the kids and get your buns out here."

"You know I can't do that."

"Why not? You can live with us until you find a job. It'll solve your problems with Mom and Pop. They can't drive you half as crazy when you're sixteen hundred miles away. If Colin gets out of hand, you can sic his Uncle Greg on him."

Dani laughed and shook her head. "Hey, you find me a big, handsome cowboy like Greg, and I'll be out there in a flash."

"You mean that?"

"Sure. Why not?"

"Now, *that* sounds like my sister," Micky replied with a chuckle. "Gotta go, hon. My big, handsome cowboy is waving his arms and making time-out signals. Honestly, why does every American male think it's his God-given duty to ward off big phone bills?"

"I don't know, but tell him I appreciate the call."

"Will do. Talk to you next week, Dani."

Dani hung up the phone, then looked around the small kitchen of her apartment, and felt as if the walls were starting to close in around her. Three days' worth of dishes were piled in the sink. Colin's books were stacked on the counter. She'd bet her evening's tips he hadn't opened one of them. There was an orange puddle in front of the refrigerator, and what was left of the casserole she'd prepared for the kids at six o'clock that morning sat in the middle of the stove.

Rolling up the sleeves of her barmaid's uniform, she waded into the mess, telling herself that things would look better in the morning. She'd gotten by on her own for the past three years. Somehow, she'd get by for the next three.

Four days later, Dani rushed home, ready to commit homicide on her son. Mr. Ames, the counselor at Colin's school, had phoned her at work, and reported that Colin had been absent for the past three days and that it was school policy to contact the parents. What was the nature of his illness?

That's what Dani intended to find out. Since it was her night off from the tavern, she intended to find out a few other things, as well.

She shoved open the apartment door, and nearly gagged on a cloud of smoke. Then she tripped over a small mountain of high-topped sneakers piled inside the door. Three gangly adolescent boys, each puffing on a cheap cigar, sprawled over her furniture. The raucous sound of MTV turned up full blast assaulted her ears. What looked like the remains of a potato chip fight littered every available surface. God, she had a headache.

"Colin!" she shouted.

Of course he didn't hear her. Who could hear anything over those screaming guitars? And what teenage boy could be expected to tear his eyes away from that . . . girl, writhing on the screen in her underwear?

Dani stormed across the room, yanked the television's cord from its socket and slammed it on the floor. The boys jerked upright, gaped at her for a second, then hastily stubbed out their cigars in an empty tuna-fish can they were using for an ashtray.

"Yo, Ma," Colin said, scrambling to his feet. "You're home early."

"Yeah, and you're in big trouble, mister," Dani replied before turning on his friends. "You two get out of my living room. Get out of my apartment. And stay away from my son."

Snickering and nudging each other with their bony elbows, the other boys strolled to the door. "Hey, Col," the taller one with the purple Mohawk said, "let us know when your mommy lets you out to play again."

"Get out!" Dani screamed.

"Hey, Ma, chill out, will ya?" Colin whined. "Jeez, did ya have to embarrass me in front of the guys?"

Trembling with rage, Dani closed her eyes and envisioned wrapping both hands around her son's neck. How long would it take to choke him to death? she wondered.

"Go to your room, Colin," she said as quietly as she could manage. "And don't come out until I tell you to. Is that clear?"

"Yeah, sure," he replied with a cocky smirk. He turned away from her, his shoulders slouched in that I-don't-give-a-damn posture that never failed to send Dani's blood pressure through the ceiling. "In case you're wondering, the little geek's in her room."

Hands clenched at her sides, Dani waited until she heard his bedroom door close. Then she opened the windows to clear out the cigar smoke, muttering every obscenity she'd ever heard at Johnny's Tavern. She left the rest of the mess for Colin to clean up, and went to her own room to change into more comfortable clothes before starting dinner.

She turned when a soft tap sounded on her door, and her nine-year-old daughter, Kim, entered the room. Carrying a cup of tea in her hands and the mail under one arm, the little girl gave her mother a tentative smile.

"I thought this might help calm your nerves," she said, carefully setting the cup and a stack of envelopes on the bedside table.

Dani smiled, sat on the edge of the bed and held out her arms. "You're an angel, Kim. How was life in the fourth grade today?"

Kim shrugged and snuggled against her mother's side. "It was okay. I don't like Colin's friends, though."

"I'm sorry, honey," Dani replied, stroking her daughter's long, black hair. A horrible thought crossed her mind. "They didn't... do anything to you, did they?"

Kim smiled with a wisdom beyond her years and wrinkled her nose. "Relax, Mom. They're just nasty. And Colin's nasty, too, when they're around."

"I'll talk to him tonight."

"Do you think you'll have time to sew my Halloween costume this year?"

"I'll make time," Dani promised. "But it's only the first week of September. Aren't you worrying about Halloween a little early?"

Kim stood and put her hands on her hips. Adopting Dani's lecturing tone, she said, "Well, Mother, you always say to give you plenty of warning about stuff."

"Fair enough." Dani chuckled, then playfully swatted Kim's bottom. "Now scram, and let me drink my tea and read the mail in peace."

Kim ran from the room, giggling. Piling up the pillows on her bed, Dani leaned back, sipped her hot drink and sighed with pleasure. She flipped through the envelopes, setting aside the bills and tossing the junk mail at the wastebasket. When she came to a large manila envelope bearing Micky's return address in Missoula, however, she smiled and eagerly ripped it open.

She pulled out a thin magazine of some sort. A yellow Post-It note covered the title. She read her sister's message on it. "Check out the guy on page twenty-five. Too bad he lives in Wyoming."

"What in the world?" Dani murmured, peeling the note away. "*Cupid's Arrow.* Good grief, it's a personal-ad magazine."

She flipped open the cover and skimmed the first couple of pages, laughing at one man's description of himself until her sides ached. " 'Slightly bald and a little hefty, but plenty of horsepower left in this old tractor's engine to please a lady, if ya know what I mean.' "

Her curiosity aroused, Dani turned to page twenty-five. "Oh, my," she whispered, gazing at the photograph of a man who looked as if he'd walked straight out of a Marlboro ad.

He wore a cowboy hat tipped back on his head, exposing a thick shock of dark hair. Bold dark brows arched above intelligent eyes with attractive laugh lines radiating from the corners. His nose had a bump along the bridge that somehow fit with the rugged line of his jaw and chin. A neatly trimmed mustache followed the curve of his wide smile, making Dani wonder if it would tickle when a woman kissed those generous lips. And he had the cutest little dimple in his left cheek.

Suddenly feeling warm and a bit breathless, Dani fanned herself with one hand while her gaze lowered to take in a thick, muscular neck that disappeared into the collar of a Western-cut shirt. The man had a pair of shoulders broad enough to fill a doorway, and the arm he had propped up on the top rail of the fence bulged with muscles. He looked as if he could play defensive tackle for the Chicago Bears.

Dani sighed with disappointment that the photo had been cropped in the middle of his chest, then read what the man had written about himself.

Single white male, early forties, six feet, four inches and two hundred pounds of solid muscle. Dark hair, brown eyes, have all my own teeth. Friends say I'm a good-lookin' son of a gun, but you'll have to judge that for yourself.

"I'd say your friends are right, pal," Dani muttered before reading on.

Don't like to hang around bars, and am on the shy side, but I'm a true-blue guy you can depend on. Like to snuggle in front of a roaring fire on a cold winter night. Run a large family ranch in northern Wyoming. Lots of animals and room for kids to run free. Want kids of my own, but if you've already got some, that's fine by me.

"Holy Toledo, is this guy for real?" Dani yelped, sitting up straight while she eagerly read the rest.

Not rich, but am pretty comfortable. Enjoy a cold beer after a hot day's work, but no heavy drinking. Nonsmoker, nonchewer. Want an honest, healthy, mature woman who likes to cook and doesn't mind pitching in with chores when needed. Sweet disposition and a good sense of humor required. Would appreciate a photo, but let's don't quibble about age or looks. Want something permanent and I know my dream woman is out there somewhere. Come on and write to me now, honey. We've got nothing to lose but loneliness.

Dani groaned and flopped back onto her pillows. "Be still, my heart. I think I'm in love." She hugged herself around the middle, envisioning what it would feel like to be held in that wonderful, gorgeous man's strong arms. If he could turn her on this much with a picture and a few paragraphs, what would he do to her up close and personal?

She wished the magazine had published his name, although she could understand why they would want to protect their advertisers' privacy. With an ad and a picture like his, this man would be utterly besieged.

Chuckling and shaking her head, she climbed off the bed. There had to be a catch somewhere. The guy probably snored like a freight train or chewed with his mouth open or had terminally bad breath. Real men simply weren't that wonderful or that gorgeous. No woman in her right mind would answer an ad like that. Still, it was fun to dream.

Unfortunately she didn't have time to dream anymore this evening. She had children to feed, bills to pay and a rebellious son to talk to. The phone rang as she walked into the kitchen. She answered it, then sank onto one of the battered chairs at the table when she heard her mother's voice on the other end of the line.

"Yeah, Mom, I'm home for a change. It's my night off....The kids are fine, but they're starving, so can we make this quick?...No, they're not really starving, it's just time for dinner and I haven't even started cooking yet....Of course, there's food in the house....No, Mom, I don't want you and Pop to come over tonight. I've got things to do....That's none of your business, Mom. Look, I've got to go. I'll talk to you later, okay?...Fine. Bye, Mom."

Dani hung up the phone and opened the refrigerator, hoping for inspiration she doubted she would find. Deciding Colin might as well be cleaning up the mess in the living room while she cooked, she went to his room and banged on the door.

"Are you finally gonna let me out now?" he asked.

"Only to clean up the living room. After dinner, you and I are going to have a talk about the phone call I got from Mr. Ames this afternoon."

"Get off my case, Ma. I don't need this hassle."

"Don't push your luck, Colin. Now get busy or Kim and I will eat without you."

"Yeah, yeah, yeah," Colin grumbled.

Dani exhaled a silent sigh of relief when he stomped to the closet for the vacuum cleaner. He already topped her five-foot-two-inch height by six inches, and she honestly didn't know what she would do if he absolutely refused to obey her. It was a hideous worry, and a real one.

She finally settled on grilled cheese sandwiches and tomato soup for dinner. A dark cloud of tension hovered over the small kitchen. Except for Colin deliberately slurping his soup, the meal was silent. Afterward, Kim escaped into the living room to watch television.

Dani cleared the table and stacked the dishes in the sink, bracing herself for an ugly scene with her son. Ignoring his insolent stare, she took the chair across from him.

"You promised me you wouldn't cut school again," she began quietly. "I want to know why you did."

"School's dumb, Ma."

"Stop calling me that, Colin. You can call me Mother or Mom."

"All right, *Mom*. School's dumb and I hate it. I want to work with computers, not sit around and read some dumb history book."

"You can't have one without the other, Colin. We've been over this before. You need a college degree to get into the computer field, and you're never going to get to college if you don't even pass junior high school."

"You're talking about years of my life," Colin protested. "I can't wait that long."

"What do you want me to do about it, son? I can't wave a magic wand and make you eighteen years old."

"You could let Granddad buy me a PC."

"No."

"He's offered a thousand times."

"And there'll be a thousand strings attached to it. You know that. Do you want me to get a third job so I can buy you a computer?"

"Why not? You're never here anyway."

"Dammit, Colin," Dani shouted, banging her fist on the table. "I'm doing the best I can for you and Kim. What do you think your dad would say if he could hear you talking to me this way?"

"Why bring him up? He's dead, Mom."

"Yes. He is," she replied, struggling to moderate her voice. "And it's not my fault or his fault. That's just the way life is sometimes."

"Gimme a break."

"No, you give *me* a break," Dani demanded, thumping the table with her index finger. "I need your help and your cooperation. I'm scared to death you're going to get into so much trouble you won't be able to get yourself back out. I can't just sit back and watch you destroy your whole life."

"It's my life, isn't it?"

"Not until you're old enough to support yourself, it isn't."

"Yeah, well, I think you're jealous because I'm still young and I've got a future. All you ever do is work and bitch at me. Why don't you get a life, Mom?"

His bitter words ringing in her ears, Dani stared at the hostile young man across the table. What had happened to that dear, sweet little boy who used to climb onto her lap asking for a story? The one who used to bring her dandelions and beam with pride when she put them in a juice glass and set them on this very table as a centerpiece?

"You know, Colin," she said, scraping the legs of her chair across the linoleum as she stood, "I just might do that. In the meantime you're grounded for the next two weeks. That means no friends in the apartment, no phone calls, no TV. If you violate the rules, you'll be grounded for another two weeks."

"Come on, Mom—"

Dani cut him off midwhine. "I'll get a list of your as-signments from your teachers and check your homework every night. I'll be calling Mr. Ames every day. If you're not at school, I'll leave work and come looking for you. If I get fired, then we'll either move in with your grandpar-ents or go to Montana to live with Micky and Greg."

"You'd never do that," Colin scoffed.

"Don't be too sure about that. No matter what you think, I love you and I'm *not* going to give up on you."

With that, Dani left the room. After spending an hour with Kim, she tucked her daughter in bed and went into her own room. She scooped up the stack of bills and wrote checks for the ones she could, putting the others aside un-til her next payday.

Finally she took a shower and crawled into bed. Of course she couldn't sleep. Her argument with Colin re-played itself inside her head over and over again. Was there something else she could have said—should have said—that would have reached him this time? How much longer could she handle him if his attitude didn't change?

Why don't you get a life, Mom? Now, *there* was an in-teresting concept. But now that she thought about it, why *didn't* she get a life? A life with a warm, strong, wonderful man who would share her worries—like that guy in *Cu-pid's Arrow.* She'd love to see Colin try to take on "six feet, four inches and two hundred pounds of solid muscle."

Dani sat up, turned on her bedside lamp and opened the magazine to page twenty-five. So, no woman in her right mind would answer an ad like that. Who said Dani Smith was in her right mind? Lately it seemed as if her whole life was crazy anyway.

Flipping back the covers, she carried the magazine to the small desk where she paid her bills. She wouldn't *really* have to marry the man like a mail-order bride would. He probably wouldn't even write back to her. But what would it hurt if she wrote him a letter? She would be completely honest about herself and her situation. She'd even send him a picture of herself and the kids.

And if he answered? At best, she might have another option to consider. At worst, she'd be out a couple of dollars. Dani's mother had always said she was too impulsive, but being impulsive wasn't *always* a bad thing. Was it?

Chapter Two

"You know, it's not too late to turn back, Mom," Colin said, darting nervous glances through the window on his side of the car.

Dani shot him a sympathetic smile, then whipped her gaze back to the narrow, bumpy two-lane road ahead. Except for the headlights, the complete and utter darkness surrounding them was starting to unnerve her, too. They hadn't passed another vehicle or even a lighted house for the past fifteen minutes. She'd never realized just how wide and open the spaces between towns out west really were.

It hadn't been so spooky while they'd stayed on I-80; at least there'd been lots of signs and the ever-present eighteen-wheelers for company. Now, however, it felt as if her little red Fiesta held the world's entire population. Thank God that nice mechanic in Cheyenne had noticed her worn fan belt.

"Mom, I'm serious," Colin said more forcefully. "If you'll take us home, I won't cut school anymore. I'll stay away from Brian and Eddie, and I'll never touch beer again until I'm twenty-one. I'll even be nice to the little geek.''

"I've heard those promises before, Colin."

"But this time I really *mean* it."

"I've heard that before, too."

"I know, but I never thought you'd do something like this. It's crazy! You can't marry some strange guy because I was acting like a jerk. Are you trying to drown me in guilt?"

"You were a big part of the decision, Colin, but it wasn't just you," Dani admitted, although she was happy to see that something had finally broken through his hostile shell. "Your grandparents have been driving me nuts for years. When the landlord raised the rent again, I knew it was time for a change."

"But for all you know, this Dawson guy could be a real psycho, Mom. Why don't we go to Montana and stay with Aunt Micky?"

"We will if Sam and I aren't compatible," Dani assured him, "but I've been writing to him for a month now, and I want to meet him. I think his suggestion about our living at his ranch for six months was a good one. We won't do anything rash. Try to look at this as an adventure."

"Hah! Some adventure. There's nothing out here but cows and sagebrush."

"You could have stayed with your grandparents."

"Grandma's a worse nag than you are," Colin grumbled.

"Remember that. And give Sam a chance. You just might like him."

"I might if he doesn't try to boss me around."

Colin settled into a sullen silence. Dani heaved a sigh of relief when a faint glow appeared on the horizon. Her neck and shoulders ached from hours behind the wheel. She probably should have stayed in Cheyenne for the night as she'd originally planned. But she'd been so eager to see

Sam, and since she'd already committed the most impulsive act of her life, what was one more?

"Look, Mom," Kim said from the back seat five minutes later. "There's a sign for Pinedale."

"Yeah, Population: 1066," Colin muttered, rolling his eyes in disgust. "Does that even qualify as a town?"

"Help me watch for a phone, kids," Dani instructed, trying to drive and take in everything at once. "Sam's last letter said to call him when we arrived and he'd come to town and guide us out to the Circle D."

"King Cone. Home Of The Road-Kill Burger," Kim read from a sign in front of a drive-in. "What's that?"

"I don't know," Dani admitted with a laugh. "We'll have to ask Sam. Look, there's a big grocery store. And the buildings all look old-fashioned. Isn't this a cute little town?"

"Oh, *real* cute, Mom," Colin grumbled.

"There's a library. That must be the courthouse," Dani said, ignoring her son.

"There's a bank," Kim added.

"Nothing's open but the bars," Colin complained.

"It's after midnight," Dani reminded him. "This isn't Chicago. Lots of things are going to be different here."

Deciding Colin was right about the bars being the only businesses open, she made a U-turn, drove back down the street and parked in front of the Cowboy Bar. She shut off the engine and rested her head against the seat for a moment. Lord, she was tired.

"Mom, I have to go to the bathroom," Kim said, smothering a yawn with one hand.

"All right, honey." Dani straightened up, then dug her purse out of the back seat. "Let me call Sam first, and I'll ask the bartender if I can bring you in to use the rest room. Both of you stay in the car and keep the doors locked. I'll be out as soon as I can."

Grabbing her jacket, Dani stepped out onto the street. The air was fresh and crisp with a late-October chill. A country-and-western song blared from inside the building. Otherwise the town was quiet. Almost too quiet.

Before she could lose her courage, she crossed the sidewalk and entered a dim, smoky room. A mahogany bar lined with men stretched down the left side. Dark wooden tables filled the rest of the space. Doorways draped in red velvet opened off to the right at both the front and rear of the room. Though the decor was strictly Western, the place had the same jovial atmosphere as Johnny's Tavern. It was definitely a workingman's hangout.

"Hey, kid," a big, burly man with thinning gray hair shouted from behind the bar, "we don't serve minors in here, so take a hike."

Since the man appeared to be looking at her, Dani glanced over her shoulder to see if Colin or Kim had come in behind her. No one was there. She looked at the bartender again and pointed at her chest, as if to say, "Are you talking to me?"

"Yeah, you, shorty. Ya gotta be twenty-one to come in here."

Dani laughed with delight, then quickly made her way across the room. She flipped open her wallet, exposing her Illinois driver's license, and gave it to the man.

"That's the nicest compliment I've had in a long time," she told him.

Giving her a sheepish grin, the bartender handed the wallet back to her. "Sorry, ma'am."

"That's all right. I used to work in a place like this. You can't be too careful about serving teenagers."

"That's the way I look at it," the man agreed. "How about a beer on the house?"

Dani smiled and shook her head. "I just came in to use the pay phone if you have one."

The man reached under the counter and produced a telephone. "Be my guest."

After taking the slip of paper with Sam's phone number out of her wallet, Dani reached for the receiver, then hesitated as Colin's words came back to haunt her. *It's not too late to turn back, Mom. . . . For all you know, this Dawson guy could be a real psycho, Mom.*

"Is something wrong, ma'am?" the bartender asked.

Dani looked up into his friendly, concerned face, and decided he might be a good source of information. Hitching one hip up onto a bar stool, she said, "Do you happen to know a man named Sam Dawson?"

"You bet. Everybody around here knows ol' Silent Sam."

The nickname surprised Dani. Sam had certainly been chatty enough in his letters. "Do you know him very well?" she asked.

"Well enough. Why do you want to know?" the bartender replied, wiping down the bar with a rag.

"I came out here to see him. Is he nice?"

"Oh, sure. All the Dawsons are great folks. Sam's brother used to be one of my favorite customers before he got hurt. He's a lot of fun."

"What's Sam like?"

The bartender rested one elbow on the bar and studied her curiously for a moment. "Let me get this straight. You came all the way from Illinois to see Sam, but you've never met him?"

Realizing she wasn't going to get any more information out of the man unless she told him the whole story, Dani quickly explained her reasons for coming to Pinedale. "So, you see," she finished, "I just want to know if he's a good man. Or should I go to my sister's house instead?"

"Nah, you'll be sorry if you do that," the bartender replied with a broad grin. "Sam Dawson's as solid as they come. Tell you what. Let me call him for you while you go check on your kids. You can bring 'em in to use the rest rooms if you like.''

Dani offered her hand across the bar for a handshake. "Thank you, uh...oh dear, I don't even know your name."

"Just call me Bob, ma'am," the man said, pumping her hand vigorously. "Everybody does."

"All right, Bob. I'm Dani."

"Please to meet you, Dani. Go on now, I'll call Sam."

When the door closed behind Dani, Bob motioned a few of his friends over to the bar.

"Hang on to your hats, boys," he said with a chuckle. "We're gonna have some *real* entertainment tonight."

Then he picked up the phone and started to dial.

The first ring of the telephone brought Sam Dawson out of a sound sleep. He squinted at the green numbers on his bedside clock and shook his head to clear it. Nobody would call him this late at night unless they had bad news. Oh, God, had something happened to Becky and the baby? Or to Grandma D?

A tendril of fear curling deep in his gut, he grabbed the receiver. "Hello."

"Sam? This is Bob at the Cowboy."

"For God's sake, do you know what time it is?" Sam snarled, rubbing one hand over his face.

"Yeah. Sorry about that, but you need to come into town right away. Got a personal emergency for ya."

"What kind of an emergency?"

"I don't think you'd want me to say over the phone, Sam."

"What the hell are you talkin' about? Does this have anything to do with my family?"

"In a way," Bob replied. "Nobody's dyin' or anything, but, well . . . I mean, it's *really* personal, and this ain't exactly a private spot. Know what I mean?"

"Are you tryin' to pull my leg or what?" Sam demanded. "If this is some kind of a prank—"

"Have I ever done anything like that to you before?" the bartender asked.

"Well, no, but—"

"Do whatever you want, Sam. If it was me, I'd get my butt down here pretty damn quick."

Sam heard a click in the receiver and the line went dead. Thoroughly mystified, he flipped back the covers and got out of bed. He yanked on some clothes, then hurried downstairs, grabbed his Stetson and a coat from the mudroom and went outside to his pickup.

His Australian shepherd, Bear Dog, came out of the barn to investigate, barking softly and hopefully wagging his tail when Sam opened the truck's door.

"Wanna go for a ride, boy?" Sam asked, patting his leg in invitation.

The dog raced across the yard and jumped into the vehicle. Sam climbed in beside him and scratched the shepherd behind his ears before starting the engine and driving away from the house. All the way into town, one question echoed repeatedly inside Sam's head. What the hell did Bob mean by a "personal emergency"?

By the time he parked across the street from the Cowboy, he had convinced himself that this was nothing but a fool's errand. He shoved the bar's door open with the palm of his hand and stomped inside, ready to tell Bob Williams exactly what he thought of people playing practical jokes in the middle of the night.

Every head in the room—there were more than Sam would have expected, even on a Saturday night—swiveled in his direction. An expectant hush fell over the crowd. Uncomfortable to find himself the object of undivided attention from so many folks, Sam crammed his hands into his jeans pockets.

Bob walked out from behind the bar. He tossed a towel onto the counter, then approached Sam.

"It's about time you got here, Dawson," he grumbled. "Follow me." He led the way to a table near the doorway to the rest rooms, saying over his shoulder, "Your future bride's gettin' mighty anxious."

Sam halted dead in his tracks. "My *what?*"

Bob stepped to one side and held out his arm, indicating that Sam should take the lead. Then a colorful blur launched itself at Sam. The next thing he knew, two arms wrapped around his middle, a pair of soft breasts pressed into him above his belt buckle and a head full of black, glossy curls collided with his chest.

"Oh, Sam, I'm so glad you're finally here," a husky feminine voice said from somewhere down around his sternum as those arms squeezed him in an enthusiastic hug. "I was beginning to think you'd decided you didn't want to meet me after all."

Sam opened his mouth to speak, but before he could get a single syllable out, the woman pulled away a few inches, tipped her head way back and smiled up at him. Lord, but her eyes were a deep, smoky blue. He couldn't remember having anyone look at him with such absolute delight before.

"My goodness," she said, her words coming as rapidly as flashes from the strobe light on the dance floor in the next room, "you really are a big man. And you're even more handsome than your picture. Oh, I'm *so* glad you're here."

As if she couldn't help herself, the woman hugged him again. Putting his hands on her shoulders, one of which was bare because her sweater or whatever the hell that thing was she was wearing had slipped down, Sam peeled her off him and held her at arm's length.

She laughed and gave him another one of those pixie smiles. "Hi, I'm Dani. I'm sorry we got here so late, but I just couldn't wait another day to see you."

Sam studied her in confusion. He knew damn well he'd never seen her before. He wouldn't forget eyes like hers. No way. Or clothes like hers, either.

She wore a big, purple colored top that reached the tops of her thighs. A skinny black belt at her narrow waist emphasized the smooth curve of her hips. Beneath the top, she wore black skin-tight pants that revealed, in intimate detail, her short, but nicely shaped legs. He'd have swatted his little sister's rear end but good if she'd ever tried to wear pants like those when she was growing up.

And now that he really looked at it, except for a mass of curls on top and feathery bangs that practically covered her eyebrows, her hair was damn near as short as his. Long, spangly gold earrings dangled to her shoulders, and if those weren't false eyelashes, he'd eat with Bear Dog for a week. A stack of gold bracelets stretched from her left wrist halfway to her elbow.

As if the rest of her getup didn't beat all he'd ever seen, she wore a pair of high-topped sneakers with purple and black laces intertwined. Was she planning to try out for a midget basketball team or just ready to run if he didn't have a sense of humor over whatever sick joke she was tryin' to pull on him? Shoot, she didn't look a day over eighteen.

Her smile faltered under his intense scrutiny. "Is something wrong, Sam?"

"Yeah, lady. I don't know who you are or what the hell you're talkin' about."

A vivid blush colored her face for a moment, and her mouth fell open. Then she shook her head, as if that action could erase what he'd said. "But your letters—"

"*What* letters?"

"The ones you wrote to me," she said earnestly, her eyes big as the silver dollars in the glass case mounted on the wall behind her. "Six of them in the last month."

Muffled snorts of laughter from nearby tables brought a hot flush to Sam's neck and ears. He shot a quick glance at Bob, and found the bartender hiding his mouth behind one hand, his brawny shoulders shaking. Taking the woman's arm in a firm grip, Sam marched her back to the only empty table in the place.

She collapsed onto a chair as though her legs couldn't hold her up another second. Even beneath all that makeup, Sam could see she'd gone pale. He sat across from her, and after giving the gawking people around him a warning scowl, he signaled Bob for a drink. He had an awful feeling he was gonna need one mighty soon.

"All right, uh, Dani," he said quietly. "Why don't you tell me what's goin' on?"

"You really don't know?" she whispered.

"Nope. How do you even know my name? I've never heard of you before."

There was a huge black purse slung over the arm of the next chair. Dani pulled it onto her lap, rummaged around in it for a moment, then pulled out a dog-eared magazine. She opened it to a page marked with a paper clip, and laid it on the table.

"That certainly looks like you," she said, shoving the magazine across the scarred wood to Sam.

He stared at the photograph in disbelief, blinked his eyes and stared again. That was him, all right. The reporter from *Ag World Today* had taken it four months ago. His gaze moved to the text beside the picture. After reading the first five lines, he slammed the magazine shut and gaped at the cover.

"*Cupid's Arrow?*" he read, his voice taking on an incredulous tone. Where had he heard that phrase before?

"That *is* you, isn't it?" Dani demanded, two hot red spots coloring her cheeks now, her chin set at a challenging angle.

"Yeah. It sure is," Sam agreed. "But I didn't put that ad in that magazine."

Dani rummaged in her purse again and tossed a handful of envelopes held together with a rubber band to Sam. "Right. And I suppose you didn't write those, either."

Sam caught the packet. One look at the handwriting on the top envelope told him everything he needed to know. "Aw, Hank, no," he groaned.

Bob delivered a bourbon on the rocks for Sam and a Coke for Dani. Sam gratefully picked up the glass and downed half of its contents in one gulp.

"Who is Hank?" Dani asked when Bob had left.

"My brother. But he's a dead man, now," Sam answered. "When I get my hands on him, I'm gonna wring his damned neck."

"Is he the one who…" She gestured at the magazine and envelopes.

Sam nodded, then polished off the rest of his drink. "Afraid so, ma'am."

"But why?" Dani asked. "Why would he do such an awful thing?"

Sam had a pretty good idea of the answer to that question, but he wasn't going to share it with Dani. God, he hoped she wasn't gonna burst into tears or anything. The whole situation was already embarrassing enough.

"I reckon he thought it'd be a pretty good joke on me," Sam replied gruffly.

Suddenly Dani sat up straight, and an expression of horror crossed her small face. "Are you married?"

"Nope."

"Engaged?"

"Nope."

"Seeing anyone seriously?"

"Nope. Lady, I hardly ever date at all."

She relaxed slightly at that. "Why not? Don't you like women?"

"Well, of course, I do," Sam answered indignantly, glancing around to see if anyone else had heard *that* question. Grinning faces quickly turned away on three sides. "Wouldja *please* keep your voice down?"

"Oh. I'm sorry." She reached out and covered his fist with her hand. Then, as if realizing what she was doing, she jerked her hand back and wrapped it around her glass. "It's just that I'm trying to understand. I had such high hopes for us. The ad and your letters—"

He shot her a dirty look and she immediately corrected herself. "I mean, the letters I thought you wrote... You seemed like the perfect man."

"Believe me, honey," Sam drawled, feeling exasperated and flattered at the same time, "I'm not even close to perfect."

Chuckling, she shrugged, exposing a slender, bare shoulder. "So who is?"

Sam gulped and looked away from her. She looked awfully small and soft and vulnerable in that moment, but dammit, he just couldn't get involved with her.

"Well, I'm sorry if you've been inconvenienced, but I guess there's no real harm done." He scooted back his chair and started to rise. "It's been nice meetin' you, ma'am."

Her eyes narrowed with anger. "Wait just a minute, cowboy. What makes you think no real harm has been done?"

Sam eased himself back down. "What do you mean?"

"I came halfway across the country on the basis of some very specific promises your brother made in his letters."

"Such as?"

"Such as, my children and I could live on your ranch for the next six months to find out if we were compatible."

"Children?"

"Yes. Two of them. They're waiting for me in the car."

"My God, they're probably freezing to death."

"They're bundled up in blankets," she assured him. "Anyway, I've already pulled them out of school, and I gave up my apartment and two jobs, and spent most of my savings to get here."

"What do you expect me to do about it?" Sam asked, feeling the hair at the back of his neck stand up.

"I expect you to honor that promise." She grabbed the letters and the magazine and stuffed them back into her purse.

"C'mon, lady. Let's save ourselves a lot of grief. You're not my type and you never will be."

"From what you've told me about your social life, I don't think you know if you've got a type or not. Why don't you give us both a chance and find out? The letters said you've got plenty of room."

"That's the nuttiest idea I've ever heard," Sam muttered. "Look, if what you really want is money, I'll give you enough to get home on—"

"No. *You* look," Dani replied, leaning across the table and thumping his chest with her index finger, "I just told you I don't *have* a home anymore. And I've been driving since seven o'clock this morning and I'm exhausted."

"Okay. Fine. I'll take you to a motel for the night and we'll talk again in the morning. You can spend the whole damn night figuring out how much money you can get out of me."

"Hmmph! You'll probably take off and I'll never see you again."

"Are you callin' me a liar?" Sam asked, not sure whether he wanted to laugh or get mad or what. He'd give her this much, she sure didn't seem to feel intimidated. She was cuter than hell when she was furious, too. Reminded him a little of Becky in that regard.

"If the boot fits, mister. Anyway, I can't afford a motel."

"I'll pay for it."

"When you already think I'm some kind of a . . . gold digger? Forget it. I wouldn't accept a penny from you. Besides, don't you think I at least deserve to meet Hank?"

Sam scratched his left earlobe and studied her for a moment. She had a point there. Might be good for Hank to see what his damn scheming had done to this woman. He wouldn't mind watching her tear a few strips off his brother's mangy hide with that sharp tongue of hers, either.

On the other hand, if he let her come out to the Circle D, would she ever leave? Six months could be one helluva long time. But then, if worse came to worst, he'd be out working most of the time. Hank would be the one stuck in the house with the gabby little woman and her kids. That would sure as hell serve him right, now wouldn't it?

"All right, you can come out to the ranch," Sam finally agreed. "But just for tonight. We'll thrash out some kind of a plan tomorrow."

Chapter Three

Gulping at a huge lump in her throat, Dani slung her purse over her shoulder and followed the big, angry man making his way between the crowded tables to the door. She started when a hand patted her shoulder, and paused to find Bob standing beside her.

"Keep your chin up, kid," the bartender said quietly. "He'll come around."

Dani gave him a shaky smile, then shrugged as if she didn't feel like a first-class fool for getting her hopes up so high. "Thanks for being...nice to me and the kids."

"No problem. Let me know if you need anything." He nudged her gently between her shoulder blades. "Go on now. Sam's waitin' for you."

Looking toward the door, Dani noted that Sam certainly was waiting for her. Not very patiently, either, judging by his thunderous expression. At the moment it was hard to believe that face had ever produced the wonderful smile in the *Cupid's Arrow* photograph.

A shiver of fear raced down her spine. She could almost hear her mother crowing, "I *told* you so, Danielle. You should have listened to me." The thought was enough to stiffen Dani's resolve. Raising her chin, she marched over to Sam and out onto the sidewalk when he opened the door for her.

Colin scrambled out of the car. "Jeez, Mom, it took you long enough. Can we go now?" He gazed over the top of her head, his mouth dropping open in surprise. Then he gulped. "Is that him?"

Dani nodded, saw that Kim was sound asleep in the back seat of the car, then glanced over one shoulder at the man standing behind her. The brim of his hat blocked the illumination from the streetlights, leaving his face shadowed. His massive size and the air of suppressed anger surrounding him added sinister elements to his appearance.

Turning back to Colin, she saw the teen widen his stance, prop his hands on his hips and pull himself as tall as he could. A fierce, protective scowl crossed his boyish features, and Dani felt a warm, sweet glow of pleasure deep inside at her son's reaction.

"Yes, Colin, this is Sam Dawson," she answered, moving to stand beside him while she finished the introductions.

Sam stepped directly under a streetlight and reached out to shake Colin's hand. His gaze darted over the boy, his eyes taking on the same expression of surprise and disbelief he'd worn when he'd first studied Dani. His mouth twisted into a sardonic smile as he noted Colin's earring, the Don't Have A Cow, Man slogan on his T-shirt, the hightops with untied laces dragging on the ground. He didn't say anything derogatory, however, for which Dani was extremely grateful.

Instead, he nodded toward a dusty red pickup across the street. "That's my truck. Watch out for deer on the road, and when we hit the gravel, don't follow too close or you'll lose your windshield.''

Dani and Colin climbed into the car and fastened their seat belts. Even behind their closed windows, they could hear Sam furiously gunning his engine. Colin turned to Dani as she switched on the ignition.

"He's one mean-looking dude, Mom. Why was he so mad?"

Sighing, Dani quickly explained what had happened inside the bar. Then she put the car in gear and followed Sam out of town, heading west.

"Oh, *jeez,* Mom," Colin said with a groan. "I *told* you this was a crazy idea. We've got to go home, now."

"Don't start with me, Colin. You sound like your grandmother," Dani replied. "When Sam has a little time to get used to the idea, maybe he'll change his mind. If someone had done that to me, I suppose I would have been . . . upset, too."

"Upset?" Colin yelped, his voice cracking. "He was practically frothing at the mouth. He doesn't like you. Or me.''

"He doesn't know us yet."

"Do you like *him?*"

"I don't know him well enough to answer that."

"For God's sake, Mom, will you listen to me? This isn't going to work. I mean, like, I can't protect you from a guy that big without a bazooka."

"You won't need to, honey," Dani answered with more confidence than she felt.

Five miles out of town, Sam turned north onto Highway 352. Dani ignored her son's dire muttering and executed the turn. The road gradually narrowed and yard lights on both sides appeared less frequently. When they left the highway for the graveled road Sam had mentioned, the darkness crowded around her little car like a giant fist, forcing her doubts and fears closer to the surface.

She gritted her teeth, clutched the steering wheel harder and focused on the red taillights ahead. She might well be making the biggest mistake of her life, but she'd promised herself and her children a new life, and that's what they were going to get. Giving up was not an option.

After what seemed like hours of bouncing from one pothole to another, they passed under an arching sign supported by huge posts, announcing their arrival at the Circle D ranch. Dani wished she could see more than the lane in front of the headlights. Then they rounded a final curve, and her breath caught in her throat when a yard light revealed a stately red barn and a white two-story farmhouse.

Big, solid and old, though obviously well cared for, the house looked just as wonderful as she had imagined it would from Sam's—no, Hank's—letters. Four dormer windows graced the front of the second floor, and a chimney protruded from the sharply slanting roof. Before she could admire any more of the building, however, Sam drove around to the back door.

Dani followed, parked behind his pickup and turned to waken Kim before climbing out of the car to face him. A dog leapt out of the pickup and charged toward her, teeth bared, hackles raised, low, fierce snarls coming from his throat. Dani grabbed for the car door, but at a curt command from Sam, the animal stopped and waited for his master to catch up with him.

"You'd better come and meet Bear Dog," Sam said, crouching down to pat the animal's head. "He's pretty protective, but he won't bother you once he gets to know you."

When her heart resumed its normal rhythm, Dani led Colin and Kim over to meet the dog and cautiously held out one hand for him to sniff. Bear Dog eyed her for a moment, as if considering whether or not he should take a bite of the juicy tidbit dangling before his snout. Sam murmured something to him, however, and the animal dutifully sniffed her hand.

"He's a cow dog, not a pet like a cocker spaniel," Sam said.

Kim giggled while she held her fingers out to the animal. "That sounds funny. How can he be a cow dog?"

Sam grinned and his tone softened, as if he was used to talking with little girls and enjoyed doing it. "He helps me herd cattle, honey. He bites at their heels and makes them go where I want them to. To do that, he's gotta be feisty. He's not real friendly with most people."

"Does that mean I can't play with him?" Kim asked.

"I wouldn't recommend it. He'll chase a stick if you throw it for him, but that's kinda frustrating, because he never wants to give it back. I'd rather you steered clear of him unless I'm around."

Fascinated, Dani watched the exchange between her daughter and the big man. Kim loved animals, but she was usually excruciatingly shy with strangers, especially men. Had the dog broken the ice for her? Or was there something about Sam that made her trust him instinctively?

His manner was gruff, but not unkind as he helped them unload the luggage they would need for the night and ushered them all inside. Dani blinked against the sudden brightness when he switched on the light, then gasped in dismay.

Any self-respecting cook would love this kitchen. It had miles of cupboards, state-of-the-art appliances and counter space to die for. After struggling with the cramped kitchen in her apartment for the last three years, Dani would cheerfully kill to call this spacious, well-planned room her own.

Unfortunately at the moment it looked as if a large crowd of savage children had been having the time of their lives in it. Mountains of dirty dishes, pots and pans were stacked so high on every conceivable surface that all of those gorgeous cupboards had to be empty. The trash can in the corner overflowed with used paper plates and enough beer cans to keep a recycling center busy for weeks. The floor was sticky underfoot and so grimy, Dani couldn't tell exactly what color it was.

Though his neck and ears had flushed a dull red, Sam shot her a challenging look, daring her to comment. Dani clamped her mouth shut and forced a smile. Without a word, he turned and led the way through a living room that looked almost as bad as the kitchen. A long flight of stairs to the second floor opened on to a hallway with hardwood floors sporting dust bunnies as big as jackrabbits.

Ignoring them, Sam marched down the hall, opening doors to indicate which rooms the Smiths could use for the night. Then he pointed out the bathroom, said an abrupt "Good night" and walked back the way they had come, his big boots clomping on every stair.

Though a thick layer of dust covered the furniture, the bedrooms Sam had assigned them were neat and comfortably furnished. Dani helped Kim and Colin get settled and trudged back to her own room. She opened her suitcase and sat on the floor beside it. While digging out her nightgown, she heard deep angry voices coming through the heat grate at her feet from the room below.

"For God's sake, Sam, it's the middle of the night. Can'tcha see I'm sleepin'? Turn that light off and get outta here."

"Well, you'd better wake up, you sorry son of a bitch, before I break your damn neck."

Dani gulped at the mental picture Sam's furious tone created. She wouldn't want to be Hank right now. She supposed a truly ethical person would close the grate and let the two men argue privately. Considering the spot she was in, however, her ethics didn't stretch quite that far. She rolled onto her stomach and rested her hands on her chin in order to hear more clearly what they were saying.

"What the hell's the matter with you?" Hank demanded.

"We've got company," Sam said. "From Chicago. A woman and two kids. Get the picture?"

Dani held her breath during the moment of utter silence that followed Sam's question. She envisioned the other man going pale, then judging the distance from his bed to the door, perhaps giving his brother a sick smile.

"You mean Dani's here already? Now?"

"Now. Upstairs. In Becky's old room."

Hank's reply was too muffled for Dani to understand it. Judging from the tone of his voice, she assumed that was probably just as well. Sam's next remarks came through loud and clear, however.

"You're not usually this stupid, Hank. What the hell did you think you were tryin' to do?"

"Get you a wife."

"Did I ever say I *wanted* one?"

"Hey, one of us has to get married before we starve to death. I've been down that road twice with lousy results, so I figured it was your turn."

"You could've at least said somethin' about it and given me a chance to find a woman on my own."

"Seein' as how you're so bashful with the ladies and all, I thought you might need a little help."

"I'm not *that* bashful. I'm just not in any hurry."

"At the rate you've been workin' on findin' a woman, we'll be a couple of skeletons before you have any luck. So, uh, how'd you like Dani? Cute little thing, isn't she?"

"Well, she's little, all right."

Dani's eyebrows drew together at the scathing note in his voice.

"You didn't like her? She sounded like a real lively little gal in her letters."

"Hell, Hank. Get serious, will ya?"

Sam let out a snort of laughter that made Dani sit up straight. Just who did that...cowboy think *he* was? Prince Charming?

"She practically molested me in the Cowboy, right in front of God and everybody. She talks too damn much and she left her kids outside, freezing in the car while she cozied up with ol' Bob. She wears the weirdest clothes I've ever seen on a woman and enough makeup for three whores."

"Aw, c'mon, Sam—"

"No, I mean it, Hank. Wait'll you see her. The way she dresses, I'll bet she's got the morals of a mare in heat. And that boy of hers looks like a real punk. Her daughter seems all right, but we don't really know a thing about any of 'em. Do you think her last name's even Smith?"

Seething, Dani climbed to her feet and walked slowly down the stairs, her mind racing to find the exact phrases she would use to tell that big jerk what she thought of him. An open doorway on the right side of the living room told her where to find him. She approached it quietly and studied the scene inside.

Sam sat at the foot of a hospital bed, his Stetson tipped back on his head, exposing that unruly, dark shock of hair she had liked so much in his photograph. The other man, who looked a lot like Sam, except that he was much thinner and his features were more finely cut, reclined against the raised head of the mattress. He was bare to the waist, a sheet and blanket draped over his lap. A pair of crutches leaned against a built-in bookcase beside the bed.

Neither man had noticed her, and since they were now discussing what they should do with her, Dani decided she might as well listen a bit longer. She crossed one foot over the other and propped her shoulder against the doorjamb.

"I don't care what you promised her or how you do it, I expect you to get rid of her," Sam said.

"Give her a chance, Sam," Hank argued. "The least we can do is offer her a job as a housekeeper for six months and let her earn enough money to go somewhere else."

"Everybody knows Grandma D's stayin' at Becky's now. It wouldn't be decent for us to live in the same house with a single gal like that."

"So, let Dani and her kids live in the old foreman's house. That oughtta be decent enough."

"There's only one bedroom, Hank, and with winter coming on, it'll be too cold. Besides, I couldn't let somebody as irresponsible as that woman live out there. She'd probably burn the place down."

"Dani's not irresponsible or anything else you've accused her of. She's a real nice little gal, and she had damn good reasons for wanting to leave Chicago." Hank rummaged through a drawer in his bedside table, pulled out a stack of envelopes and tossed them in his brother's lap. "It's all right there in the letters she sent me. Read 'em and see for yourself."

Sam shook his head and dumped the letters onto the blanket. "How do you know she told the truth? Anyway, it doesn't matter what her reasons were. What kind of a nitwit would give up her job and her house to run off halfway across the country, planning to marry a man she's never even met?"

"A nitwit who loves her children," Dani replied from the doorway.

At the sound of her voice, both men jerked around hard enough to give them whiplash and stared at her in consternation. Dani pulled herself up to her full height, small though it was, and advanced into the room. Hank recovered first. A broad smile spread across his face and he held out a hand to her.

"Come on in, Dani. I've been anxious to meet you."

"I'm sure you have," Dani replied, ignoring his hand.

"Anybody ever tell you it's not polite to eavesdrop?" Sam asked.

Dani shrugged and met his heated glare with one of her own. "Under the circumstances, I thought I might learn something important. Just add 'rude' to your long list of my sins and shortcomings."

"He was mad at me, Dani," Hank said. "He always exaggerates when he's riled up. He didn't mean half of what he said."

"Don't apologize for him, Hank. I admire honesty in a man, as long as he can take it as well as he dishes it out."

"Be my guest," Sam said.

"I thought I was coming here to meet a kind, decent man who had some of the same hopes and dreams I did. Obviously I was wrong."

She was so angry, her thoughts refused to come out in any rational fashion. Dani paused, fearing she would make an even bigger fool of herself than this man already thought she was.

"Go ahead," Sam said. "Get it all off your chest."

"All right. You can relax, Mr. Dawson. I wouldn't marry a narrow-minded idiot who judges people by their appearance...you know, you'd look pretty strange where I come from, too. Maybe you need to get out and see a little more of the world before you pass judgment."

Sam looked away, his lips tightening to a grim, hard line. "I'm sorry I hurt your feelings."

"I'll get over it," Dani assured him. "Unfortunately that doesn't help my situation much. Or yours."

"What's that supposed to mean?"

Dani inhaled a deep breath and glanced at Hank. He winked at her and gave her a thumbs-up gesture. She couldn't resist giving him a wry smile.

"Besides wanting to leave Chicago, one of the reasons I came here," she said, turning back to Sam, "was that I thought you needed me." She ignored the way he rolled his eyes toward heaven. "From the condition of this house, it's obvious you need *somebody*. I would gladly accept a job as a housekeeper. I think you owe me that much."

"She's right about that, Sam," Hank said, his eyes glinting with amusement.

Sam shot his brother a quelling look, then eyed Dani from head to toe, making her painfully aware of just how tight her spandex pants were.

"How much experience have you had as a house-keeper?" he finally asked.

"Enough to know I can do a better job of it than either of you," Dani retorted. "Not that it would take much. I'm not looking for charity, Mr. Dawson. I've supported myself and two children for the last three years without help from anyone. Believe me, I'm not afraid of hard work."

"Look, Ms. Smith—"

"That's *Mrs.* Smith, Mr. Dawson. For your information, I'm a widow."

"Pardon me. As I was saying, people around here love to gossip, *Mrs.* Smith. It won't do your reputation any good if you live out here with two bachelors."

"At the moment I'm more worried about being homeless than I am about my reputation. Now that we've got that settled, do I have a job, or don't I?"

A grudging smile tugged at the corners of Sam's mouth, and he studied her thoughtfully for a long moment. Then he nodded his head once, as if making a decision.

"All right. We'll give it a six-month trial. You'll get room and board for you and your kids and eight hundred dollars a month. In return, you'll do the housework, cooking and laundry around here, with Sundays off. Fair enough?"

"Fair enough," Dani replied, suddenly feeling weak with relief. She'd die before she would let Sam Dawson see that, however. "If you gentlemen will excuse me, I'll go un-pack."

She turned and left with as much dignity as she could muster. Once inside the privacy of her own room, she collapsed onto the bed and clutched a pillow to her breasts. It could have been worse, she told herself, trying to ward off the cloud of depression settling over her.

She had a place to live and a job. The terms were more than fair and she'd be home for Colin and Kim all the time. She would have six months to decide what to do next.

Still, she couldn't help feeling bitterly disappointed. If only Sam had written those letters himself, things might have turned out... Well, there was no use wishing for things that would never happen. Sam Dawson was not the man she'd thought he was. She should have known he was too good to be true.

Sam waited until he was sure Dani was out of earshot before turning back to Hank. The damn fool was grinning at him like a man who'd just been told he wasn't going to be executed after all. Well, one of these days Hank was going to pay for this stunt. Sam would see to that.

"She's got a lot of grit for such a little gal," Hank said.

Sam shrugged. "I don't know if that was grit or stupidity."

"Don't give me that," Hank chided him. "You like her more than you're lettin' on. If you'd just unbend a little, I think you'd like her a lot."

"I might," Sam conceded. "But don't get your hopes up that I'm gonna marry her."

"Never say never. Once she gets over your pigheaded remarks about her looks, I think she'll fall right in love with you. You're exactly the kinda guy she's lookin' for."

Sam climbed to his feet and put his hands on his hips. "You're forgettin' something, Hank," he said. "*You're* the one who wrote those letters she liked so much that she came all the way to Wyoming. If she falls in love with anybody, it's gonna be you."

"Nope," Hank said with supreme confidence. "You may think that little gal is a flake, but she's determined to give those kids of hers some stability. And you're just the man to provide it. She'll figure that out pretty damn quick."

"Now look, I let her stay because you got her into this. The way I see it, that makes her *your* responsibility. I expect you to keep an eye on her and those kids. I'm goin' over to Becky's in the morning, so you'll have to show her where things are and tell her what to do. You're on your own, little brother."

With that, Sam turned to go, then paused in the doorway when Hank called to him. "Sam? Don't run too hard from Dani. You might miss out on somethin' special."

Sam shook his head, left the room and climbed the stairs two at a time. He shucked off his clothes and crawled into his big bed, settling under the cold covers with a tired sigh. Damn, what a day. And what a mess.

He wondered if he *had* misjudged Dani Smith. Whether he had or not, he still felt rotten that she'd heard him say all those mean things about her. Somebody ought to warn her never to play poker.

Those big blue eyes of hers gave away her feelings no matter how hard she tried to hide them. It bothered his conscience something fierce that he'd hurt her, when Hank was really the guilty party from the get-go. Well, maybe Hank wasn't completely to blame.

Being the housekeeper for the past three months had been rough on his brother's ego. Sam supposed he hadn't helped matters much by griping about Hank's cooking and complaining when he turned all their underwear pink with that damn red sweatshirt. And, Sam had to admit, Hank hadn't been able to get out and stop in at a restaurant for a decent meal once a day the way he had.

But, *Jeeeez*, wasn't sending off for a modern-day mail-order bride taking matters just a little too far?

Maybe Dani wasn't as bad as she'd seemed at first. She'd stood up to him with no trouble at all, and despite what he'd said to Hank, Sam did admire the woman's spunk. All right, so she *was* kind of a cute little thing, once you got used to her clothes and hair, and the whole damn town of Pinedale wasn't breathing down your neck.

Remembering that scene in the Cowboy Bar, the way she'd looked at him with such delight, the feel of her wrapped around him in an exuberant hug... And all those people watching the whole thing with avid interest... And when everybody found out she was staying at the Circle D, no matter what the reason...

Sam groaned and pulled the extra pillow over his face. It'd be one helluva long time before he could show his face in town again without getting ribbed. He should have just given Dani some money and sent her on her way. Dammit, he was *not* going to get involved with the woman or her kids.

Hank had finally succeeded in pushing him over the edge of sanity. It was the only thing that made any sense at all in this ridiculous situation.

Chapter Four

The next morning, Dani woke up to the sound of a pickup's door banging shut. She groaned and rolled onto her side. An engine roared, then gradually faded away, leaving a deep silence in its wake.

She pulled the covers up around her neck, settling back into sleep. A moment later, she found herself straining to hear traffic outside the window, the sound of footsteps or water running in the neighboring apartments. But the silence continued, as if all of her neighbors and the city of Chicago had vanished during the night.

She opened one eye. A massive, antique mahogany dresser came into focus. This wasn't her bedroom. She bolted upright, her heart racing until she saw her suitcase spread open on the floor, and the memory of the previous night penetrated her sleep-fogged brain.

Yawning, she rubbed her eyes with her fingertips and stretched before climbing out of the big old bed, whose headboard matched the dresser. Sunlight peeped under the bottom of the miniblinds at the window. Dani opened them, and blinked at the panorama spread before her eyes.

While driving across Wyoming on I-80 yesterday, she'd seen plenty of mountains off in the distance—beautiful, but remote. These mountains were different; they rose from the ground before her very eyes and scraped that cloudless, blue sky with jagged, snow-capped peaks. Dani reached out and touched the window, wanting to trace the sharp granite edges with her fingertips.

Now she knew why it was so quiet here. Every part of nature must have stood in awe of those mighty structures. The mountains touched an elemental part of her that yearned for permanence and safety and peace. She felt sheltered by them, as if they could block out all the bad things that happened in this world in the way they blocked out the horizon.

Her stomach chose that particular moment to announce it was empty. So much for poetic thoughts about the scenery, Dani told herself with a chuckle. She put on her bathrobe and hurried down the hall for a quick shower. After dressing in a pair of jeans, sneakers and a Chicago Cubs sweatshirt Colin had recently outgrown, she headed downstairs to cook breakfast.

The kitchen looked worse in the light of day than it had the night before. The optimism produced by her moments communing with the mountains shriveled at the prospect of cleaning the room. Shaking her head in denial of those self-defeating thoughts, she pushed up her sleeves and went to work.

An hour later, she finally unearthed the coffee maker. While waiting for it to finish dripping, she soaked another load of dishes in the sink. The aroma of the fresh brew made her stomach rumble again. She poked her head into the refrigerator and found three gallons of milk in big glass jars, enough eggs to clog every artery in Illinois, butter, half a loaf of bread and not much else.

"See anything interesting?" a deep, hopeful voice asked from the doorway to the living room.

Dani straightened and saw Hank making his way to the coffee maker on the crutches she had noticed the night before. Though his hair was wet and he'd obviously shaved, his shirt looked as if it had spent the past few weeks wadded up on the floor and his jeans were stained in several places. Oh, dear, was the laundry as backed up as the kitchen?

"I could make French toast if you've got syrup or jelly," she said.

He nodded toward the door beside the refrigerator. "Check the pantry."

Following his suggestion, Dani discovered a treasure trove of canned goods, cleaning supplies and God only knew what else stored on the shelves above her head. Promising herself she would explore later, she grabbed a gallon can of syrup and lugged it into the kitchen. Hank saluted her with his mug.

"This is great coffee, Dani. How soon can we eat?"

She scowled at him for a long moment. "Not until I can make enough room to clear the table and the stove."

Hank gazed around the room, his eyebrows raising as if he were surprised to see such a mess. Then his neck and ears flushed. "Oh. Sorry. I don't like washin' dishes much."

"I never would have guessed."

He gave her a boyish grin. "I was plannin' to do 'em before you got here, but I didn't expect you 'til this afternoon."

"I wanted to meet Sam."

His grin faded at the frosty tone of her voice. "Yeah. Look, Dani, I'm real sorry he reacted that way. I meant to tell him about you, but there just never seemed to be a good time to do it. How mad are ya?"

She turned away and started unloading the dishwasher. "I was awfully embarrassed last night, but I guess I'm more disappointed than angry this morning. Would you mind answering a few questions?"

"Not at all." Hank poured himself a second cup of coffee and leaned back against the counter. "Shoot."

"Was I the only one who answered your ad?"

"Heck, no. I got at least two dozen letters from gals all over this part of the country. Yours was the only one I answered, though."

"Why did you choose me?" she asked. "It's obvious Sam wouldn't have."

Hank tipped his head to one side and thought about that for a moment. "You were the most honest," he finally said. "You didn't try to make yourself or your kids sound like you were perfect, and I didn't think you'd expect Sam to be perfect, either. I thought you'd be good for him."

"How could you possibly think—"

"Sam's been in a rut for a long time," Hank interrupted, talking more rapidly. "He needs somebody to blast him out of it. Shake him up a little."

"And you thought *I* could do that?" Dani asked incredulously.

Smiling, he nodded. "Your letters had a nice sense of humor and you seemed like a real spunky little gal. If you can ignore his bark, you'll find out he never bites unless you threaten our family or the ranch. You know, you've already got him runnin' scared."

"Hah! I don't believe that."

"Well, you should. He took off for our sister Becky's house this morning, and I'll bet you five bucks he doesn't come back before supper."

"So what? Maybe he just wanted to see her."

"Nah. He's hopin' you'll get so disgusted tryin' to clean this house, you'll give up and go away."

"But why? Other than the way I was dressed last night, what is there about me that's so awful? I mean, I know I was a little . . . overly affectionate, and he wasn't expecting me, but—"

Hank laughed, then reached out and patted her shoulder in a brotherly gesture. "You're a female, Dani. A young, good-lookin' one. That's what's got him shakin' in his boots."

She shook her head in confusion. "That doesn't make sense, Hank. I asked him if he didn't like women last night in the bar, and—"

"You asked him *what?*" Hank threw back his head and roared with laughter until tears squirted out the corners of his eyes. "God, I wish I'da been there to see his face."

"I was just trying to understand why he was so horrified to meet me," Dani said, defending herself. "He said he hardly ever dated."

"That's true enough." Hank wiped his eyes with the back of one hand. "You know, Sam used to be quite a charmer back when he was in high school. I don't know what happened to him, but somewhere along the way, he kinda turned in on himself. Now it seems like the only women he's really comfortable with are Becky and Grandma D."

Dani walked over to the table and brought back a load of dirty dishes. "Then why did you put him in such an uncomfortable position? Why didn't you advertise for yourself?"

Hank's eyes narrowed, and his mouth twisted into a bitter imitation of a smile. "I haven't had much luck with women."

Dani would have loved to question him about that statement, but the finality in his tone told her he wouldn't discuss it. "You think Sam will?"

"Somebody's gotta carry on the family name. It's Sam's turn to try. That's another reason I chose you." His expression softened and his lips twitched at the corners. "With those two good-lookin' kids of yours, I figured you were a proven breeder. You and Sam oughtta produce some—"

"*Proven breeder?*" Torn between shocked laughter and outrage, Dani gaped at him. "Like one of your cows?"

Hank shrugged. "The biology's the same. Sam's not gettin' any younger. I wouldn't want to hook him up with some gal who can't have kids, now would I?"

Though his tone was completely serious, his eyes had taken on a wicked twinkle. Dani put on her best mother's glare and shook her finger at him. "Well, get this straight, Hank Dawson. I am *not* one of your cows. From now on, I'm your housekeeper and that's all."

"Yes, ma'am."

"No more matchmaking."

"No, ma'am."

"Why don't I believe you?"

"Beats the heck outta me," he answered.

Perhaps it was fatigue after her long trip to Wyoming, or the stress she'd been living with for so long, or simply the bizarre situation she now found herself in. Whatever the reason, Hank's oh-so-innocent expression tickled Dani's funny bone. A giggle escaped her throat, followed by an unladylike snort from trying to suppress her mirth. Finally, she gave in and laughed until her stomach hurt and she had to gasp for breath.

Hank joined in, and by the time they finally settled down, she felt as if she had found a new friend. She looked around the kitchen, and suddenly the mess didn't seem quite so depressing. She switched on the dishwasher again and brought a load of pots and pans from the stove to wash in the sink. Hank dried them for her, talking constantly as if he'd been starved for conversation.

Colin and Kim came downstairs half an hour later. After breakfast, Dani put Hank and the kids to work picking up the living room while she finished cleaning the counters and tackled the god-awful kitchen floor. Stripped of the layers of dirt and grease, it turned out to have a pretty powder-blue and yellow design that complemented the café curtains at the windows.

The rest of the day sped past in a flurry of work. How two grown men could have trashed such a lovely old home so completely, Dani didn't know, nor did she want to. As long as she was here, however, she vowed this house would never be treated with such blatant disrespect again.

By late afternoon, Hank declared he needed to rest and disappeared into his room. The kids rebelled against any more housework. Dani sent them outside to explore, giving multiple warnings to be careful, then searched the pantry shelves and the huge freezer Hank had shown her in what he called the mudroom, hoping to find something interesting for dinner.

She settled on a chicken-and-rice concoction she could put together in her sleep. After defrosting the chicken in the microwave, she dumped it into a casserole dish with the rice and cream of mushroom soup, and slid it into the oven. Then, fortifying herself with a deep breath, she went downstairs to check out the laundry situation.

A pile of clothes and soggy towels as high as her head dominated the center of the room like a shrine. Shaking her head in dismay, Dani walked around the edges of it. In the southeast corner of the room, she discovered a heavy-duty washer and dryer, a shelf filled with detergent, bleach and stain removers, a big double sink, a rod for hangers and a table for folding. The radio bolted to the wall under the shelf suggested that at one time, someone had spent many hours in this room.

Ignoring the danger of causing an avalanche, she yanked out the closest pair of jeans and started sorting. The kids tromped down the stairs half an hour later, full of stories about everything they'd seen. Dani listened with interest, wishing she could go out and look around for herself. Well, there would be plenty of time for that once she caught up with the housework. *If* she ever caught up with the house-work.

Sam drove toward the Circle D, wishing he didn't have to go home. It was so much more pleasant at Becky's house. Everything was neat and clean, and he'd enjoyed being with his sister, her husband, Peter Sinclair, Grandma D and Tina. Of course, they'd all had a good laugh when he'd told them what Hank had done. Now that he'd had a little time to cool off, he was ready to admit the whole thing *was* kinda funny.

He wouldn't be one bit surprised if he found out Dani had packed up and left. What did surprise him, however, was that he was starting to hope she hadn't. Not that he was the least bit attracted to her, mind you, but the day with the Sinclairs had made him realize just how sick he'd become of Hank's surly company.

Dani might be a little flaky, and her son might turn out to be a royal pain in the butt, but as she'd pointed out, it wouldn't take much to do a better job of keeping house than Hank had done over the past few months. And, if Dani stayed awhile, maybe he could finally convince Grandma D to come home and bring Tina with her. He missed those two, and he wanted his family back together. Besides, Becky and Pete deserved some time alone before the baby was born.

After all, just how much trouble could one pint-sized woman and two kids get into?

He got his first clue when he rounded the last curve and saw at least half of the Circle D's horse herd grazing in the front yard and trampling his mother's rose bushes. Dammit, couldn't he leave for even one lousy day without coming home to a disaster? Where the hell was Hank?

Sam parked next to the barn and got out. With Bear Dog at his heels, he stomped into the tack room and got a bri-dle, then went back outside and whistled for Smokey, his big gray gelding. The horse obediently trotted over to him and submitted to the bridle. Grabbing a handful of mane, Sam swung himself up onto Smokey's bare back.

As if reading his master's mind, Bear Dog raced to the front yard, barking at the other horses, but staying well out of kicking range. Sam rode after him, shouting and waving one arm to get the animals moving. Three curious faces appeared at one of the kitchen windows. Sam ignored them.

Everything was going along just fine and dandy until the back door banged shut. The entire Smith family ran around the corner of the house, their sudden appearance spooking the lead horses. The small herd scattered in a dozen directions.

"Get back in the house and stay there," Sam bellowed, scaring the horses even more.

Dani and her kids beat a hasty retreat. Sam counted to ten, then reined Smokey around to start over again. Skittish as all get-out now, the animals shied away every time he approached. He finally gave up and went back to the barn for a rope.

It took him a solid hour to get all of the damned critters back where they belonged. He took care of Smokey, then marched into the house with blood in his eyes.

"Who left the pasture gate open?" he demanded.

Wide-eyed and wary, Dani, Colin and Kim looked at each other, then up at him. Finally Colin stepped forward. "Kim and I did."

"Then you two get your coats and come with me."

"Wait a minute," Dani protested, moving in front of her children. "What are you planning to do to them?"

There was no mistaking the fear in her big, smoky blue eyes. To her credit, she raised her chin another notch and put her arms out at her sides like a mother hen sheltering her chicks.

"Do to them? What do you *think* I'm gonna do to them?"

"I know they made a mistake," she said, her voice quavering slightly as she pushed the children back a step. "And I'll admit you have a right to be angry, but—"

Appalled by her defensive stance, Sam rubbed one hand down over his face and sighed. "Good Lord, lady. Do you think I'm gonna *beat* 'em or something?"

"Aren't you?"

"Of *course* not."

She relaxed slightly at that. "Oh. Well, um, what did you have in mind?"

"I'm gonna give 'em a wheelbarrow and a couple of shovels and let 'em clean up the horse manure in the front yard. That way, they'll always remember to shut any gate they open. Unless you think that's an unreasonable punishment."

"Oh, uh, no. That's not unreasonable at all." She glanced over her shoulder at the kids. "Get your coats on."

"Aw, Mom," Colin grumbled.

"No arguments, Colin," Dani said sternly. "Dinner's almost ready."

She watched her children trudge from the room before turning back to Sam. "I'm sorry. I didn't mean to imply that I thought you would hurt them. But I don't know you very well and you seemed so angry...."

On occasion, Sam didn't mind having certain men approach him with a healthy dose of caution, but he would never lay a hand on a woman or child in anger. Despite her apology, it hurt to have Dani's gaze darting around the room, looking everywhere except directly at him. He'd always felt big and awkward around women, and Dani's small stature made him feel even more so.

Was he really that terrifying? He'd been mad as hell last night, and it hadn't seemed to bother her much. Well, who could figure out a woman's thought processes? Not him, that was for damn sure. This arrangement just wasn't going to work.

"Forget it," he said gruffly. "Have the kids meet me in the front yard." Then he turned and marched out the back door.

Dani had a sinking sensation deep in her stomach. Rats. She'd worked like a slave all day, hoping to make a better impression on Sam when he finally came home. Instead, she'd insulted him, had practically called him a child abuser.

But she'd never had anyone shout at her the way he had when he'd ordered them all back into the house. She didn't know much about horses, except that they cost a great deal of money and that cowboys were supposed to be awfully fond of them. After what Hank had said about Sam biting if someone threatened the ranch, she hadn't known what to expect.

Dani looked out the window and winced at the rebellious expression on Colin's face as he scooped manure into the wheelbarrow. Where was Sam? Oh, there he was, crouched beside Kim, showing her how to use a shovel that was taller than she was. The little girl glanced up at him with a shy smile. He smiled back and playfully tousled her hair, and Dani's heart promptly turned over.

Sighing, Dani turned back to the kitchen and put the finishing touches on dinner. The one useful piece of advice her mother had ever given her about men was that feeding their stomachs tended to brighten their moods.

When they'd all gathered around the big table, Hank dug right in, but Sam suspiciously eyed the steaming casserole Dani had prepared. He helped himself to a piece of chicken and a tiny portion of rice, then looked over at the counters as if hoping to see something else.

Dani checked the table and couldn't think of anything she'd forgotten. They had the casserole, the green beans she'd found in the freezer and small dishes of canned peaches from the pantry. Milk and water to drink. What more could the man want?

The already-strained atmosphere in the room rapidly degenerated. Colin's sulky expression was enough to spoil anyone's appetite. Hank tried to start a conversation with Kim, but the little girl retreated behind bashful shrugs and one-word answers until he gave up. Sam pushed the food around on his plate and demonstrated the reason the bartender had called him Silent Sam.

A tidal wave of discouragement crashed down on Dani's head. She and the kids were like aliens dropped onto a strange planet without any lessons on fitting into the local culture. This was never going to work.

The abrupt scraping of Sam's chair across the tile interrupted her thoughts. Without so much as an "Excuse me," he left the room. Bewildered, Dani looked to Hank.

Hank shrugged. "He's just goin' up to his office. Does paperwork most every night."

"But he didn't eat anything. What did I do wrong?"

"Not a darn thing," Hank assured her, scraping the contents of the casserole dish onto his plate. "Sam doesn't like chicken much, but don't worry about it. Becky probably stuffed him to the gills. You might take him a pot of coffee, though. Grandma and Beck always kept a pot goin'."

Dani sighed and went to fill the coffee maker. "I'll be glad to do it, Hank, but I don't think it's going to help much."

"Give it up, Mom," Colin said. "Let's go to Aunt Micky's house."

Hank turned on the boy. "Why in the world would she want to do a fool thing like that? You think she's such a coward she'll turn tail and run at the first sign of trouble? I don't think you know your mom very well. Why, I'll bet you five bucks she'll have Sam eatin' out of her hand inside of two weeks.''

"Mom?" Colin smirked and shook his head. "No way."

It was blatant manipulation on Hank's part. Still, when both children turned and looked at her with speculation in their eyes, Dani knew she couldn't refuse the challenge. She gave Hank a wry smile and braced both palms on the counter.

"You're on."

Chapter Five

Sam walked through the living room, headed for his office in what used to be Hank's bedroom. Something nagged at the back of his mind as he climbed the stairs, however. A feeling that something was...out of place. He turned and looked over the hallway banister to the floor below. Then it hit him.

The room looked the way it used to before Becky had married Pete. A faint odor of lemon polish drifted to his nostrils as his gaze took in the shine on the coffee table and the bookcases. The magazines were neatly stacked. The carpet had been vacuumed. Hank's newspapers and beer cans were gone. So were his smelly socks.

Leaning one hip against the railing, Sam absently scratched his right earlobe. Now that he thought about it, the kitchen had been pretty darn close to spotless, too. No overflowing garbage can. No dirty dishes stacked all over the place. The floor hadn't even felt sticky.

Considering the terrible shape both rooms had been in when he'd left that morning, he realized Dani must have worked her little butt off to accomplish so much in one day. The kitchen alone would have kept him busy for a week.

Turning down the hall, Sam noticed the dust balls had vanished. He poked his head into the main bathroom, and was nearly blinded by the light reflecting off sparkling chrome and porcelain fixtures. Man, would Grandma D love to see this!

Still marveling, he walked into his office. He sat behind the desk, leaned back in his swivel chair and propped his feet beside the stack of ledgers he'd have to get to in a minute. Fingers laced behind his head, he remembered the disheartened expression in Dani's eyes when he'd left the table.

Damn. If she could only cook, she might just turn out to be a great housekeeper. Come to think of it, maybe she *could* cook. How was she supposed to know he hated any kind of casserole and despised rice even more? She'd used those nice place mats. He figured that showed a certain amount of effort to serve a decent meal.

And what had he done to encourage her? Not one blessed thing. In fact, he'd shown her a surly side to his personality that would have surprised most people who knew him. The problem with the kids leaving the gate open wasn't that big of a deal, and it was Hank's fault for not warning them the way he should have.

The truth was, he owed the woman an apology. Apologies never came easy for Sam, but he gave them when they were due because he was a fair man. At least he tried to be. So why did the prospect of telling Dani he was sorry for being rude to her rankle so darn much?

Was it because he still resented Hank's manipulation? Or was he afraid that if he let his guard down for a second, he might actually like her? He never got the chance to figure it out.

A quiet "Ah-hem" brought him out of his reverie. He looked up to find Dani, a loaded tray in her hands, standing in front of his desk. Feeling like an idiot, Sam swung his feet to the floor. She grinned and set the tray beside the ledgers he hadn't opened yet.

His eyes widened and his stomach rumbled when he saw the thick, fried egg sandwich sitting between the salt-and-pepper shakers, the catsup bottle and the thermal coffee carafe. He raised his gaze to meet Dani's, noting with disappointment that she had assumed a more somber, businesslike expression. She lifted the plate onto his desk and poured a mug of coffee with brisk, efficient movements.

"If you'll give me a list of foods you don't like, I'll avoid them in the future, Mr. Dawson. I'd like to talk with you, if you have a moment."

Sam gestured toward a straight-backed chair beside the door. "Pull up a seat, Dan—I mean, uh, Mrs. Smith." He turned and grabbed the empty cup he'd left on the credenza behind his desk the night before, then pushed the mug she'd already filled toward her. "Have some coffee with me?"

Dani nodded in acceptance of his invitation, and he found himself admiring the curve of her trim little backside as she dragged the chair over in front of his desk. Then she plunked herself down and after exhaling a weary sigh took a sip of coffee.

"Please," she said, waving her free hand at the sandwich, "eat that before it gets cold."

"All right." He pulled the plate closer with one hand and reached for the catsup with the other. Hank must have given her a hint or two, because she'd toasted the bread and fried the eggs crisp around the edges, just the way he liked them. "What did you want to talk about?"

She examined her fingernails for a moment, then shrugged and folded her hands in her lap as if the chips in her nail polish didn't bother her a bit. "We've, um, had a rough start, but I don't want the next six months to be miserable for everyone, Mr. Dawson. So, I thought it might help if we set some ground rules."

That sounded like a pretty reasonable idea to Sam. In fact, everything about her seemed more reasonable now than it had the night before. Her sweatshirt was too big for her, and her jeans were on the tight side, but he had to admit they looked damn good on her. Without the elaborate makeup and gaudy earrings, her face had a healthy, natural glow. He still wasn't sure he liked her hair that short, but it framed her face in a pleasant way, and maybe she thought all those curls up on top gave her a little extra height.

"Mr. Dawson?" she prompted, looking at him expectantly.

What was the question? Oh, yeah. Ground rules. "I'm listening, Mrs. Smith."

"I need to know more about what you expect from a housekeeper. For example, is there a particular day you're used to having the laundry done? And how do you want to handle buying groceries? What kind of a budget will I be working with?"

She paused to take a breath. Her earnest expression touched Sam, and he couldn't help smiling at the way words tumbled from her mouth, as if she needed to get them out to make space for more. If she cleaned house as fast as she talked, it was no wonder the place looked so good.

"Another thing I need to know, is whether there are any places in the house or outside that are off-limits to me and my children. We don't want to invade your privacy or create more problems like the one today with the horses. You see, we've never been on a ranch before, and—"

"I understand, Mrs. Smith, and I'm sorry I hollered at you about that. We'll all have to make some adjustments, but I think we can work things out all right."

She gaped at him for a second, as if surprised by his apology. Then her eyes brightened with enthusiasm. A dimple appeared in her right cheek as her mouth curved into a smile that made Sam's heart skitter around in his chest.

"Oh, I do, too, and—"

He raised one hand to cut her off. God only knew when he'd get another word in edgewise if she really got rolling again. "There's one thing I think we should clear up right away."

"What's that, Mr. Dawson?"

"Do we need to be so formal with each other? You called me Sam last night."

Her gaze dropped from his like a hawk shot out of the sky. A blush spread over her cheeks, and she spoke so softly, he had to lean forward to catch what she said. "That was when I thought we were going to be . . . friends. Now that I'm an employee, I didn't want to seem too forward."

The nasty accusations he'd made about this woman in a fit of temper ran through Sam's mind, and he felt heat rush to his own face. Damn, he hated situations like this, when he didn't know what to say and feared whatever came out of his mouth would only make matters worse.

"Dani, I, uh . . . well . . . I feel real bad about what I said last night. I'm not a guy who likes surprises, and it . . . takes me a while to get used to changes."

She nodded, but didn't look up at him. "I can understand that."

God, she looked so small and hurt, sitting there with her shoulders hunched. Made him want to haul her onto his lap and comfort her the way he did Tina when she scraped her knee or banged her head. Then Dani raised her head and pierced him with a fierce, indignant glare. That was all right with Sam. He'd rather face a woman's fury than tears any day.

"I'm not what you said, you know. My husband was the only man I've ever slept with."

"I was just ticked off, Dani, and I was lookin' for an excuse to dislike you. I didn't really mean any of it."

"That's not the way it sounded to me. And for your information, I work hard at being a good mother. We've had some problems—it's not easy raising kids by yourself."

"I understand—"

"I doubt that, Mr. Dawson. I really do." She thumped her index finger on the desk to punctuate each sentence. "When my husband died I had no job, no job experience and only one year of college. I knew I couldn't earn enough to keep up the house payments, so I sold the house and banked his life-insurance money for my kids' education. Since then, I've been working two jobs to pay the rent and keep food on the table."

"You don't have to tell me all of this," Sam muttered, starting to feel desperate.

"Yes I do. Because there's one thing I *do* want you to understand. I didn't come here looking for some man to take care of me. I can do that myself."

"Then what *did* you want?"

"Two things. The most important was a decent role model for Colin. He's had a rough time since he hit puberty, and my dad...well, his answer to everything is to buy Colin whatever he wants."

Her voice softened then, and she sighed, as if her anger had already spent itself in that one rapid outburst. "And I wanted to be able to spend more time with Kim before her hormones start raging."

"Didn't you want anything for yourself, Dani?"

She tipped her head to one side for a moment, then wrinkled her nose at him and gave him a crooked, yet somehow wistful smile. "Yeah, I did," she admitted.

"What?"

"I don't think you really want to know, Sam. It was awfully...romantic."

By golly, she was gonna tease him, Sam thought, noting the hint of amusement creeping into those big blue eyes. And she'd said his name without even seeming to think about it. "Go on. I can take it. What did you want?"

"Companionship. Somebody to hold me in the night when I'm scared or lonely or worried. Someone to share my problems and let me share his."

"That doesn't sound very romantic," Sam said.

"It depends on how you look at it." She chuckled and shook her head at him. "But don't worry, I won't molest you again. From now on, I'll save my hugs for the kids."

"I don't have anything against hugs."

"Hah! You should have seen the terrified look on your face last night, Sam."

"There were too many people around. I'm a private kinda guy."

Dani's voice took on a sympathetic tone, but her eyes still danced with mirth. "I don't suppose you're ever going to live that down."

He shrugged and heaved a long-suffering sigh. "I doubt it. But that's the way it is in a small town."

They shared a chuckle, and a comfortable silence settled over them for a while. Sam finished his sandwich and Dani refilled their coffee cups. Finally she brought the conversation back to business.

"About my job, Sam. I know there's a lot to be done here, but I'd like to take tomorrow morning off and enroll the children in school."

"No problem. You were supposed to have today off. I'll come along and we'll set up a household account at the bank so you can buy groceries and whatever else you need."

By the time he'd answered the rest of her questions, Sam had gained respect for Dani Smith. As far as he could tell, she wasn't the least bit flaky. No, she came across as an intelligent, practical little gal who would whip this house into shape in short order.

She stood and cleared away his empty plate and the condiments. "I'll let you get on with your work, Sam. I'm glad we had this discussion."

"So am I, Dani. It *is* okay if I call you that now, isn't it?"

"Of course, it is," she said with a surprised laugh that told him she wasn't one to hold a grudge.

"Good. Then I have one more thing to say."

"What's that?"

"The house really looks great. I appreciate your diggin' right in like that."

She flushed at his praise. "Thank you, but there's still a lot to do. I didn't even get to the bedrooms today."

"Well, don't kill yourself trying to get it all done at once, okay? We don't expect miracles, so take your time and do whatever you need to do to get your kids settled in. If you need some help, don't be afraid to ask."

"All right, Sam. I won't."

When Dani left the room, Sam stared at the chair she had occupied, a confusing combination of emotions churning inside. Relief that somebody might finally bring order and sanity back into his home life. Amazement that he could talk to Dani as easily as he could to Grandma D or Becky. Gratitude that she'd had the guts and the common sense to come in here, confront him and get the air cleared between them.

If it had been left up to him, well, they wouldn't have talked at all. He'd have avoided her as much as possible and, every time he looked at her, he'd have gone on feeling guilty about the rotten things he'd said. Then he'd have avoided her some more.

He hated talking about feelings and expectations, but she'd made it seem like a simple, straightforward deal. What had she said she wanted?

Companionship. Somebody to hold me in the night when I'm scared or lonely or worried. Someone to share my problems and let me share his.

That didn't strike Sam as an awful lot to ask. Shoot, he wouldn't mind having somebody like that in his life. But most of the women he'd met over the years had wanted more than that from him. It seemed like they were always wanting to get inside a man's head and stomp around at will. Then they wanted pretty words and romantic gestures and dynamite sex.

The sex he could provide. But the rest of it—forget it. He *was* a private kinda guy. He wasn't about to expose his most secret thoughts and emotions as though he were playing a damn parlor game, just to satisfy some woman's curiosity. Not many men and fewer women kept their mouths shut when they ought to, and he had more than his share of things he didn't want blabbed all over creation.

And that was one thing about Dani Smith he knew he'd never really be comfortable with—the woman could talk the ears off a deaf horse. Still, as long as she did her job and kept her manner businesslike, there was no reason they couldn't get along. Maybe they'd even be friends someday.

With that settled in his mind, Sam grabbed a ledger, but paused before opening it when he heard a rhythmic thumping coming down the hallway. A second later, Hank propelled himself into the room on his crutches and lowered himself into the chair opposite the desk without waiting for an invitation.

"What're you doin' up here?" Sam asked, warily noting his brother's broad grin.

"Just gettin' a little exercise."

"Well, get it someplace else. I've got work to do."

Hank reached out with one of his crutches and pushed the door closed. "Dani was up here for quite a while. Have a nice chat with her?"

"It was okay." Sam opened the book and pretended to study a column of figures.

"So?" Hank prodded.

"So what?"

"So, do you still think she's some kind of a wicked woman?"

"I may have misjudged her a little," Sam admitted, turning a page.

"A little?" Hank rolled his eyes in disgust, then laid one forearm across the corner of the desk. "You shoulda seen her today, Sam. Give that woman a mop or a vacuum cleaner, and she's hell on wheels."

"That's her job."

"Well, you shoulda seen her doin' it." Hank winked. "Just now she seemed pretty dang pleased when she came back downstairs."

"That's nice."

Hank drummed his fingers on the desktop for a moment, then reached over and flipped Sam's ledger shut. Sam glared at him. "Whaddaya want, Hank?"

"Whaddaya think? I wanta know what you said and what she said and what you really think of her. I mean, are we gonna have a little romance here, or not?"

"We're not."

"Why? She's a *nice* little gal, Sam. How can you not like her?"

"I like her fine, but I didn't ask for any of this. She's here—and you won't have to eat your own cookin' anymore unless you drive her off, so don't push your luck, okay?"

"Oh, all right," Hank grumbled, climbing to his feet. "But you're makin' a big mistake. Once the other studs around here find out about Dani, she won't stay single long. If you don't get your brand on her before it's too late, we'll be right back where we started."

"For God's sake, Hank, she's not a heifer." Sam opened the book again, banging the cover on the desk. "Now, wouldja let me get some work done?"

Hank fished in his back pocket, then dropped a pile of envelopes onto the open pages and headed for the door.

"What am I supposed to do with these?" Sam asked.

"Read 'em. They're the letters Dani sent me."

Knowing he would never hear the end of this if he gave Hank one iota of encouragement, Sam picked up the envelopes and dumped them into the trash can. "Forget it."

"Jeez, Sam! There's some things in those letters you oughtta know before you make up your mind about Dani."

"I already have. Mind your own damn business and get the hell outta here."

Sam waited until he heard Hank thumping his way down the stairs. Then he inhaled a few calming breaths and turned his attention back to his paperwork. At the rate he was going, he'd still be sitting here at midnight.

He worked steadily for the rest of the evening. Once in a while he could hear Dani or one of the kids talking, but he forced himself to concentrate. By the time he was ready to pack it all in, the house was so quiet, he figured everyone else had gone to bed.

After stretching the kinks out of his shoulders, he pushed back his chair and glimpsed the stack of envelopes lying in the wastebasket. Seeing his own name written in Dani's small, precise handwriting tempted him to grab the stack, but he squared his shoulders and told himself she hadn't really sent those letters to *him*. If she ever wanted him to know any of those things Hank had mentioned, she could tell him herself, right? Right.

He made it as far as the door before his feet refused to budge another step. He looked back over his shoulder, then cursing under his breath, he turned around and rescued the envelopes from the trash. There were only six of them, but their weight told him Dani was just as talkative on paper as she was in person. Lord, she must have really poured her heart out.

Before his curiosity could get the better of him, Sam opened the bottom desk drawer and tossed the letters inside. He wouldn't read them because he wasn't all that interested. Still, you never knew what might come up in the future. It wouldn't hurt to keep those letters for a little while. Just in case.

Dani put away the last of her clothes in the closet, then closed her empty suitcase and shoved it under the bed with the others.

"Jeez, Louise, what a day," she muttered, wiping the back of one hand across her forehead.

Her back and shoulders ached, and she still had to unpack all the miscellaneous junk that had ended up in her tote bag. Oh, and she'd better figure out what to wear in the morning and take off her chipped nail polish. Heaven knew she didn't want to make a bad impression on the kids' new teachers.

She hauled the heavy bag over to the dresser and set her toiletries on the top. A flash of color caught her eye as she started to bend over again. Straightening, she found an old photograph stuck between the mirror and the wooden frame.

Dani pulled it out and studied it with interest. A family, obviously the Dawsons, was grouped in front of a Christmas tree. The parents appeared to be somewhere in their forties. The daughter, who must be Becky, couldn't have been more than fourteen or fifteen. Dani chuckled when she noticed Hank's cocky grin, shaggy hair and black leather jacket. But Sam was the one who captured her attention.

She guessed he would have been nineteen or twenty when the picture was taken. He was smiling like everyone else, but there was a hint of sadness in his eyes and he held himself a little apart from the others, as if he wasn't quite sure he really belonged. His extremely short hair and rigid posture made Dani wonder if he'd been in the military.

If she held the picture one way, he looked virile and handsome and confident. But if she tipped it a little more toward the light, there was something painfully young and vulnerable about his expression that stirred an answering ache in Dani's chest.

She glanced from Sam to Hank and back to Sam again. Both had matured into extremely good-looking men. It was funny. From what little she'd seen of the Dawson brothers, Hank was more charming, more congenial and definitely more happy to have her and the kids around than Sam was.

Dani liked Hank and had enjoyed his company today, but she could honestly say with absolute certainty, that she would never fall in love with him. Her husband, Ray, had had that same kind of devil-may-care charm. He'd dazzled her with it, and swept her off her feet at the ripe old age of nineteen. The last thing either of them had thought about was birth control.

There had been good times during her almost fourteen-year marriage, lots of them. She certainly didn't regret those years with Ray, and she would always love him for the children he had given her. But given a choice, she wouldn't marry him again. The fun and excitement he'd brought to her life would never make up for the constant burden of stifling her own impulsiveness because somebody had to be the practical one, the responsible one, the strong partner in the relationship.

As she'd told Sam, Dani wasn't looking for a man to take care of her. She didn't want to be dominated or to dominate anyone else. But it would be so nice to be able to lean on someone, just once in a while. A woman couldn't lean on men like Ray and Hank. They were good at heart, but they needed more excitement and stimulation than the daily grind of family living could ever hope to provide.

Change a few details in the stories Hank had told her today about his travels on the rodeo circuit, and she could have been hearing about Ray's passion for stock-car racing. No, she would never fall in love with another man like Ray.

However, Sam... Well, Sam might be a different story. There was no question about which man was in charge of the Circle D. She couldn't count the times she'd asked Hank a question today, and his response had always been "You'll have to ask Sam about that" or "Sam takes care of that. Better check with him."

Now that she'd actually seen the nice guy Hank and the bartender had told her about, she found herself feeling as attracted to him as she had been when she'd first seen his photograph in *Cupid's Arrow*. Unfortunately, although they had parted on friendly terms, Dani knew Sam would expect her to prove herself time and again before completely accepting her.

He'd apologized for what he'd said the night before, and she appreciated that. But her feminine pride still smarted every time she remembered his scathing description of her. The thought of making Sam like her and find her attractive presented a challenge that was hard to resist.

Chapter Six

At 7:25 the next morning, Dani herded two extremely reluctant children out the door and into the back seat of Sam's burgundy-colored Lincoln Continental. He shot a wry grin over his shoulder at Colin and Kim, then executed a U-turn and drove off toward town.

Attempting to calm her own jangled nerves, Dani mouthed a silent "Whew," smoothed the slim skirt of her favorite navy-blue suit over her knees and gazed at the scenery she hadn't been able to see on Saturday night.

The sun was just starting to peek over the tops of the Wind River Mountains to the east. A thick coating of frost glistened on the sparse brown grass and clumps of sagebrush beside the gravel road. The car climbed to the crest of a hill, revealing a deep, broad valley, ranch houses, barns and haystacks. Curving lines of trees marked the paths of creeks. Another mountain range jutted up out of the earth and touched the sky to the west.

"Hey, Mom, look," Kim called from the back seat. "Antelope!"

"Big deal," Colin muttered.

"They're a big deal to me," Kim said defensively. "We didn't have them in Chicago."

"Shut up, you little geek," Colin replied.

"That's enough," Dani said. "Colin, I know you're scared, but don't take it out on your sister."

"I'm not scared."

"You're not?" Sam shook his head as if in amazement. "New school. New teachers. New kids. That'd be enough to scare the whey outta me."

"Oh yeah?" Colin asked.

"You bet," Sam answered. "Of course, I'd do my best not to let it show."

"That's for sure," Colin agreed fervently. "Everybody would think you're a wimp. What are the kids like around here?"

Sam shrugged. "Like kids everywhere else, I guess. But we don't get a lot of new kids, so you're liable to make quite a splash, especially since you're from a big city. Play your cards right, and you'll fit right in."

"How do I do that?"

"Just be yourself. Don't feel like you have to impress everybody right off the bat. And you might keep in mind that most folks around here are pretty proud of their hometown and their school."

"You mean, don't make any rotten remarks about hick towns?"

"Might be a good idea."

Colin fell silent then. Dani smiled at Sam with heartfelt gratitude. She had spent most of the night tangling with her covers, worrying over how the kids would cope with their first day of school in Pinedale.

She'd been especially concerned about Colin's attitude, fearing he would alienate his new teachers and classmates in the first five minutes. She'd tried to talk to him about it last night, but as usual, her son hadn't been interested in anything she'd tried to tell him.

The rest of the trip into town passed quickly. At the middle school, Sam waited in the car with Kim while Dani took Colin inside to register. Mrs. Johnson, an attractive gray-haired woman, greeted them at the main office and gave Dani a stack of forms to fill out.

The noise level increased dramatically when the other students began filtering into the building. Four girls trooped into the office to speak to Mrs. Johnson. They all shot curious glances toward Colin, then huddled together at the opposite end of the counter, whispering and giggling.

A dull red color flooded Colin's face. He shifted his weight from one foot to the other and fiddled with his earring. The giggling and whispering continued. As the secretary explained the school's routine, he nodded in the appropriate places, but the distant expression in his eyes made it doubtful he would remember a thing the woman said to him. He nudged Dani with his elbow and gave her a desperate look that clearly said "Would you *please* hurry up?"

By the time she finished the last form, Colin looked as if he were ready to bolt for freedom. Dani tried to give him a reassuring smile along with his lunch money. He glared at her in return and muttered, "I'll never forgive you for this," before Mrs. Johnson escorted him out of the office to find his locker.

Dani gulped as he disappeared down a long hallway, then hurried outside before the tears stinging the backs of her eyes could fall. Colin would be all right, she told herself. Kids changed schools every day and survived.

Approaching the car, she saw Kim leaning forward with her elbows propped on top of the front seat, deep in conversation with Sam. *Oh God,* Dani thought as she reached for the passenger door latch, *Kim's probably more scared than Colin.*

Her eyes wide with fright, the little girl violently shook her head and wailed, "What if I get a mean teacher?"

"Aw, we don't have any mean teachers around here, honey," Sam said. "No siree, to get hired in this town, a teacher's gotta be pretty darn nice."

"Really?"

"You bet."

"What if the other kids don't like me?" Kim demanded.

Both of Sam's eyebrows shot up, almost to the brim of his Stetson. "You? Why, I don't see anything not to like about you, Kimmy. Before the day's over, all the boys'll have a crush on you, and the girls'll be fightin' about who gets to be your best friend."

Kim giggled at that remark and finally noticed her mother sitting in the front seat. Anxiety invaded her smile and her voice. "Hi, Mom."

"Hi yourself," Dani answered. "Are you ready to go?"

The little girl heaved a heartrending sigh. "I guess so."

Sam started the engine and drove them to the elementary school. To Dani's surprise, Kim asked Sam to come inside with them. He agreed, and talked to the little girl in a low, reassuring tone while Dani filled out another set of forms. Though still apprehensive, Kim marched into her classroom without the tears or clinging that Dani had expected.

When they returned to Sam's Continental, Dani turned to him. "Thank you for helping Kim."

Looking straight ahead, he started the engine with a quick, angry twist of his wrist. "Forget it."

Intending to argue the point, Dani leaned toward him and opened her mouth, but the dark scowl he shot in her direction changed her mind.

"Let's get some coffee while we wait for the bank to open," he said.

Confused and miffed by his suddenly gruff tone, Dani settled back against the seat and crossed her arms over her midriff. What in the world was bugging him? Jeez, Louise, it wasn't even nine o'clock yet, and she'd already been through an emotional wringer.

She hadn't asked him to come with her and she didn't need any more to cope with from him, either, she thought resentfully, gazing at the main street without really seeing it.

"You want coffee or not?" he demanded.

"Fine. Whatever you say... *boss*."

Silently fuming, Sam drove to the grocery store, though he'd have really rather gone back to the elementary school and given Esther Bingham what for. The old biddy had been downright rude to Dani, shooting all those sly glances at her, as though she were no better than a tramp. Dani hadn't seemed to notice, thank God. Maybe being from a city and all, she was used to dealing with rotten manners.

He'd thought and said some pretty awful things about her on Saturday night, but he'd been madder than a sow grizzly with a cub to protect, and... well, Dani just didn't deserve that kind of treatment. Especially when she'd gone to so much trouble to look nice this morning. Why, that suit she had on was conservative enough for a church service. So where the hell did Esther Bingham get off?

Stopping in front of the store, Sam slammed the gearshift into Park, climbed out of the car and headed for the entrance. Since his legs were about three times longer than Dani's and she was wearing high heels, he had to wait for her to catch up. The strained, mutinous expression on her face made him realize he'd been acting like a jackass.

He sighed and gestured for her to precede him through the automatic door, wincing inwardly when she sailed past him like an indignant princess with her nose in the air. Oh, brother. He'd really ruffled her feathers. Well, maybe a cup of coffee and a doughnut would sweeten both of their dispositions.

Inside, the aroma of freshly baked bread surrounded them. Sam sniffed appreciatively, giving Dani a moment to look around before escorting her to the bakery section. The lively chatter at the tables grouped in front of the L-shaped display case halted as if someone had switched off an electrical current.

Sam cursed himself for forgetting what a hotbed of gossip this place usually was, then trudged after Dani. Oblivious to all the attention they were receiving, she oohed and ahhed over the assortment of sweet rolls behind the glass until he wanted to choke her. To make matters worse, Betty Collins came out of the kitchen to wait on them, her voice booming loud enough to reach the courthouse two blocks away.

"Hi there, Sam. Who's your friend?" she asked, wiping her hands on the white apron tied around her broad girth.

Deliberately pitching his voice in a quiet tone, Sam grudgingly introduced the two women. Of course Betty didn't take the hint.

"Glad to meet you," she bellowed, pumping Dani's hand across the counter as if she expected to strike oil if she repeated the motion enough times. "I might as well admit I've already heard a lot about you," she added, placing their selections on paper plates.

"Oh, dear," Dani replied with a self-conscious grin. "I guess people really do talk in a small town."

Betty let out a shout of laughter that practically ruptured Sam's eardrums. "Yeah, you'd better believe that. But don't worry about it. Far as I can tell, most folks are on your side. They're betting two to one you'll get ol' Silent Sam to the altar before Christmas."

Ignoring Sam's muttered expletive, Betty leaned closer and raised one hand to the side of her mouth, as if preparing to make a confidential statement. Of course, everybody in the whole damn store heard every word. "That is, if he doesn't wind up in prison for wringing Hank's neck."

Dani glanced up at Sam as if seeking guidance, but he had none to give her. "Yes, well ... um, I don't think he'll do that," she said.

"Well, there's *not* gonna be any wedding," Sam informed busybody Betty and the rest of the regulars, smacking a five-dollar bill beside the cash register. "Dani's gonna be our housekeeper and that's *all* there is to it."

Counting out his change, Betty scolded him goodnaturedly. "Aw, stop lookin' like you sucked on a sour pickle. The talk'll blow over in a few days and you finally got another housekeeper. Seems to me like you came out ahead on this deal."

"Yeah, right. Come on, Dani."

Without waiting to see if she followed him, Sam stomped to the only empty table, turning away amused glances with a glare hot enough to melt lead. Dani joined him a moment later, and for once didn't say a word. She sipped her coffee and studied the other customers as if she weren't the least bit uncomfortable.

While Sam envied and admired her composure, it irritated him, too. Well, he'd warned her about ruining her reputation by living with two bachelors. If she wasn't going to worry about it, why should he?

A slight movement in his peripheral vision caught Sam's attention. He turned to see Andy Johnson, the sheriff of Sublette County, and Hal Baker, the county attorney, smiling and nodding at Dani. Of course the idiot woman had to go and smile and nod in return.

"Would you knock it off?" he whispered at her.

"Knock *what* off?" she whispered back.

"That damn flirting."

"That wasn't flirting."

"Some of these guys don't need a helluva lot of encouragement."

Dani's eyebrows drew together in a perplexed frown, but as if to prove his point, the two men dragged their chairs over and joined them. Determined not to let these jokers rile him again, Sam doggedly bit into his doughnut and let them handle their own introductions. The get-acquainted chitchat flowed with surprising ease, not that there would ever be any lags in a conversation with a talker like Dani.

Andy and Hal puffed up like a couple of strutting peacocks beneath the warmth of her friendly smile. Watching them fall all over themselves trying to impress her, Sam almost snorted in disgust. The only thing that stopped him was the knowledge that, given half the chance, he'd probably act the same stupid way.

He wanted to see her as a conniving bitch like Hank's ex-wife, Christine, but he knew he was only fooling himself. Dani Smith had about as much guile as a cocker spaniel puppy. No, there wasn't anything premeditated in the way she turned those big blue eyes on a man and listened as if every word he said were worth listening to. But she sure packed a helluva wallop just the same.

When he couldn't stand it another second, Sam shoved back his chair and stood. "Hate to break this up," he lied, "but we've gotta get going."

"Yeah, guess you're right," the red-haired sheriff agreed with obvious reluctance.

"It was a pleasure meeting you, Dani," Hal said, shaking her hand a whole lot longer than Sam thought necessary.

Sam cut him off with a brusque "See you around, fellas," then hustled Dani outside to the car.

"Is there some reason you don't like those guys?" she asked on the way to the bank.

"Nope. They're both friends of mine."

"I see," she answered, though the doubtful look she shot him indicated she didn't see anything at all.

Sam didn't try to explain his behavior because he didn't understand it himself. Andy and Hal weren't just friends, they were *good* friends. When some ruthless neighbors, who ran a corporate ranch known as the Executive Cattle Company, had tried to force the Dawsons off the Circle D last year, both men had responded above and beyond the call of their respective duties.

Andy had discovered the ECC's link to organized crime and had accompanied federal drug agents on a raid at considerable risk to his own hide. Hal Baker had helped to prosecute the criminals, and had given the Dawsons more free legal advice about filing a civil suit against the ECC for monetary damages than the American Bar Association would approve.

In spite of all that, Sam still felt irritated as hell that two of Pinedale's most popular bachelors had zeroed in on Dani so damn fast. Arriving at the bank, Sam stepped out of the car with a disgruntled sigh and braced himself for the next round of curious stares.

By the time they'd finished setting up Dani's household account and stopped at Frannie's Fine Fabrics so she could make Colin a new shirt, Sam felt about as conspicuous as a five-legged heifer at the county fair. Honest to God, if he had to listen to one more damn comment about Saturday night and his relationship with Dani, he'd... Unable to finish that thought with any degree of satisfaction, he turned the car toward home and raced out of town as if there were no such thing as a speed limit.

As the space between houses lengthened and the miles ticked off on the odometer, however, his tension gradually drained away. He suddenly realized Dani hadn't said a word since they'd left Pinedale. He glanced over at her, and felt his heart plummet to the toes of his boots.

She was staring straight ahead, her posture so rigid, she looked as if she might shatter with a single touch. Her eyes were dry, but he could see a fine trembling in her stubborn little chin, and he suspected she wasn't far from tears. Worst of all, she was huddled against the door as if she was afraid he might lash out at her.

"Are you all right, Dani?" he asked quietly.

"I'm fine."

"You don't look fine."

"Well, I am."

"Well, good. I'm glad you're fine," Sam answered, wondering if he should say something else or shut his mouth. "Kinda rough in town today, wasn't it? I, uh, hope you weren't too embarrassed by all those remarks. People can be kind of blunt around here."

"Everyone was just trying to be friendly," she retorted, shooting him a frosty glance. "What embarrassed me was your behavior."

"What did *I* do?" he demanded.

"You acted like we had some big guilty secret, Sam. Like you were ashamed to be seen with me."

"Ashamed to... I did not!"

"Yes you did."

"Well, I didn't *feel* that way."

"Oh, right. Tell me another one."

"For God's sake, Dani, I didn't enjoy hearing over and over again about how I acted like a jerk Saturday night."

"So you thought acting like a jerk today would improve matters?"

"Forget it, okay? Just forget I said anything."

"Don't worry. I will."

Sam cursed under his breath and shook his head. In the future, he'd have to remember that whenever Dani Smith looked defenseless, she was liable to come out swinging. After ten solid minutes of excruciating silence, he dropped her off at the rear of the house.

She slammed her door hard enough to rattle his back teeth. When he drove away to put the car in the garage, his ears were still ringing. He switched off the engine, but sat behind the steering wheel for several minutes, willing his blood pressure to drop back to normal.

He hadn't been this upset since the day one of the ECC's hired thugs had burned down the barn. And all because of some feisty little she-cat, who...

Tossing his hat onto the passenger seat and raking both hands through his hair, he muttered, "Oh, hell and damnation."

The truth was, Dani was right about the way he'd acted this morning. The truth was, he wanted her to like him. In fact, the truth was, he'd been jealous, just plain old, green-eyed jealous of the way she'd smiled and talked so easily with everyone in town. Everyone but him.

If he was really in the mood to be honest with himself, he might as well admit that it had stroked his ego some to have folks thinking a pretty little gal like Dani might be interested in him. And maybe, somewhere in the back of his mind, he'd kinda started hoping that someday they would get together. Maybe as more than friends. All right, as lovers.

Was that why it had bothered him so much to see her with Andy and Hal? Probably. Hank had been right about one thing. It wouldn't be long before every damn stud in the county would find an excuse to come out to the Circle D and sniff a little flank.

Sam climbed out of the car and banged the garage door shut, then told himself it wasn't any of his business if other men started courting Dani. As usual, he'd already blown any chance he might have had with her.

From now on, she was nothing more to him than a housekeeper. Still, he felt responsible for her, maybe even more responsible than he did for all the other ranch employees, because she was out of her element here. It wouldn't hurt to keep an eye on her and make sure she didn't get mixed up with the wrong kind of a guy.

Unfortunately, at the moment, every other man he knew, including his own brother and two of his best friends, suddenly seemed like the wrong kind of a guy.

Later that afternoon, Dani finally managed to put thoughts of Sam out of her mind. She had a pot of stew simmering on the stove for dinner, a cake in the oven and the washer and dryer chugging away downstairs. With everything under control for the moment, she set up her sewing machine on the kitchen table and started putting Colin's new shirt together.

Since Hank had gone out with Sam in the pickup, she turned on the radio for company. Though she'd never listened to country music much, before long she was wailing away with Hank Williams, Jr. and the Judds, and enjoying herself immensely.

In the middle of belting out the chorus of a raucous song about a man who had "friends in low places" she looked up to find two women standing by the back door, studying her with blatant curiosity and more than a little amusement. Her face flaming, Dani shut her mouth and snapped off the radio, then jumped to her feet.

The younger woman, who appeared to be about Dani's age, stood close to six feet tall and was obviously pregnant, chuckled and walked farther into the room. "Hi. Sorry we startled you. We knocked, but I guess you didn't hear us. I'm Becky Sinclair. Sam and Hank's sister."

Still too mortified to speak, Dani forced a stiff smile in return.

"Somethin' smells mighty good in here," the much shorter, elderly woman said. Her eyes keen behind big red glasses, she glanced around the room, then gave a quick, decisive nod of her head and approached Dani with one hand outstretched. "I'm Amelia Dawson, the boys' grandma. Everybody calls me Grandma D. You might as well, too."

Dani shook hands and introduced herself, trying not to stare at the fluorescent orange sweatshirt and pants Amelia wore under a bright purple ski jacket. The old woman looked her up and down without any attempt at subtlety. Knowing she probably didn't look like much of a housekeeper, Dani tugged at the hem of her favorite old sweater and wiped her damp palms on the seat of her spandex pants.

"Love your high-tops," Amelia said cheerfully, lowering herself onto one of the kitchen chairs. "They comfortable?"

"Oh, uh, yes," Dani answered, tearing her startled gaze from Amelia's hot pink Nikes to watch Becky approach the table.

Finally collecting her wits, Dani started to offer her guests coffee or tea, but at that moment, the dryer buzzed downstairs and the stove's timer dinged.

Becky laughed and reversed directions. "Go ahead and get the dryer. I'll check the oven for you."

Dani hesitated, then shrugged and hurried down the stairs. By the time she got back, her cake was cooling on a rack and both women sat at the table with coffee mugs in front of them. Amelia held the back section of Colin's shirt up to the light, studying the construction.

"My, but you do fine work, Dani," she said. "These seams are straight as a yardstick."

"Thank you," Dani replied. "That's, um, for my son. He just started school in Pinedale today, and when I saw how many of the other boys were wearing Western shirts, I thought he might need one." Jeez, she knew she was babbling out of nervousness, but she didn't know how to stop herself. "It's important for him to fit in, so—"

"Dani," Becky broke in with a tentative smile, "we're really glad you're here. We just came over to get acquainted and see if you need anything."

"You are? I mean, you did?"

"Land sakes, yes," Amelia said. "But I gotta admit, I feel bad about it." At Dani's quizzical look, she quickly explained how she'd given Hank a copy of *Cupid's Arrow*.

Dani showed them her copy of the magazine, and they all shared a good laugh over Hank's ad. Then Dani explained her reasons for coming to the Circle D. Becky and Amelia automatically reached for more pieces of the shirt and pinned them together, insisting that Dani continue with her work while they visited.

The room took on a cozy atmosphere of acceptance and shared confidences. When Amelia asked how Dani was really getting along with "the boys," she answered honestly.

"Oh, Hank's been very nice. I think he still feels a little guilty."

Becky nodded. "And he should, that stinker. What about Sam?"

Dani sighed, then raised one hand and wobbled it back and forth. "He's more difficult to understand. He was wonderful with the kids this morning, but after we left them, he was awfully tense and irritable."

"More just like plain awful, you mean," Becky said, guessing.

"Now that you mention it . . . yes," Dani replied.

"That doesn't surprise me," Amelia said. "He gets pretty uptight whenever he's around a bunch of people. He'll do just about anything to avoid going to town. And knowing he was gonna get ribbed wouldn't have helped him much, either."

"But why?" Dani asked. "Everyone seems to like him."

"They do," Becky told her. "Oh, they tease him and call him Silent Sam, but whenever somebody's got big trouble, he's the one they come looking for."

"He impressed a lot of folks when his dad died," Amelia added. "He wasn't much more than a kid, but he dug right in and took over the ranch, supported his mother, helped Hank with his rodeo career and practically raised Becky through her teens. There aren't many young men who'll take on that kind of responsibility."

"Is that why he's never married?" Dani asked. "Because he had too many other responsibilities?"

"Partly, I think," Becky answered, her eyes narrowed thoughtfully. "But if I remember right, it seems like after he got back from the service, he kinda lost interest in dating. He didn't even mess around much in college that I know of. Got through in three years and came right home."

Amelia sadly shook her head. "I've always thought that year in Vietnam did somethin' to him, but he would never talk about it. Not to me, anyway."

She tipped her head to one side and studied Dani with a speculative gleam in her eyes. "And it's too bad. The way that boy loves kids, he'd make a wonderful father. Probably be a damn good husband, too, if a woman knew how to make him happy."

"I don't suppose you'd have any suggestions," Dani said in a dry tone.

"Oh, it wouldn't take much." Amelia leaned forward and gave Dani a conspiratorial wink. "You know, Hank's a slob at heart, but Sam likes things orderly, so he can find what he wants without havin' to spend a lot of time lookin'. Other than that, all you'd have to do is wash and iron his clothes, feed him right and give him *lots* of lovin'."

"Behave yourself, Grandma," Becky scolded. Then, grinning at Dani, she said confidentially, "Watch out for this old bat. She has no shame when it comes to sex."

One eyebrow raised, Amelia stared pointedly at Becky's protruding belly. "Look who's talkin'."

Dani chuckled at the old lady's deadpan expression. "That reminds me, what does Sam like to eat? He hardly touched my casserole last night."

Becky and Amelia exchanged amused glances before answering in unison. "Meat and potatoes, and lots of 'em."

"That's all? Hasn't he ever heard of cholesterol?"

"Don't mention that word to a cattleman," Becky said, rolling her eyes. "My husband's a doctor, and it drives him nuts to see how much beef Sam and Hank put away."

"How much is lots?" Dani asked.

"I always figured both of the boys eat about three times more than a normal person would," Amelia replied. "You're on the right track with the baking. Sam's got a terrible sweet tooth."

Dani shot a worried glance toward the stove. "I'd better add some more potatoes."

"Sit still, Dani," Amelia said, scooting back her chair. "We'll do it for ya."

Becky joined her grandmother and dug a huge kettle out of the cupboards. For the next twenty minutes, the two women continued chatting while they transferred Dani's stew to the kettle and prepared more meat and vegetables to fill it to the brim. Then they left, admonishing Dani to "Keep in touch and holler if you need any help."

Dani waved them off from the back door, and couldn't help thinking they would make awfully nice in-laws. It was too bad Sam was such a... toad.

Chapter Seven

Dinner that night was a quiet affair at first. Sam and Hank dug into their bowls of stew as if they hadn't eaten for weeks. Dani found herself jumping up to bring them refills at amazingly brief intervals and silently thanking Becky and Amelia for their advice about quantities.

The men's hearty appetites gave Dani a sense of accomplishment, even though her children picked at their food with as much enthusiasm as if she had served them liver and pickled beets. Colin ate a bite, scowled at his mother, then ate another bite. Kim listlessly stirred the contents of her bowl as though she didn't have enough energy to raise the spoon to her mouth.

Dani wasn't sure which child worried her more, and couldn't force anything past the guilt-laden lump in her throat. Had she been unfair in uprooting the kids and taking them so far away from everything they'd ever known? Their exciting new lives weren't exactly working out the way she had envisioned.

Of course, their old lives hadn't been all that terrific, either. She'd felt she had to try *something*. But was this the *right* something? At that moment, Hank broke into her troubled thoughts.

"So, guys," he said, smiling at the children, "how was your first day of school?"

Kim shrugged, but didn't look up. Shooting another glare at his mother, Colin was less reticent.

"It was dumb," he said bluntly. "Even dumber than my old school."

Hank leaned back in his chair, his mouth quirking at one corner. "Now that surprises me. The elementary school won some kind of a presidential award last year, and the middle school's been nominated for one this year."

"Who cares?" Colin sneered. "It's still dumb."

"No pretty girls?" Hank asked.

"A few."

"Gonna go out for basketball? Tall as you are, I'll bet the coach would be glad to have you."

"I'm not very good at sports," Colin mumbled.

Hank gestured toward Sam with his thumb. "This ol' boy here was the center on a championship team. He might give you a few pointers. Whaddaya think, Sam?"

"If Colin wants to," Sam said.

"I might," the boy said cautiously.

Dani slipped out of her chair and collected the dirty dishes, listening intently while she served the dessert.

"Ya know, Colin," Hank drawled, winking at Dani as she set a generous slice of cake in front of him, "it's pretty normal to feel outta place for a while when you move to a new town. Did anything in particular happen today that upset you?"

Colin shook his head. "Not really. There was a lot of talk about cattle and stuff, and I didn't understand any of it. And some of the kids had driver's licenses already, and they thought I was pretty dorky when I admitted I've never driven a car."

"Nobody would give a fourteen-year-old kid a driver's license," Dani said.

"Colin's right, Dani," Sam said. "They can't drive anywhere they want because it's only a provisional license, but it sure helps kids who live way out on a ranch get to school or to the bus stop."

Hank nodded in agreement. "A lot of kids around here start driving tractors and pickups when they're ten."

Colin bolted upright in his chair. "Could I get a license? Then you wouldn't have to drive us to the bus stop all the time, Mom?"

"I don't mind driving you," Dani said.

"I'd be glad to teach him to drive," Sam offered.

"Man, that'd be totally cool," Colin crowed. "Can I, Mom? Please?"

Dani gave Sam an are-you-out-of-your-mind? look. "Oh, honey, I don't know. You're still awfully young."

His eyes flashing with anger, the boy jumped to his feet and slammed both palms on the table. "Aw, Mom! Stop treating me like a baby. Why can't you ever—"

"Hold on there a minute, Colin," Sam interrupted. "There're a few conditions attached to that offer. Your mom's worried about your safety, and I don't blame her. You'll have to prove you're responsible enough to handle a vehicle before I'll let you get anywhere near one."

"Oh, right," Colin muttered, subsiding onto his chair. "How can I do that?"

"It's not all that hard," Sam said. "Keep your nose clean at school. Obey the rules here at the ranch. Do your chores without being told."

"Chores?" Colin yelped. "Nobody said anything about chores."

"Everybody's got chores on a ranch. I just haven't gotten around to figurin' out what yours are gonna be yet. Wouldn't you like to earn a little pocket money?"

Colin's face brightened at that question. "You mean you'd pay me?"

"Last I heard, they outlawed slavery over a hundred years ago," Hank said.

Sam shot his brother an amused glance, then looked back at Colin. "How does two dollars an hour sound for starters?"

"What would I have to do?"

"I'd probably start you out milkin' Gertie and helpin' me feed the stock. There's all kinds of things you could learn if you wanted to. Do a good enough job, and I'll raise you to minimum wage. Interested?"

"Yeah," Colin answered, an eager grin erasing the sullen expression that never failed to raise Dani's blood pressure. "Yeah, I'm interested."

"What will my chores be?" Kim asked.

Sam smiled and reached a long arm across the table to ruffle her bangs. "You can help me with the chickens until Tina comes home."

"Who's Tina?"

"My daughter," Hank told the little girl. "She's stayin' at my sister's house for a while. She's a couple of years younger than you, but I'll bet you two will be good buddies before long."

"Won't she get mad if I do her job?" Kim said.

"I doubt it," Hank replied with a chuckle. "One thing about a ranch, there's always plenty of work for everybody."

Sam pushed back his chair. "Speaking of work, I'd better head upstairs and get going on the books."

"Why don't you use that computer Pete and Becky bought you?" Hank asked. "It's supposed to save you all kinds of time and drudgery."

"You've got a PC?" Colin asked, excitement making his voice crack.

"Yeah," Hank answered, rolling his eyes at the ceiling. "But it's still in the box, 'cause Sam's afraid he can't figure out how to work it."

"I'll help you set it up," Colin offered with no attempt to hide his enthusiasm. "I know a lot about computers. And Mom used one all the time at work."

Sam looked at Dani, his eyebrows raised in query. She nodded in reply. "I kept books for a trucking company. Colin learned how to use one at school."

"Come on, Sam, let's go," Colin urged, practically dancing from one foot to the other. "It'll be easy."

"How much homework have you got?" Sam asked.

"I don't have any."

Pursing his mouth, Sam studied the boy for a long moment. "Who'd you get for teachers?"

Colin's face turned red, and he muttered a few names.

"Uh-huh," Sam replied.

"Okay, so I've got some math and English," the boy admitted with a sheepish grin. "But I can finish in an hour."

"All right, but school comes first in this house," Sam told him. "I'll check your papers before we open that box."

"Yeees!" Colin shouted, punching one fist into the air. Then he ran from the kitchen, and a second later his footsteps thumped up the stairs.

Dani stared after him for a moment, then turned to the men and asked in astonishment, "Who *was* that kid?"

Hank laughed. "That was a teenager."

"I don't have any homework," Kim said, hesitantly smiling at Sam. "Can I come watch you set up the computer?"

"Of course you can. I'll holler when we're ready to get started," Sam answered, before heading out of the room.

He paused at the doorway and looked back over his shoulder. "Great supper, Dani. Thanks."

Still unable to comprehend the abrupt, but welcome change in her son's attitude, Dani sat at the table, slowly shaking her head until Hank asked for another piece of cake. She hurried to the counter with a new spring in her step and a surge of hope blossoming in her heart. Then she remembered the implied bargain she and Sam had made with Colin, and shuddered at the mental image of him sitting behind the wheel of a car.

"Why so glum?" Hank asked. "I thought you'd be tickled to see the kid so happy."

"I am. I'm just not sure he's ready to drive."

"Aw, don't worry about it," Hank said. "Sam's had experience at keeping a tight rein on boys like Colin."

"How did he get it?" Dani asked.

"We have a lot of 'em working for us during the summer. And since my dad and I didn't get along too well, Sam kinda stepped in and rode herd on me."

"That must have been quite a challenge," Dani said dryly.

Hank grinned, as if at a fond memory. "That's for sure. Wild as I was, I mighta ended up in jail. When it comes to teenagers, Sam knows what he's doing. He'll lay out an incentive, something a kid wants real bad, like Colin learning to drive. Then he'll make the kid work his butt off to get it and enjoy doin' it in the meantime."

"But how does he do that?" Dani asked. "No matter what I try with Colin, he seems to resent me more every day."

"That's because you're his mom, Dani. Boys that age are tryin' to break away from their moms, but they crave approval from an older man. Sam's a demanding boss, but he's fair and consistent, and real good about dishing out praise along with the work."

"He won't give Colin any dangerous jobs, though, will he?"

"Not until the kid's ready to handle them," Hank assured her. "Our dad died in an accident, so Sam's a real stickler for safety."

"Then why is your leg hurt?" Kim asked.

"That wasn't Sam's fault. A guy took a shot at me and hit my horse instead. My leg got busted when he fell," he said in a matter-of-fact tone. Patting his stomach as if it was pleasantly full, Hank grinned at the little girl. "Wanna come help me do my exercises while you're waiting for Sam?"

"Okay."

When the two of them walked into the living room where the weight-lifting equipment was stored in the far corner, Dani cleaned up the kitchen, then went back to work on Colin's new shirt. Her hands moved automatically, stitching and pressing, but her mind focused on Sam. Earlier today, she'd been ready to kill him, and neither of them had tried to apologize after their argument.

After learning more about him from his family and watching him deal with her kids, however, she couldn't help seeing him in a more favorable light. Bracing one elbow on the table, she rested her chin on her palm and closed her eyes.

A picture of him, smiling and relaxed, formed in her mind. Her lips curved in response. Then the picture shifted focus, and she saw him gazing at her intently, as if he might be considering what it would be like to kiss her. Her stomach did a funny little flip-flop and her pulse rate zoomed for a moment.

Sighing, Dani sat back in her chair, her emotions more unsettled than she wanted to admit. Despite the conflicts she'd had with him, she *was* attracted to Sam Dawson. During the weeks between seeing his ad and coming to Wyoming, she'd daydreamed about him constantly.

It had been easy to envision herself falling head over heels in love with him. The impulsive part of her still wanted to do just that. But the voice of her conscience urged caution.

Would she be falling in love with Sam himself? Or with the security and stability he represented?

A deep, permanent relationship with him would certainly benefit her children. But she'd married one man to provide a home and father for her son, and it hadn't been fair to either her or Ray.

And what about Sam? Could he ever love someone like her? Or would he be settling for a permanent housekeeper and a chance to have children of his own?

"This is ridiculous," Dani muttered. "What makes you think the man might be interested? He's never even looked at you like he wanted to kiss you, much less marry you."

Ignoring a dash of disappointment at that thought, she forced her attention back to Colin's shirt. She finished it at nine o'clock, then carried it upstairs. A deep, booming laugh came out of Sam's office as she approached.

Dani paused in the doorway, and felt her stomach do another one of those funny little flip-flops. Sam sat in the chair behind a computer table with Kim on his lap, his arms reaching around her to work the keyboard. One hand braced on the back of the chair, Colin leaned over Sam's right shoulder, and pointed out something on the monitor.

"Now hit the Enter key again," he ordered.

Sam searched the keyboard with the seriousness of a first-year typing student, then poked the appropriate key with his index finger. His eyes widened when he saw the result.

"If that doesn't beat all," he said, a delighted smile breaking across his face that matched Colin's for boyish appeal. "You're a genius, kid."

Colin straightened, his chest puffing out with pride. "Hey, it's nothing. You should see the awesome stuff Mom can do."

"Thank you, Colin," Dani said walking into the room.

The three of them looked up in surprise at her entrance.

"Hey, Mom, come see Sam's system. It's totally excellent. He's got a mouse and a modem, and he said I can use it whenever I want."

"That's great, honey," Dani replied. She held out the hanger holding his shirt. "Can you tear yourself away long enough to try this on for me?"

"You finished it already?" Sam asked, clearly impressed.

Dani smiled at him and shrugged. "It was an easy pattern."

Colin stripped off his sweatshirt and shoved his arms into the sleeves of his new shirt. While he fastened the snaps down the front and at the cuffs, Dani stroked the shoulder seams, checking the fit.

"What do you think, Sam?" Colin asked, holding his gangly arms out at his sides.

"That's one good-lookin' shirt, bud. I wouldn't mind having one just like it."

"Mom'll make you one," Kim offered. "She can sew anything. Even coats."

Sam looked at Dani, amusement dancing in his dark eyes. "I'd appreciate it. I can never find shirts that have long enough sleeves. That's why mine are always rolled up."

She met his gaze and held it, and, to her consternation, discovered she couldn't look away. Lord, but he was handsome when he wasn't scowling. His smile faltered and his pupils dilated slightly, as if he suddenly felt the same pull of attraction. Oh, my, she thought, maybe he *is* interested, at least in kissing.

Her lips tingling at the thought, she struggled to make her voice function. "You buy the material, and you've got a deal."

Kim let out a jaw-cracking yawn. Dani glanced at her, then at the clock on the wall. "Okay, you two, time to get ready for bed."

After the obligatory protests, both kids left the room. When their bedroom doors banged shut, an awkward silence hovered between Sam and Dani. He moved over to sit behind his desk. Then his gaze slowly roamed over her from head to high-tops, a smile lurking at the corners of his mouth as if he liked what he saw. A sudden, primitive urge to flee overcame her, making her wonder if Sam might not be more man than she could handle.

To cover her sudden nervousness, Dani scooped Colin's sweatshirt off the floor, turned it right side out and folded it over her arm. "Well, um, I'll let you get back to work."

"Wait a minute, Dani," he said, his voice sounding rougher than usual. He waited until she faced him again before continuing. "I owe you an apology."

"If you're referring to this morning, don't bother. I was so nervous, I'm sure I overreacted."

"Well, you weren't the only one." Sam gave her a crooked smile. "I just hate having people pokin' around in my business."

"I don't like it much, either, but I don't think anyone meant any harm."

"Aw, I know they didn't. Anyway, I'm sorry."

"Apology accepted."

"Thanks." He sighed as if he had just completed an ordeal. Then he leaned back in his chair and studied her for a long moment. "I'm sorry for what I said about Colin, too. You know, the night you came here?"

Dani chuckled and rested one hip against the corner of his desk. "Well, he does act like a punk sometimes."

"Yeah, but once he stops bein' defensive, he's a good kid. Damn smart, too."

"You'd never know it from his report cards," Dani replied.

"Maybe he hasn't been challenged enough."

"He's always complained about being bored," she said thoughtfully. "I've been so worried about him lately."

"Most boys get pretty testy at his age. We'll keep him so busy around here, he won't have the time or energy to get in trouble."

"That's really kind of you, Sam." Her eyes misted, and she had to swallow hard. "I'll be grateful for any attention you can give him."

"Aw, jeez," Sam said with a groan, his ears turning pink. "Don't start that again. I've gotta live with the kid too, ya know."

"Why does it embarrass you to have someone thank you?"

He shrugged one shoulder and looked away. "Makes me feel silly. 'Specially if you get all gushy when you do it."

"Oh, now I understand," Dani said, wisely nodding her head. "You big tough cowboys don't have emotions. At least, you're not supposed to show them."

"That's right."

He shot her a sheepish grin, then looked away again. On the surface, it was a small gesture, but it touched Dani more deeply than anything else he could have done. That glimpse of vulnerability was all it took to free her impulsive side. Concerns about her motivations and his motivations and being cautious, slid from her consciousness like gelatin from a warmed mold.

Sam Dawson was the man she wanted, and she was going to have him.

"Go on ahead and laugh at me," he grumbled. "I can see you're just dyin' to."

"I'm not going to laugh at you, Sam."

"Then what are you starin' at me like that for?"

Dani walked around to the other side of the desk and stood as close to him as she could get, chuckling inside at the wary look in his eyes. When she reached out to touch him, he tipped back in his chair, clearly trying to ward her off. That didn't stop her.

Cupping the side of his face with her palm, she leaned down and gently forced him to face her. Then she kissed him. He didn't move so much as a whisker in response. That didn't stop her, either.

She pressed her lips more firmly against his, smiling when she discovered that his mustache *did* tickle, just a little. She raised her other hand to the back of his head, stroking his thick, glossy hair while she experimented with different angles for their first kiss. She touched the tip of her tongue to the center of his upper lip, and a stifled moan escaped his throat.

His hands slowly released their death grip on the chair arms and grasped her shoulders. She felt tension in his hands, as if he wasn't sure whether he wanted to pull her closer or push her away. But at last, his mouth began to cooperate with hers.

Arousal rushed through her, so fast and strong it left her breathless. When she started to pull away, he slid his hands down her back to her hips, anchoring her in place. His tongue probed its way into her mouth, searching hungrily for hers. She was losing control of the kiss, but she didn't care. Sam was doing just fine on his own.

She wrapped her arms around his neck and pressed her breasts against his chest. His arms closed around her waist, warm and hard, fulfilling her need to be held. Oh, God. It had been so long, so damnably long since she'd felt such sweet excitement.

Suddenly, as if some internal alarm had sounded, Sam jerked back his head and released her. Chests heaving, they stared at each other for a moment. Then Dani removed her arms from his neck and stepped away.

"What the hell did you do *that* for?" he demanded.

Her brain felt as mushy as her knees. She shook her head in an attempt to clear it, and finally smiled at him. "You wouldn't let me *say* thank you, Sam."

With that, Dani turned and walked out of the room. Halfway down the hall to tuck Kim in for the night, she heard Sam mutter something that sounded like "Oh, horse apples!"

Chapter Eight

Three weeks later, Sam rode in from checking the herd in the north pasture. His gelding, Smokey, walked along at a brisk clip, eager to get back to the barn for a ration of oats. The sharp November wind carried a hint of snow, and the gray, overcast sky matched Sam's mood.

The weather didn't concern him at the moment, however, although it sure as hell ought to have. Instead, his thoughts whirled like a tornado, all of them centered on that blasted woman back at the house. How anyone so small could invade every corner of his life in less than a month, he'd like to know.

The problem was, he didn't have the faintest idea of how to go about stopping what was happening. For that matter, he wasn't at all sure he understood exactly *what* was happening. But ever since the night she'd given him that thank-you kiss, he'd felt more and more like a hunted man.

He muttered an explicit curse under his breath, then snorted in disgust at the way that memory lingered in his mind. It popped out at the strangest times, like when he was out vaccinating the heifers, for God's sake. And it wasn't like he'd never been kissed before. But shoot, that hadn't been any innocent little peck.

Oh, no. She'd given him a full-fledged, openmouthed, belly-whompin' smooch. Since then, she hadn't made one overt advance toward him, but he couldn't forget that damn kiss. Hell, he'd enjoyed it too much to even want to forget it. Worse yet, he suspected she knew how he felt, and was enjoying his discomfort.

Well, she might not be all that blatant about it, but there wasn't a doubt in his mind that Dani was in hot pursuit of him. He was running as fast as he could, but it didn't seem as though he was making any more progress than Kim's pet gerbil ever did, running around on his little exercise wheel. No matter how hard he tried to avoid her, somehow she was always just sorta *there*.

When he came downstairs in the morning, she'd be in the living room, wearing a skimpy leotard and flailing her legs around to a Jane Fonda video tape. She claimed she needed the exercise, but there wasn't any fat on her that he could see, and, brother, could he see plenty. For such a slender little gal, she had enough chest on her to make a man's hands itch and his mouth water.

Despite all that exercise, she must have mighty weak hands and wrists. She was always asking him to open a jar for her. Then she'd smile up at him with those big, gorgeous blue eyes of hers, and he'd feel like some big macho stud, which was completely ridiculous, because the damned jar lids always popped right off.

If he tried to hide in his office, in she'd come with a pot of coffee and a plate of home-baked cookies—cookies that melted on his tongue and made him close his eyes in pleasure.

He'd go out to the barn for a little peace and quiet, and before he could get the door closed, she'd be tracking him down and asking all kinds of questions about the stock.

Yeah, she was after him with the determination of a pit bull, and he didn't have one decent weapon to use against her.

He couldn't even bellyache about the way she did her job. Oh, the house wasn't always neat as a pin, not with two kids and Hank and Dani around. They all tended to leave little messes here and there. But underneath the clutter, the house was clean.

She did the laundry on time and ironed his work shirts. She'd made both him and Hank new shirts that really fit well, and replaced all the buttons missing from their old ones. Hell, she'd even started helping him with the bookkeeping for the ranch. Man, she could work that computer like nobody's business.

Her cooking wasn't bad, either. She still made casseroles, but she always had a steak and a baked potato for him in case he didn't like what the others were eating. And he had to admit her lasagna and enchiladas weren't half bad.

So how could any reasonable man complain about a housekeeper who did all that, and did it so damned cheerfully?

Smokey snorted and broke into a trot. Sam looked up and noted in surprise that they were almost back to the barn. He exhaled a disgruntled sigh, then hunched his shoulders against the blustery wind. When he'd taken care of the gelding and turned him loose in the pasture, Sam headed for the house.

Dani's car was gone and he found a note taped to the back door saying she and Hank had gone to town for groceries because Becky, Peter, Grandma D and Tina were coming for dinner. Sam smiled at the news and went inside. The aroma of something chocolate, still warm from the oven, tantalized him while he shucked off his coat and wiped his boots.

He stepped into the kitchen, poured himself a cup of coffee and cut a generous slab from the pan of brownies cooling on the stove. Settling at the table, he stretched out his legs and gazed around the room.

In the corner, Dani's current sewing project cluttered the table that he'd brought her from the old foreman's house. A picture Kim had drawn at school decorated the refrigerator, along with a math test Colin had aced. A vase full of flowers Dani and Kim had made from brightly colored tissue paper and pipe cleaners graced the countertop.

That was when the worst realization of all, the one that really graveled his drawers, hit him.

Dani didn't even have to be there to *be* there. She'd brought children and laughter, warmth and comfort and excitement into this big old house. The woman had so much energy, he never knew what to expect when he walked in the door, only that he'd find something good cooking on the stove and something interesting going on.

Since Dani had come to the Circle D, whenever he was headed home after a long day, his heart always beat a little faster with anticipation. If she wasn't there, his spirits took an immediate nosedive. He'd never felt that way about anyone before.

An introvert for as long as he could remember, he used to enjoy the rare occasions when he had the house all to himself. But now, without Dani's bubbly presence, it seemed quieter than a graveyard in January. He didn't just feel alone. He felt lonely.

Dammit, he *liked* the woman. More than he'd ever liked any female outside his family. That scared him a whole lot more than the physical attraction he felt for her did.

He was a normal man with normal needs that had been denied for a helluva long time, but it didn't bother him that Dani could get him all stirred up without half trying. He wasn't some randy kid who couldn't control his hormones. What worried him was adding the physical attraction to the liking.

That combination could get downright dangerous. When a man felt both of those things toward a woman, he could wake up one morning and find himself in love. Sam shuddered at the thought.

"Dammit," he muttered, smacking his fist on the table. "Why can't she be like every other woman and go after Hank?"

Unfortunately he knew that wasn't going to happen. Dani and his brother kidded each other all the time. But Sam had never seen her look at Hank the way he'd caught her looking at him once or twice when she thought he wasn't watching—like she wanted to haul him off to bed and have her way with him. It was confusing, embarrassing and flattering as hell all at the same time.

Sam shoved his chair away from the table and went back outside to work. He couldn't afford to waste any more time stewing over Dani Smith. Thank God Hank was around to act as a buffer.

Dani glanced around the dinner table that night and felt a warm glow of happiness swell inside her chest. Her chicken enchiladas were a hit. Kim was chattering away with Hank's daughter, Tina. Colin and Peter Sinclair were engaged in a friendly debate about computers. Becky and Grandma D were laughing over some story Hank had told them. Even Sam, who had been looking haggard lately, seemed happy and relaxed.

The past three weeks had been a revelation to Dani. She hadn't thought of herself as the housewife type since Ray's death had compelled her to join the work force, but she was enjoying her new job immensely. Of course, she would have gone insane with boredom staying at home all day in her old apartment in Chicago. But here at the ranch, there were so many new things to see and do, she hadn't had time to be bored.

"All right, Hank," Becky said, breaking into Dani's thoughts. "Time to tell us the big news."

Sam frowned and looked at his brother. "What big news?"

"That's what we'd like to know," Grandma D told him. "He said he had something important to tell us when he called to invite us for supper."

Everyone else quieted down. Obviously enjoying being the center of attention, Hank leaned back in his chair and grinned.

"Come *on*, Dad," Tina demanded.

"I got a check from the ECC folks today," he said. "This busted leg cost them plenty."

"Well, it's about time," Grandma D muttered.

"And," he continued before anyone else could speak, "I wanted you all to know I'll be taking off for Oklahoma City tomorrow."

Tina's smile faded. "Why?"

Hank ruffled her dark auburn hair affectionately. "One of my old buddies called me the other day and told me he's starting a stock-contracting business for the rodeo circuit. He wants me to come in with him on it, so I'm gonna go check it out."

"Can I come with you?" the little girl asked.

"Not this time, honey. You've gotta go to school."

Tina's chin started to quiver, and a fat tear slid down one cheek. "But I haven't seen you for a long time already, Dad."

"Aw, sugar," Hank said, pulling her onto his lap. "I know the past couple of months have been rough on you, but I'll only be gone a few weeks. And you'll still have Aunt Becky and Grandma D, and your Uncle Sam and Uncle Peter. Why, I'll be back before you even notice I've been gone."

"I still don't want you to go," Tina insisted.

Sam shoved his plate aside and braced one forearm on the table. "I don't, either. I could use some help around here."

"I can't help you that much right now, Sam," Hank replied. "I won't be able to drive for another three weeks, and it'll probably be another six months before the doc'll let me get back on a horse."

"Won't traveling be awfully hard on you until your leg's completely healed?" Becky asked.

"He's a big boy, Becky," Peter said, softening his warning tone with a smile.

Becky flushed and shook her head. "I know he is, honey, but—"

"But nothing," Hank interrupted. "Look, I've been cooped up for months, and I've got a bad case of cabin fever. I need to get outta here for a while."

"What about the ranch, Hank?" Grandma D asked. "It sounds to me like you'd rather do something else. Permanently."

Hank ran the fingers of one hand through his hair in frustration. "I love the Circle D as much as the rest of you, Grandma. But I've had a lot of time to think about it since I got hurt, and I don't want to spend the rest of my life here. I need more excitement. I need to see new people and new places once in a while. Sam can have my share of the ranch."

"The rodeo circuit's no place for Tina, Hank," Sam argued.

"It won't be like it was when I was competing, Sam. I wouldn't have to be involved in the travel, at least not after the first couple of years. And when I do have to hit the road, Tina can come with me if she's not in school." Hank smiled down at his daughter. "You'd like that, wouldn't you, hon?"

She glared at him, her chin set at a mutinous angle. "No! I like it right here. I don't ever wanna leave Aunt Becky an' everybody." With that, she pushed herself off his lap and ran from the room.

"Nice goin'," Sam said to his brother.

"Aw, she'll get over it," Hank muttered. "Kids can adapt to anything. Look at Colin and Kim. They're doin' all right."

Grandma D pushed back her chair and stood, then shook a finger at him. "You mark my words, boy. You're askin' for trouble with that little girl."

"Well, what about me?" Hank demanded. "I gave up rodeo when she was born." He held up his thumb and index finger, half an inch apart. "I was this close to a national title, but I didn't mind quittin' because I wanted her to have a stable home."

"And you were right to do it, Hank," Grandma D said. "So why are you jerkin' the rug out from under her now?"

"Because, dammit, I'm suffocating here, and I don't think that's doing Tina any favors. Wouldn't she be better off with a dad who likes his work?"

"I don't know," Grandma D answered with a shake of her head. "Sometimes it don't seem like I know anything anymore. I'm gonna go make sure she's all right."

"I wish you'd think about this, Hank," Becky said quietly. "Tina needs you more than you realize. She couldn't wait to see you today."

Hank grabbed his crutches out from under his chair, then pulled himself to his feet. "I don't even know if I want to get into this business. All I'm gonna do is go find out. I'm goin' to Oklahoma and I don't want to hear another word about it. I'll be back by Christmas."

Everyone else remained silent until they heard the door to his room slam. Finally Dani couldn't stand the tension any longer.

"Who's ready for some strawberry cheesecake?" she asked.

Hands went up around the table and conversation gradually resumed while Dani and Becky cleared away the dirty plates.

"I'm sorry you and your kids had to hear all that," Becky said with a sigh.

"Don't worry about it. My family argues, too."

"I guess most families do," Becky replied. "Unfortunately a lot of Hank's problems with Tina are my fault."

"How can you say that?" Dani asked. "I think you're awfully generous to take care of her so much for him."

"That's just it," Becky said. "I've been too generous. You see, Tina's mom took off when she was three weeks old."

Dani nodded. "Hank told me about that."

"Well, instead of letting him fumble along with a baby and learn how to take care of her himself, I jumped right in and took over. Pete says that's my worst fault—not letting other people take care of themselves."

"I've got news for you, Becky. There are plenty of faults worse than that one."

"That may be true, but Tina's so attached to me now, it's put Hank in a bad position. He adores that kid, and I think he does the best he can with her, but he doesn't really know how to be a father."

"As much as he seems to like women, I'm surprised he hasn't remarried," Dani said thoughtfully.

"He almost did last year, but his fiancée sold us out to the ECC and darn near got him killed. I don't know if he'll ever get involved with a woman again."

Dani cut into the cheesecake and served the pieces onto dessert plates. "That's a shame. He's an awfully nice guy."

Becky gave her a sly grin. "Yeah, he is, but Sam might be better husband material."

Dani glanced across the room at Sam. He was leaning toward Kim, a gentle, indulgent smile curving his mouth while he listened to something she was telling him quite earnestly.

"What are you thinking?" Becky whispered.

"I think you're absolutely right about that," Dani answered with a chuckle. "At least for me he is." Then she picked up the biggest piece of cheesecake and delivered it to Sam.

Sam fought a rising sense of panic for the rest of the evening. The minute the Sinclairs, his grandmother and his niece left, however, he marched into Hank's room, shutting the door behind him with a sharp crack. Hank stood beside the bed, balancing on his crutches while he awkwardly folded a shirt and dropped it into an open suitcase.

"Dammit, Hank," Sam snapped, "you can't leave."

"Tina will be just fine," Hank said.

"Well, I won't." Sam lowered his voice to a furious whisper. "You brought that woman here, and you can't go off and leave me alone with her."

"You mean Dani?"

"Who the hell else would I mean? What'll people say when they find out I'm livin' with her by myself?"

Hank snorted with laughter. "I don't give a rip what they'll say, Sam. The ones with dirty minds probably think we're both sleepin' with her. My leavin' oughtta help her reputation."

"Will you be serious for once in your rotten, miserable life?"

"I *am* bein' serious," Hank replied, his expression sobering. "But I don't think you care about gossip any more than I do. You look like you're scared to death."

"I am," Sam grumbled. "That woman's after me!"

"So let her catch you. I'm sure she'll be gentle."

"Damn you, Hank—"

Hank held up his hands as if to ward off a blow. When Sam turned away and rammed his hands into his pockets, Hank continued. "Aw, c'mon, Sam. I've seen you lookin' at her like a starvin' man at a buffet table. So relax and enjoy her company and let nature take its course. What you two do together is nobody else's business."

"She's not like that, Hank. I can't sleep with her and then expect her to walk away when her six months are up."

"What makes you so all-fired sure you'll want her to? Seems to me you guys could have somethin' pretty special together. You're still not thinkin' she's not good enough for you, are ya?"

"Of course not. Maybe I'm not good enough for her."

"My brother, the saint?" Hank yelped. "What did you ever do to make you say a fool thing like that?"

"That's none of your business," Sam told him. "But trust me on this, will ya? It just wouldn't work."

"Why not?"

"She talks too damn much."

"Well, you don't talk enough, so you'll come out even. Quit hidin' from her and give it a chance."

Hank's wicked, knowing grin told Sam this conversation wasn't going anywhere. Without another word, he turned and stalked out the door, his brother's laughter grating on his ears. Then he stomped up the stairs and went into his office, praying he'd be able to think straight.

He sat behind his desk, drumming his fingers and willing his blood pressure to come back down. Finally he dialed Becky's number in desperation. Grandma D and Tina would have to come home. Becky answered on the second ring.

"Hi, Sam. I was just about to call you," she said.

"Oh? What's up?"

"Grandma's cousin Mamie had a stroke. The message was on Peter's answering machine when we got home. I'm gonna drive Grandma to the airport in Jackson Hole tomorrow, so I thought Hank could come with us and save you a trip.''

Sam closed his eyes and shook his head. No! This couldn't be happening to him. Dammit, he needed Grandma D.

''Sam?'' Becky asked. ''Are you still there?''

''Yeah.''

''Well, what do you think?''

''I'll appreciate it, sis. Thanks.''

''Are you all right?'' she asked.

Sam rolled his eyes toward heaven. There was no way in hell he wanted his little sister getting involved with this god-awful mess.

''Yeah, I'm fine. Just a little tired.''

They chatted for a few more minutes. Becky praised Dani's cooking and how the house had looked so nice and what a nice person she seemed to be, until Sam thought he would punch his fist through a wall. When she finally hung up, he slammed down the receiver, stomped across the room and yanked open the door to his office.

Dani stood on the other side, one hand raised as if she'd been ready to knock. She laughed in surprise. Then she looked up at Sam with a smile that hit him like a fist rammed square into his gut. Her big blue eyes held a special sparkle he knew was just for him.

''What can I do for you, Dani?'' he asked gruffly.

''I'm about ready to call it a day. Do you need anything before I go to bed?''

How about another one of those kisses? he thought, staring at her lips. Lord, he was getting hard just looking at her. He cleared his throat and realized she was still gazing at him expectantly.

''Oh, uh, no. Thanks, Dani.''

''Good night, then. See you in the morning, Sam.''

Gulping, he watched her little fanny sway down the hall. She paused at the door of her room and looked back over her shoulder at him. Then she shot him a sweet, seductive smile and went inside.

Sam felt cold drops of sweat break out on his forehead and bolted down the hall to his own room. He shut and locked the door. Leaning back against it, he muttered, "Damn you, Hank. I'll never forgive you for this."

Chapter Nine

When the phone rang, Dani had just finished chopping onions for the stuffing she would serve the next day for Thanksgiving dinner. She wiped her streaming eyes with the backs of her hands, sniffed, then grabbed the receiver and tucked it between her ear and shoulder.

"Dawson ranch."

"Why haven't you called or written to me?" her sister's voice demanded.

"Happy Thanksgiving, Micky," Dani replied with a grin. "How's the weather in Montana?"

"All right, brat, so that wasn't a very polite greeting. But I've been worried about you, and Mom's going absolutely bonkers. Will you *please* call her and get her off my back?"

"She's still blaming you for leading me astray?"

"Of course." Micky chuckled before continuing. "And all that hysteria is contagious. So tell me, how are you and the kids?"

"We're all fine, sis. In fact, I don't think any of us has ever been better. You won't believe this, but Kim's going to be in a school play and Colin's doing his homework without complaint. He might even make the honor roll this term."

"Good grief, what's happened to them?"

"Sam Dawson. He's incredible, Mick."

"He must be. What's his secret? Maybe I can use it on my three hellions."

"I'm not sure I can explain it. For one thing, he's so darn big, nobody in his right mind would argue with him without a good reason."

"You mean he intimidates the kids into submission?"

"No, not at all, but he does command respect. He just tells them what he expects, and then dishes out a ton of encouragement and rewards for appropriate behavior. The kids love him."

"What about you, Dani? How do you feel about him?"

"I'm not sure," Dani answered quietly. "I like him tremendously, and sometimes I'm convinced I'm in love with him...."

"But..." Micky prompted.

"But he just won't let me get very close to him."

"Physically or emotionally?"

"Both. When Hank left last week, I thought Sam would have to give in and open up a little."

"Hank left?" Micky squawked. "You mean you and the kids are living there alone with Sam?"

"Yes."

"Oh, cripes, Dani, if Mom finds out about that, she'll be on the next plane west."

"So don't tell her. Nothing's going on between Sam and me she wouldn't approve of. At least not yet."

"I don't believe this," Micky muttered. "What have I gotten you into?"

"You didn't get me into anything. I made the decision myself and I don't regret it one bit. I'm still hoping that Sam and I will get together."

"Are you sure that's what you want?"

"Ninety-eight percent and the other two don't count. Oh, Micky, he does such sweet things with the kids, and he's *so* gorgeous. I practically hyperventilate just looking at him."

"That sounds like hormones talking."

"Hey, they're not talking, they're yelling. And I know he feels the same way about me. Sometimes I catch him watching me, and his eyes look kind of wistful and lonely, and I just want to hug him and smother him with kisses. I don't know why he's being so darn stubborn."

"Maybe he's got some common sense," Micky retorted. "You haven't known each other that long, Dani. You rushed into things with Ray and look where it got you."

"Quit trying to sound like Mom."

"That was a low blow."

Dani sighed and shook her head. "Well, so was yours. But I hear what you're saying. Don't worry, I'll be good."

"Why don't I believe you?"

"You have a nasty, suspicious mind," Dani told her.

"No, I think it's because you've been alone for a long time and I remember that picture of him in *Cupid's Arrow*. From what you've told me, I'm not sure I could resist Sam, either, if I didn't have Greg. But enough about men. Anything else going on in your life I should know about?"

"Well, I seem to be developing my own sewing business," Dani said, grabbing the opportunity to change the subject.

"How did that come about?"

Dani told her sister about making shirts for Sam, Hank and Colin. "Since they started wearing them into town, I've been getting all kinds of phone calls from people who want sewing done. I should earn enough to buy the kids some great Christmas presents for a change if this keeps up."

"It probably will," Micky assured her. "In a small town like that with decent shopping so far away and icy roads, there's a big demand for custom-made clothes. You know, you might want to make a few really fancy Western things and see if the local stores will sell them on consignment for you when the tourist season starts."

The two women chatted another ten minutes before hanging up. Dani gazed at the receiver, her mind racing. As usual, Micky had given her plenty to think about, but her remarks about the demand for sewing in a town like Pinedale deserved careful consideration.

Her children were blossoming in Pinedale, and Dani herself loved the little town. No matter what happened to her relationship with Sam, she wanted to stay in the area. Unfortunately, jobs were scarce. Was it possible she could support the three of them with her sewing and maybe some bookkeeping?

"Why not?" she murmured, turning back to the stuffing ingredients.

She would be delighted if Sam fell in love with her and together they could live happily ever after. But even if that happened, the thought of having her own business excited and challenged her. And it wouldn't hurt to establish an income separate from what she earned at the Circle D, because there was one little thing about Sam that Dani hadn't confided to Micky.

When she'd been helping him set up the ranch accounts on the computer, she'd noticed a monthly check made out to a woman named Ginny Bradford, who lived in Laramie. Sam wouldn't tell her what the payments were for. Dani wasn't terribly worried about them; as bashful as he seemed around her at times, it was hard to believe Ginny could be Sam's mistress.

However, a woman with two kids to support couldn't be too careful. She had plenty to gain and very little to lose from trying. Her decision made, Dani smiled and returned to the Thanksgiving dinner preparations she could complete in advance.

Kim had gone to bed an hour earlier, and it was time to nudge Colin in that direction. Dani sliced half a loaf of banana bread, put it on a plate and carried it across the hall to Hank's former bedroom. Since Hank had gone to Oklahoma, Sam had moved his office back to its original downstairs location. As she'd expected, Colin and Sam were hunched over the computer table, playing one of the games her son had conned Sam into buying.

Their excited whoops and laughter echoed in the hallway, then suddenly stopped. Dani hesitated outside the open door. In the past few weeks she'd developed a terrible habit of eavesdropping. She justified it by telling herself that was the only way she ever found out what was going on with the two closed-mouthed males in her life.

"What do you think, Sam?" Colin said. "Should I ask her to the dance?"

"I don't know why not," Sam replied.

"What if she says no? God, I'll be completely humiliated."

"That's a risk, all right," Sam admitted. "Those ornery women put us poor guys through some terrible ordeals."

Dani rolled her eyes in amused disgust, then leaned closer to the doorway.

"Well, how do I do it? Ask her, I mean," Colin said.

"Strike up a conversation with her, ya know, kinda soften her up a little. Maybe tell her she looks real nice or something like that. Then just come right out and ask her."

"Maybe I could get her away from the other kids," Colin suggested. "Like, catch her at her locker after school when everybody else is leaving."

"Might be a good idea."

"What if she says yes?"

"Then you set a time to pick her up. I'll drive you."

"That'd be cool. I'd hate for Mom to do it. She'd embarrass me for sure."

Dani raised an eyebrow at that insult.

"No, she wouldn't, Colin. She wouldn't mean to, anyway."

"Trust me, she would!"

Colin was silent for a moment. Dani could almost see his brain ticking over with questions. "Okay, if Julie says yes," he finally said, "should I hold her hand and stuff? Like, kiss her good-night?"

"It depends on what you're comfortable with and what she's comfortable with. There's no need to rush into anything."

Dani vigorously nodded her agreement with that piece of advice.

"But how do I know what she's comfortable with? I mean, don't girls say no sometimes when they really mean yes?"

Sam chuckled, and Dani would have bet a week's salary that he was scratching his earlobe, the way he always did when he was carefully considering what he wanted to say.

"Well, now, Colin, that's locker-room talk. Guys lie all the time about what studs they are, ya know? Kinda makes 'em feel like they're real men. But you don't ever want to force a girl to do anything."

"But how do you know what they want?" Colin insisted.

"Women have weird minds, Colin. I'm not sure a man ever really knows what they want. Ya just gotta take things nice and slow and be real gentle, kinda like you would with a skittish mare. It's not easy for them, either. The best thing a man can do is treat 'em with respect and pay close attention to their body language."

"What do you mean?"

"Well, if you're tryin' to kiss a girl and she stiffens up like a block of concrete, that probably means she doesn't want you to kiss her. So you back off."

"How do you know if she wants you to kiss her?"

"Then she'll probably lean a little closer, and her eyes'll get kind of a dreamy look in 'em. Maybe she'll close her eyes, but her face'll be tipped up toward you. Trust me, you'll know. If you're not sure, it's better to wait."

"It's all totally bizarre," Colin grumbled.

"That's a fact," Sam agreed. "Women are contrary creatures, but they're mighty special. They're weaker than us in some ways, stronger in others. You've got plenty of time to learn about 'em, so remember you can't go wrong if you act like a gentleman."

Plastering an innocent expression on her face, Dani started to enter the room. Colin's next question stopped her squarely in her tracks.

"Do you like my mom, Sam?"

"Sure, I like her."

"No, I mean, do you *really* like her? Like, do you think she's sexy?"

"That's a helluva question, kid," Sam answered with a startled laugh. "I'm not sure it's any of your business."

"Oh, come on, Sam," Colin coaxed.

Yeah, come on, Sam, Dani echoed silently.

"Why do you want to know?" Sam asked.

"When she first dragged us out here, I thought she was totally insane, you know? Like, I didn't want to leave my friends and I really didn't want a stepfather. But I think it might be okay if it was you."

"Thank you," Sam said, his gruff tone telling Dani that Colin's words had touched him as deeply as they'd touched her. "I'm real flattered you feel that way."

"So tell me if you think she's sexy."

"Well, yeah, I do. But there's a lot more that goes into a relationship than sex, Colin. Ya gotta enjoy bein' together and respect each other—"

"I know *that*," Colin informed him. "But don't you think you could have that kind of thing with Mom? She can be a lot of fun. For a mother, anyway. I know she likes *you*."

"What makes you say that?" Sam asked, his voice laced with amusement.

Dani decided this conversation had gone far enough. Striving for an interested smile, she sauntered through the doorway. "What makes you say what, Colin?"

Colin blushed and shot Sam a desperate look.

"Nothin' much," Sam replied, casually snagging a piece of banana bread from the plate she carried. "Just a little man talk."

"Oh, I see," Dani said. "Well, I'm sorry to interrupt, but it's time for Colin to go to bed."

"Jeez, Mom, I'm not a little kid anymore. I don't even have school tomorrow."

"But you still have chores. Cows don't take a day off."

"Oh, all right." Colin grabbed four slices of banana bread and shuffled to the door. "Thanks, Sam. I'll see you in the morning."

Sam left the computer table and walked around behind his desk. After seating himself, he silently studied Dani for a long moment, as if he was waiting for Colin to get out of earshot.

"How much of that conversation did you hear?"

"Most of it," Dani answered with an unrepentant grin.

"That's pretty rotten, Dani."

Laughing, she perched on one corner of his desk. "Give me a break, Sam. What mother in her right mind would miss out on hearing about her son's love life? Who's Julie?"

"A girl in his English class. She lives out this way on the other side of the highway."

"Is she nice?"

"Yeah, she's a real sweet little gal. Cute, too. Your kid's got good taste."

"I'm a little hurt Colin didn't come to me with his questions, but I'm glad he talked to you. You gave him good advice."

Sam shrugged and stuffed another piece of bread into his mouth. Dani considered outwaiting him, but she knew from experience that when Sam allowed a silence to go on this long, a rock would probably speak before he did. Finally she sighed with exasperation.

"Now look, Dawson, I'm in the mood for adult conversation. Either you talk to me or I'm going to thank you again. This is how it works. First I say something. Then you say something back. Got that?"

"Yes, ma'am," he replied, his mouth twitching at the corners before succumbing to a grin. "Fire away."

"You're wonderful with kids, Sam. Why haven't you ever married?"

He shrugged again, then laced his fingers together and rested his hands on his stomach. "I haven't really thought about it much. Guess I just never met the right woman."

Dani raised an eyebrow. "You've never been in love? Not even once?"

"I've come close a time or two," he admitted. "But... aw, I don't know. I've always felt kinda...awkward around women, and I sure don't understand 'em."

"That's not true," Dani said, chuckling at his disgruntled expression. "Everything you told Colin was right on target. I especially liked what you said about treating us the same way you would a skittish mare."

"Hey, it's not easy answerin' that kid's questions, so don't start teasin' me about what I said."

"Who, me? I wouldn't dream of it."

Sam snorted with laughter, then slid down a little in his chair, his face taking on a thoughtful expression. "I might do okay as a dad, but I'd make a lousy husband. I'm just not a romantic kind of a guy, you know?"

"Oh, Sam—"

"No, I mean it. I can't dance worth spit. I'm lousy at givin' women compliments. I hate small talk and I never remember birthdays or anniversaries. Becky always takes care of that kinda stuff for me. And, I've got a terrible temper."

Bracing her weight with one hand, Dani leaned toward him. "That's silly, and you know it. You may yell once in a while, but you've never been anything but gentle with me and the kids. You're kind and considerate. You're dependable, handsome and sexy. When you do talk, you've got something worth saying. What more could a woman want? All those other things you mentioned are icing on the cake, but the cake itself is a lot more important."

His face turned a shade redder with every sentence she uttered. He looked away and folded his arms over his chest. "Yeah, well, I don't want to be anybody's cake. What was your marriage like, Dani?"

"Do you really want to know? Or are you just trying to change the subject?"

"Both."

Dani smiled at his honest answer, then scooted farther back onto the desk and crossed one leg over the other. "Considering the way it started, I guess it was okay."

"What do you mean, considering the way it started?"

"I was four months pregnant with Colin on my wedding day," she said, darting a glance at Sam to judge his reaction to that admission. Unfortunately, his eyes didn't reveal a single clue to his thoughts.

"Go on," he said quietly.

"I was nineteen and scared to death. I wasn't sure I wanted to get married, but my parents pressured me into it."

"What was your husband like?"

She let her mind drift back through the years, remembering. "Ray looked a lot like Colin. I guess I was infatuated from the day I met him. He was always the life of the party and always had a joke."

"Sounds like Hank," Sam observed.

"He was, a little bit," Dani agreed. "He had all these plans and dreams... He wanted to race in the Indy 500 someday. When Colin came along, he got a job at the factory where his dad worked and settled for racing stock cars as a hobby."

"Is that how he died?" Sam asked.

Dani sadly shook her head. "No. There was an accident at the factory and a forklift tipped over on him. He was only thirty-four."

"But you were happy with him."

"I think content would be a better word," Dani said. "I wasn't *un*happy. I don't think Ray was, either. We had some good times together, and we loved each other, but I always thought he felt... trapped. You know, like Hank sounded the night he told all of you he didn't want to spend the rest of his life here."

"What about you? Did you feel trapped?"

"In some ways," Dani admitted. "But I loved the kids and I was so busy with them, I didn't think about it very often."

"You still miss him?"

"At times. He wasn't always responsible, and he didn't pay as much attention to me and the kids as I would have liked, but at least he was there if I really needed him."

A comfortable silence settled between them this time. The desk lamp cast a soft, golden circle of light, surrounding them with a shadowy curtain of intimacy. Dani shot a

sidelong glance at Sam and found him returning her scrutiny. With his jaw darkened by a day's growth of whiskers
and his eyes narrowed to half-mast, he looked…dangerous.
Exciting but just a little bit dangerous.

"What are you thinking?" she whispered.

"I'm not gonna tell you," he whispered back.

Dani shrugged one shoulder, feigning indifference.
"Okay."

"You're gonna badger me now, right?"

"No. You've already told me more about yourself than
I expected. I just have one more little question."

"What's that?"

She leaned toward him and lowered her voice to a
breathless, sultry pitch. "Do you really think I'm sexy,
Sam?"

His shoulders shaking with laughter, Sam groaned, then
covered his face with both hands. "Damn, I knew you
heard that," he muttered.

Dani slid off the desk and walked around to the side of
his chair. He spread his fingers and peered out between
them at her. The wariness in his eyes brought a fit of gig-
gles to the surface, but she tried to force a stern expression.

"It's okay, Sam," she said, prying at his fingers. "For
heaven's sake, would you quit hiding from me?"

Without warning, his hands jerked away from his face
and wrapped around her wrists, holding them up beside her
head. She gazed into his eyes, and the urge to laugh died
abruptly. It was all there for her to see—loneliness, fear and
stark, aching desire.

His grip loosened. His thumbs absently stroked the
tender skin at the insides of her wrists as softly as he would
stroke a baby's cheek. Her heart stopped beating. Her lungs
refused to function. She couldn't see anything but those
dark, mesmerizing eyes. Deep and hoarse, his voice shattered the silence.

"You're playin' with fire, Dani. If you've got any brains in that pretty little head of yours, you'll hightail it outta here right now."

Shaking her head slowly, Dani pulled her right arm from his grasp and combed the hair at his temple with trembling fingertips. "That's not what you really want, Sam. Is it?"

"No, dammit. Of course it isn't." He shut his eyes and inhaled a deep, harsh breath, then looked at her again. "All right, so you know I want you. It oughtta make you damn happy to know I've wanted you for a long time. That doesn't mean we should do anything about it."

"Is being close to me really that frightening?" she asked softly.

He released her other wrist and spread his big hand out at the back of her waist. "I'm not afraid *of* you, Dani. I'm afraid *for* you. I don't want to hurt you."

She framed his face between her palms. "I want you, too, Sam. It hurts when you push me away."

"Oh, God."

His broad shoulders sagged for a moment, as if all the fight had suddenly drained out of him. Then he wrapped both arms around her waist and hauled her onto his lap. Dani linked her hands behind his neck and rested her head against his chest. His heart beat a frantic tempo beneath her ear and she felt the bold evidence of his arousal against her hip.

She kissed the front of his shirt and snuggled closer while his hand rhythmically stroked the length of her back. It felt wonderful to be held in his strong arms, to smell the scent of his soap, warmed by his skin, to feel his cheek brush against her hair.

"This is your last chance," he murmured, nuzzling the side of her neck with his lips. "If we don't stop now, we won't stop at all."

"Hush up and kiss me," she answered, unfastening the top snap on his shirt.

Sam trapped her busy fingers with one hand and tipped up her chin with the other.

"I'm not making you any promises, Dani," he said, gazing straight into her eyes. "We can have one hell of an affair, but I'm not gonna be your cake."

She smiled at his warning. "Don't worry about me, Sam. I'll take my chances."

Chapter Ten

Feeling like a man released from years of solitary confinement, Sam gazed down into Dani's eyes. The utter trust, acceptance and desire he found there humbled him. She looked so small and delicate he was almost afraid to touch her. Even with her sitting on his lap, the top of her head barely reached his nose.

She squirmed around, stretching to reach his lips with hers, while her fingers went back to work on his shirt snaps. Lord, if she didn't slow down, he'd never stay in control. Just the thought of those clever hands of hers on his bare chest was enough to make him break out in a sweat.

He reached behind her and swept everything off the desk with his forearm. Then he picked her up under the armpits and plunked her down facing him. She chuckled when she realized they were finally at eye level with each other, hooked her feet in the curved arms of his chair and reeled him in.

Before she could touch him, he grasped both of her hands and lifted them to his mouth, kissing each knuckle, nibbling each fingertip. The ragged little sigh she exhaled made his heart contract. Turning her hands over, he kissed the palms, and suddenly she started to chatter.

"Maybe you shouldn't do that, Sam. I was chopping onions for the stuffing tomorrow, and—"

Knowing she was nervous, too, gave his confidence a welcome boost. "It's okay, Dani. I like onions." He smiled at her over the tops of her fingers. "Believe me, I've smelled worse."

Leaning closer, he captured her lips and cupped one hand behind her neck, supporting her head while he drank his fill. Her tongue eagerly mated with his, sending a hot surge of blood to his groin. She tasted of coffee and a hint of the Mexican spices from the tacos she'd fixed for supper. Stroking the baby-smooth skin at her nape, he decided short hair on a woman gave a man access to some mighty delectable places.

Soft whimpers of pleasure came out of her throat when he touched her breasts. The buttons on her blouse frustrated his clumsy fingers, but she didn't seem to mind his fumbling. Her hands plunged into his hair, kneading his scalp, bringing him closer.

He didn't know why the sight of her lacy, fire engine-red bra surprised him; he'd rarely seen her wear anything but vivid, primary colors. But somehow he hadn't thought of that bright rainbow extending to her underwear. Sweet, merciful heaven, a bra like that, molding full, firm breasts like hers, did things to a man's sanity.

Groaning, he buried his face in her cleavage and sucked in great gulps of air. The warm, womanly scent of her made his head spin. Her mouth brushed the top of his head as she murmured his name. A small hand slid down the back of his neck and burrowed under his shirt and undershirt, caressing his shoulders, turning up the heat another ten degrees.

Then she arched her back, reaching behind to undo the clasp on that red scrap of sin. He pulled away as it slid from her shoulders, hungry to see what he'd only imagined.

"You're so beautiful," he whispered, tracing one nipple with trembling fingertips.

"Touch me harder," she coaxed. "I won't break."

He obeyed, and her head fell back, lolling like a rag doll's. He tasted her, and she moaned. He pulled her nipple firmly into his mouth, and she cried out.

It had been so long...too long, since he'd heard that sweet sound. Urgency rushed through him with the force of a freight train out of control. His jeans felt painfully tight. His hands trembled. His heartbeat galloped.

He pushed himself out of the chair and supported her with one arm while he helped her lie back. She watched through half-closed eyelids as he stripped off both shirts and flung them aside. Then she held out her arms, as if welcoming him home.

He braced his forearms on either side of her head and claimed her lips in a gut-wrenching kiss. Without the slightest hesitation, she ran her hands over his chest, weaving her fingers through the coarse, springy hair.

"Oh, Sam," she murmured between kisses, her voice husky with delight, "you're gorgeous."

Her legs wrapped around his hips, shredding what little control he had left. He reached under her rump and peeled down those tight, clingy pants that had been driving him nuts for weeks, bringing a pair of lacy red panties with them. Of course, they wouldn't come off over her high-tops, and of course, she giggled when she understood his predicament.

Her laughter cleared his head and put the whole situation into perspective. He should have known making love with Dani would be a unique experience, and probably not a serious one. Chuckling, he braced her feet against his thighs, pushed the offending garments back up her shins and went to work on her shoelaces.

"Think it's funny, do ya, Smith?" he drawled, giving her a mock-threatening scowl.

"Yeah, Dawson, I do."

She sat up and reached for his belt buckle, getting in his way while she opened his fly. It seemed natural to laugh and kiss and caress while they shed the rest of their clothes. When they were finally naked, they silently admired each other's bodies for a long, breathless moment.

Then an awful thought hit Sam. He exhaled a shuddering, frustrated sigh and closed his eyes.

"What is it?" she asked quietly, stroking his side as if she thought he needed reassurance.

"Uh, I don't know how to tell you this," he said, feeling like a complete jerk, "but I don't have any protection."

"I wondered when you were going to think of that," she said with a teasing grin.

He shook his head in self-reproach, then reluctantly started to move away from her. "God, I'm really sorry. Maybe Hank left some—"

She grabbed his hand and hauled him back. "You'll never know how much I appreciate your being willing to stop, Sam, and, I don't want to seem calculating, but I had my doctor put me on the Pill before I left Chicago, just in case we ever made love." She paused for oxygen, then gave him a lopsided smile. "I've already had one unplanned pregnancy. I don't want another one."

Laughing with relief, Sam scooped her up and whirled her around and around. Her legs encircled his waist, her arms clung to his neck. Dizzy and breathless, he stopped spinning and tightened his embrace. He loved feeling her naked body flush against his, her quick, eager kisses along his neck and jaw, her soft murmurs of delight when he found her mouth and explored every inch of it with his tongue.

Urgency came back, stronger than before. He walked backward until the backs of his knees made contact with the swivel chair. Then he carefully lowered himself into it with Dani still wrapped around him. It took some shifting and squirming, but she finally straddled his lap with her knees on the seat cushion.

She raised herself up to look him in the eye, bringing their bodies into intimate alignment. "Now, this has some interesting possibilities."

The curls between her legs tickled his engorged shaft. He bit back a groan at the sensation and cupped her bottom with his palms. "Yeah, it does," he murmured, nibbling his way across her shoulder.

She shivered, then gently nudged his mouth toward her breasts with one hand. He gladly obliged her, suckling at her nipples while his hands made forays up the insides of her thighs. Her sighs egged him on, and at last he touched the most private part of her.

Her fingernails dug into his shoulders and she gasped, moving rhythmically against his fingers. Her responsiveness drove him crazy.

"Are you ready, babe?" he asked, his voice sounding hoarse in his own ears.

"Yes," she said, panting. "Oh, yes, *please.*"

She reached down between them and guided him inside her.

"Easy now, take it slow," he cautioned her, grasping her hips. "I don't want to hurt you."

Drops of sweat beaded his forehead as she lowered herself inch by agonizing inch onto him. Lord, but she was tiny and hot and wet, as if she'd been custom-made to shove him over the edge. Fighting for control, he flung his head back and gritted his teeth.

"Oh my," she whispered, resting her head against his chest for a moment.

"Are you all right?" he asked anxiously.

"I'm fine." She raised her head and gazed at him, her eyes filled with an emotion he was afraid to name. "It's just been a long time."

Smiling, she started to move, and the rush of sensation was so intense, he felt light-headed. The sounds of ragged breathing filled the room. He wanted to tell her to slow down, to give him a chance to please her as much as she was pleasing him, but he couldn't think, couldn't form the words.

His heartbeat hammered louder and louder and she was stroking him faster and faster, and, oh damn, she wasn't the only one who hadn't done this for a long time. He sank his fingers into her bottom, as if hanging on to her would stave off the inevitable. But she didn't stop and he couldn't hold back and the top of his head was going to blow clean off...

He came back down to earth to find Dani stroking his hair and covering his face with kisses, and he'd never felt more disgusted with himself. He hadn't lost it like that, like some selfish, horny teenager, for years. He clamped his hands on either side of her head and made her look at him.

"I'm sorry, Dani."

"For what?" she asked, giving him a puzzled frown.

"Dammit, don't try to lie about it. I know you didn't get there with me."

"Well, no, not completely. But it's all right, Sam."

"No it's not." He lifted her off his lap and set her on her feet beside the chair. Then he ran one hand down over his face. "You didn't even come close. I should have know I'm too damn big and you're too damn little for this to work."

She propped her fists on her hips and stared at him. "Are you serious?"

"Of course, I'm serious."

"You think every sexual encounter has to have fireworks and bells ringing?"

"Damn right," he grumbled, glaring down at his lap. "It should, anyhow."

Dani grasped his chin between her thumb and forefinger, and tipped his head up. "That's a wonderful sentiment, Sam, but it's unrealistic. I enjoyed what we did— immensely."

"Oh, sure. You're just trying to stroke my ego."

"I'd rather stroke something else," she said, giving him a wicked grin. "Some things take time and practice. Just pretend I'm a schoolteacher, forcing you to do it over and over again until you get it right."

"That's the oldest dirty joke in the book," he muttered.

Nevertheless, he couldn't help chuckling at it. And, he couldn't resist her when she coaxed him out of the chair, led him over to the sofa on the opposite side of the room and told him to lie down beside her. She snuggled into his arms and rested her head on his shoulder, apparently content. After a while, holding her felt good and natural, kind of like cuddling a sleepy kitten.

She talked quietly about her plans for dinner the next day and drew lazy patterns in his chest hair with one fingertip. She draped one leg across both of his and slowly rubbed the back of her heel up and down his calf. Then her hand started to wander, and he lost track of what she was saying. Before he completely understood what was happening, he was hard and aching to be inside her again.

"What are you doin' to me, woman?" he asked gruffly.

"What do you think I'm doing, Sam?"

The sultry purr in her voice raised gooseflesh along his arms. Her hand strayed below his waist, caressing him with a boldness that forced the air out of his lungs.

"I think..." He gasped, then continued in a strangled voice. "I think you're seducin' me."

"Do you mind?"

"I'm not sure, but I'll give you about two years to stop doin' that."

Then she kissed him, hot and wet and deep, and he was lost in another whirlwind of passion. This time she cried out with release twice before his own climax roared through him. Afterward, resting his weight on his elbows so he wouldn't crush her, he gazed down into her bemused, misty eyes for a long moment and felt satisfaction sink deep into his soul.

"Still think you're too damn big and I'm too damn little?" she whispered.

"No, ma'am."

"I like a man who can admit it when he's wrong."

He kissed her—just to shut her up, he told himself. He heard the grandfather clock in the living room bong twice, and reluctantly pulled away from her.

"The kids'll be up in a few hours. We'd better get to bed," he said.

He climbed to his feet, then leaned down to help her up, feasting his eyes on her luscious body as if he might never have the chance to see it naked again. She looked at him the same way, and he barely managed to restrain himself from reaching for her.

They dressed in silence. He carried his boots in his right hand and wrapped his left arm around her shoulders as they climbed the stairs together. He didn't want to leave her at her bedroom door, but he knew he should, since there were two impressionable kids in the house. Brushing one last kiss across her forehead, he murmured, "Good night," and hurried down the hall before he could change his mind.

With mixed emotions, Dani watched him go. The mother part of her knew it was the right thing to do. But the woman part of her, the lover she had so joyfully rediscovered within herself, ached to call him back and beg him to hold her.

Gulping at the sudden lump in her throat, she opened the door and slipped inside. She gazed at the empty double bed for a moment, then sighed, stripped off her clothes and crawled between the cold sheets. She listened to the sounds of Sam getting ready for bed—his belt buckle thumping on the floor when he dropped his jeans, water running in his bathroom, the squeak of the bedsprings accepting his weight.

Gradually her body warmed the bedclothes and a pleasant exhaustion crept over her. She hugged the extra pillow to her breasts, smiling at the memory of Sam's lips and hands touching her there. God, how she loved him.

Later, she would no doubt worry about whether or not making love with him had been a wise decision. But for the rest of the night, she wanted to relive the ecstasy she'd found in his arms. As slumber overtook her, she prayed that Sam would dream of her, as well.

Sam hadn't had the dream for at least ten years, but his back teeth ground together in anxiety the instant it started.

Johnny Bigelow walked in front of him, slashing away the drooping vines with a machete. With Bubba Jackson slung over one shoulder in a fireman's carry, Sam slogged through the undergrowth. The rest of the platoon, battle-weary from ten days in the jungle, brought up the rear.

Bubba's helmet banged against the middle of Sam's back with every step. A swarm of mosquitoes attacked the side of his neck, but he was so used to them and so exhausted, he barely noticed. What little energy and concentration he had left went into putting one foot in front of the other.

"Oh, sweet Jesus, we made it," Johnny said quietly, turning to flash a broad grin. "Daylight ahead. Looks like a village."

Sam nodded and picked up the pace, signaling to the men behind him. Three minutes later, he entered the clearing, blinking against the harsh sunlight. George Pearson and

Mark Wellman hurried to his side, helping him ease his unconscious burden to the ground.

The men dropped their heavy packs and set up the radio to call in a chopper. Sam knelt beside Bubba, checked his leg wound and sighed with relief that it didn't look infected.

"How's he doin'?" George asked.

"Okay for now."

Sam set his rifle on the grass and reached for his canteen, sweeping his gaze from one side of the village to the other. Though he knew the area was crawling with Vietcong, it looked peaceful enough at the moment. There were a dozen huts, maybe a few more. A small group of children played in a mud puddle. An old man sat with his back braced against a broken-down cart, smoking and sunning himself.

Knowing what was coming, Sam thrashed his head back and forth on the pillow. *Wake up, dammit,* his mind screamed, but the dream wasn't ready to let him go.

The children looked up and noticed the American soldiers. Chattering and giggling, the kids ran toward them. He dug into his pack, rooting around for some candy or gum for the little welcoming committee. When he looked up, he saw a flicker of movement on the west side of the village.

It was there and gone so fast, he wasn't sure he'd really seen anything, but he pulled his rifle closer. He hadn't survived the first eleven months of his tour of duty by being careless. With any luck at all, this would be his last patrol. He intended to go home in one piece.

The kids were only ten yards away now, and the sight of their jubilant faces warmed his heart in a way that nothing else could. But there it was again—was it only a shadow? Or a shadowy figure darting between those two huts?

Bubba groaned, claiming Sam's attention for a moment. After assuring himself that his buddy was merely regaining consciousness, he studied the spaces between huts, straining his eyes, the back of his neck prickling with primitive instincts.

There—it wasn't a shadow. It wasn't just a curious villager. Whoever it was, he wore the black pajamas and conical straw hat the Cong favored and was zigzagging his way toward the platoon with a purpose.

"Get those kids outta here, Johnny," he said quietly, picking up his rifle.

Johnny shot him a puzzled glance, then looked toward the village. "See something?"

"Yeah. Tell everybody to act normal, but be ready to hit the dirt."

He continued to watch while Johnny hurriedly followed his orders. The other men stopped talking, adjusted helmets, casually located weapons. Adrenaline pumped into his bloodstream. His gut clenched with tension.

An instant later, the shadowy figure charged into the open, one arm raised, as if ready to throw something.

Somebody yelled, "Damn, he's got a grenade!"

Without allowing himself to think or feel, he whipped the M-16 up to his shoulder, aimed and squeezed the trigger. The figure jerked, ran two more steps. He fired another round. The figure jerked again, then fell backward. The grenade sailed from nerveless fingers into a clump of bushes, exploding on impact.

Villagers poured out of their homes and came running from nearby rice paddies to see what had happened. When the dust settled and the ringing in his ears finally faded, he climbed to his feet. He shouted for everyone to stay back while he cautiously approached the body. Using the tip of his M-16 he pushed the hat away from the enemy's face.

"God almighty," he whispered, his gorge threatening to rush into his throat. He fought it down, then bellowed at the villagers, his buddies, maybe even God, "What the hell kind of a war *is* this . . . ?"

The sound of his own voice, sobbing that question again and again, finally released Sam from the nightmare. He bolted to an upright position and held his head in his hands, shaking and covered with icy sweat. He inhaled harsh, choking breaths, willing the helpless trembling to stop.

A black pit of loneliness and despair opened inside him. Over twenty years had passed since that horrible day, but the sights, smells, sounds and emotions in that damn dream were as vivid as if it had happened yesterday. Would he never find any peace, any solace for the horror and shame? And why had it all come back to haunt him now?

Shivering, he yanked the blankets he'd kicked to the floor back onto the bed and wrapped them around himself. He leaned against the headboard and closed his eyes, but he wouldn't sleep again. Dammit, he ached for someone, anyone, to hold him, stroke his hair, tell him it was all right, like his mother used to do when he was little.

Dani would do that for him. If he asked. But Dani was the reason for the dream's return. He knew that. Somewhere in the back of his mind, he'd always known that, or he wouldn't have fought his attraction to her for as long and hard as he had.

The black pit yawned wider, swallowing another chunk of his soul. It didn't matter how he tried to rationalize what had happened. It didn't matter that it had happened so long ago. It didn't matter that he'd already fallen in love with Dani or that, given a little encouragement, she'd probably fall in love with him.

She deserved a better man than he could ever hope to be. Somehow he would have to find the strength to let her go.

Chapter Eleven

During the next two weeks, Dani felt like a commuter imprisoned on a train that only had two stops—heaven and hell. It was the wrong time of the month for PMS, not that she'd ever suffered much from that particular malady. And she couldn't blame the violent mood swings on her children. They were both behaving themselves better than she could ever remember.

The source of her problem came in a six-foot-four-inch, two-hundred-pound package of solid muscle. She suspected most of that muscle was lodged between Sam's ears, because he certainly acted as if there weren't any brains in there at all.

Sometimes he would laugh and talk with her, and look at her as if he wanted nothing more in this life than to sweep her off her feet and make love to her until neither of them could move. But did he do that? Hah! Didn't she just wish!

No, one minute everything would be wonderful between them, and the next, a distant, haunted kind of look came into his eyes and he closed up tighter than a Tupperware seal. If she pushed him for an explanation, he got up and left without a word. If she went after him, touched him, he shook her off like an obnoxious insect and stayed away from her for hours.

At first, Dani had felt hurt and humiliated by his rejection. But now she wanted to whack him over the head, kick him in the shins, rip out a great big handful of his chest hair. If he honestly didn't want to pursue a sexual relationship with her, fine. All he had to do was tell her so. It would hurt and she wouldn't like it much, but she could accept it—eventually.

What she refused to accept was his disgusting lack of consistency. She'd had it up to her eyeballs with this hot-and-cold act. For God's sake, didn't the man realize she had feelings? She didn't know what the heck his problem was, but she intended to find out.

She parked her car in front of Becky Sinclair's house, killed the engine and sat there for a few minutes, inhaling deep, calming breaths. It didn't help one bit, of course. When she was this livid, nothing ever did.

Becky appeared at the living room window and motioned Dani to come inside. Sighing, Dani stepped out of the car and hurried up the walk. The front door opened as she reached for the doorknob.

"What a nice surprise. Come in before you freeze," Becky said.

"Thanks," Dani replied, rubbing her hands together. "I'm sorry to barge in on you without calling, but I'm going to murder your brother if I don't talk to someone."

Becky smiled with the serenity that happily pregnant women sometimes have, and took Dani's coat. "Well, you've come to the right place. Come in the kitchen and I'll make you some chamomile tea."

Dani cast an appreciative glance at the Sinclairs' beautifully decorated Christmas tree, then followed her hostess. Too agitated to sit, she paced from the doorway to the window and back while Becky set out cups and put a kettle on the stove. By the time the kettle shrieked, Dani felt ready to shriek right along with it.

"All right," Becky said, when they were settled at the table, "spill your guts. You can start with telling me how much you love Sam and then move on to whatever idiotic thing he's done."

"How did you know?" Dani asked, gaping at her.

"That you're in love with Sam?" Becky chuckled and pointed to a picture of Peter that sat on the windowsill. "Until he came along, I was a calm, mild-mannered woman. He's the only person I know who can make me mad enough to spit nails in less than thirty seconds."

Chuckling, Dani eyed Becky's distended abdomen. "Wait'll that baby learns to walk and tell you off."

Becky's eyebrows shot up and a look of mock-horror crossed her face. "You mean I'm gonna have another one like that to cope with?"

"I'm afraid so."

The two women grinned at each other, then sipped their tea. After setting down her mug, Becky flipped her long braid over one shoulder as if getting down to serious business.

"All right, I'm ready now. What did Sam do?"

"It's more what he hasn't done," Dani said slowly. "I thought everything was going so well, and then boom, he's withdrawn from me again."

"Have you made love with him yet?"

Dani's face heated at the blunt question, but she couldn't see any judgment in Becky's eyes. Finally she nodded. "Once. Well, twice, but on the same night. The next morning he acted as if nothing had happened."

"Oh, cripes," Becky muttered. "He's still acting that way?"

Dani nodded again. "Yesterday he came to Colin's basketball game with me, and this morning he came to Kim's play, but I could feel the tension rolling off him in waves. He was so careful not to touch me, you'd think I had lice or something. Making love with him was the most wonderful thing that ever happened to me. I thought he felt the same way, and, dammit, I just don't understand what I could have done to offend him."

"You probably didn't offend him at all," Becky replied.

"Then why is he rejecting me like this? Has there been so much gossip in town about my living at the ranch, he's embarrassed to be seen with me?"

Becky shook her head. "Not that I know of. Pete hears most of the hot poop at the clinic, and he hasn't mentioned anything about it to me. Sam's not all that straitlaced anyway. He probably wouldn't be openly affectionate in public, but—"

"I didn't expect him to be," Dani said with a disgruntled sigh. "I could handle it if he only acted that way in public, but he does the same thing when we're alone, which, believe me, isn't often."

"Why don't you ask him what's going on?"

"I've tried, but he always pulls this vanishing act. It's so irritating!"

Becky reached across the table and patted Dani's fist. "Yeah, I know what you mean. If it helps any, Sam usually retreats when he's feeling too much. Maybe he just needs more time."

"I'm scared to give him much more, Becky," Dani wailed. "My kids are really getting attached to him. I don't even want to think about how they'll react if we have to leave."

"You don't seriously think it will come to that."

"I don't know. I just don't know."

"Drink your tea, Dani."

A brief silence settled between the two women while Dani did as she was told. She drummed her fingernails on the tabletop, wracking her brain for an answer. Finally an idea glimmered through her muddled thoughts.

"Do you know a woman named Ginny Bradford?" she asked.

Becky let out a startled laugh. "Where on earth did you dig up that name?"

"It's really none of my business, so I can't tell you, but I wonder if she's important to Sam. I mean, could he be feeling that he betrayed her when he made love with me?"

"Oh, shoot. I don't think so," Becky answered, shaking her head. "Sam dated her a few times when they were in high school, before she started going with his best friend, Charlie. But as far as I know, the three of them were good buddies all the way. She married Charlie before he and Sam went to Vietnam, and Sam was the best man at their wedding."

"Are Ginny and Charlie still married?"

"Charlie passed away two years ago. I don't think Ginny's remarried. Last I heard about her, she was going to the university down in Laramie, workin' on a teaching certificate."

"What does she look like?" Dani asked, not really sure she wanted to know.

"She's kinda tall, has long blond hair, but you'll see for yourself any day now," Becky said. "I'm sure she'll come home to visit her folks for Christmas, and she always drops by the ranch to see Sam."

"Then that's *it*, Becky," Dani insisted. "He's got something going with her, and he's afraid I'll ruin their relationship."

"No way! I'm telling you, he's not in love with her. They'll sit around and drink beer and reminisce, and that'll be the end of it."

"Maybe he's just waiting for her to graduate or something," Dani suggested.

"Well, if you *really* love Sam, I'd think you might want to fight for him, even if he *is* involved with Ginny, which I don't believe for one minute," Becky said.

Dani leapt out of her chair and threw both hands up beside her head. "Would you look at me, Becky? Really look? How can I compete with a tall, gorgeous blonde?"

"I never said she was gorgeous. Oh, she's pretty enough, but she's not one bit more attractive than you are, Dani. Now, the way I see it, you're here and she's not. That gives you a pretty big advantage."

"Yeah, right." Dani exhaled a disheartened sigh and sat down again. "God, this is ridiculous. High school kids act this way."

Becky laughed. "When you're in love, you're bound to act a little wacko. I sure did." A wicked grin spread across her mouth. She leaned closer and lowered her voice, as if she feared someone might overhear. "Now, are you ready to listen to my plan, or not?"

"All right."

"I'll have you and Sam and the kids over for dinner next Friday night. Pete and I are planning to take Tina on one of those weekend trips to Yellowstone Park. You know, where you go snowmobiling and stuff? We'll invite Colin and Kim to come along with us, so you can do your Christmas shopping for them. You'll have Sam all to yourself."

"Oh, Becky, my kids would love it. But that's an awful lot for a pregnant lady to take on."

"Aw, shoot. Kim will keep Tina entertained for me, Pete and Colin will talk computers, and I'll have a great weekend of peace and quiet. You can take care of Tina for us the next weekend, if it'll make you feel any better. Whaddya think?"

"It seems kind of... devious."

"Of course it's devious," Becky answered with a laugh. "Sam's so damn stubborn, you need something a little devious to shake him up."

"Why are you doing this?"

"Couple of reasons. The first is, I think you're the best thing that's ever happened to Sam and he's just too darn blind to see it. I had a ball watching him watch you at Thanksgiving dinner."

"Oh yeah?"

"Yeah. He cares a lot about you, Dani. I can tell. The other reason is that I owe him a little payback for some things he and Hank did to me when I first met Pete. Those fools about teased me to death. So, come on now, and tell me you'll do it. It's for Sam's own good."

"Well...all right." Then Dani nodded and said more decisively, "I will."

"That's the spirit," Becky crowed. "Take no prisoners."

Laughing, Dani pushed back her chair. "I'd better get going or I'll be late meeting the bus."

Becky walked her to the door and watched her hurry out to her car. When the little red Fiesta pulled away from the house, she murmured, "Sic 'im, girl."

Late Friday afternoon, Sam watched from the barn while the little red car stopped at the end of the driveway and Dani and the kids piled out. She paused at the back door for a moment, glancing over her shoulder as if she sensed him staring at her. Feeling like an idiot, he stepped farther back into the shadows.

Still, the sight of her brought a familiar, hollow ache to his chest, and he sighed when she finally disappeared into the house. Damn. He wanted her so much, he could hardly sleep at night. When he did manage to nod off, his old nightmare came back, reminding him that he had no place in her life.

He did his best to stay away from her, but it was damn hard to avoid the woman who cooked his meals and washed his underwear. Besides that, he *was* involved with Colin and Kim, and he couldn't bring himself to disappoint them when they asked him to attend their school functions. He couldn't do things like that with the kids and exclude their mother, now could he?

Driving Dani into town for a basketball game, he had found himself torn in a dozen different directions. He was almost as proud of those kids as she was. It tickled him no end to watch her cheer on Colin's team as if they were playing in the NCAA finals. Then he'd sweated right along with her until Kim had successfully delivered her lines in the school play, too.

Dani was like a cheerful little grasshopper, bouncing here and there, curious about everyone and everything around her, striking up conversations with total strangers as easily as he brushed his teeth every morning. More often than he'd care to admit, he'd caught himself eavesdropping while he sat beside her on the bleachers, and learned some surprising things about people he'd known for years. Nobody could resist her for long.

That realization had driven Sam to miserable new depths of jealousy. The community had linked Dani to him, and he'd enjoyed feeling as if he was part of a couple for a change. But there were plenty of single guys around who would ask her out if they thought he wouldn't mind. He knew he should put out the word that she was available— let her find happiness with somebody else if he wasn't going to marry her—but he couldn't bring himself to do it.

The truth was, he would mind one helluva lot if she started dating other men. The thought of her sharing all that sweet passion with somebody else was enough to make him gnash his teeth and give him an ulcer. He was damned if he loved her and damned if he didn't, and dammit, he just didn't know what to do about her anymore.

He wished Hank would come home. He wished Grandma D and Tina would come home. Hell, at this point he'd welcome a wino into the house—*anybody* who could serve as a buffer between himself and Dani. Thank God they were all going to Becky and Peter's for supper tonight so he could have a little breathing room.

Sam finished his work in the barn, then trudged into the house to get cleaned up. When he came back downstairs, Dani and the kids were waiting for him in the kitchen. Noting a pair of suitcases sitting by the back door, Sam felt a shiver of apprehension race up his spine.

"Somebody goin' someplace?" he asked.

Colin turned to him, his face flushed with excitement. "Guess what, Sam? Becky and Pete are taking Kim and me to Yellowstone Park for the weekend. We're gonna stay at their house tonight so we can start really early tomorrow morning. Isn't that cool?"

Sam rocked back on the heels of his boots, sheer panic threatening to suffocate him. He looked at Dani, and the satisfied gleam in her eyes told him the answer to his next question.

"Aren't you going along?"

She shook her head and smiled. "Oh, no, I—"

"Don't worry about takin' an extra day off," he said in a rush. "It's no problem, at all. I can take care of myself, and you really oughta see the park in the winter. There aren't as many tourists and the snow is—"

"I'm not going, Sam," she said firmly. "I need to do some Christmas shopping without certain nosey people around."

"We're not nosey," Kim protested. Dani gave her a droll look that made her giggle. "Well, I'm not, but Colin is."

"I am not, you little geek," Colin replied automatically.

"Don't start that, you two," Dani said. "It's time to go. Take your suitcases out to the car." While the children obeyed, she turned to Sam. "Are you ready?"

Ready for what? he wanted to ask. Supper? Yeah, he was hungry. Sex? Yeah, he was hungry for that, too. A whole weekend alone with her? God, no! She'd wear him down to a nub and wheedle a marriage proposal out of him before Sunday morning. Hell, he could barely keep his hands off her right now.

She knew it, too, the little snot. He could read it all right there in those big, smoky blue eyes of hers—desire, anticipation, amused triumph. Well, he'd just have to see about that. He'd show her he was made of sterner stuff than she'd ever come up against.

Without saying a word, Sam crammed his hat on his head and stalked out the door. The kids filled the car with lively chatter during the drive to Becky's house. Sam concentrated on the icy road, but it wasn't easy with Dani's perfume wafting around his head and her bubbly laughter filling his ears.

His sister greeted him with a broad grin and a wicked, knowing sparkle in her dark eyes. He'd wondered about a conspiracy, and having his suspicions confirmed cranked his temper up another notch. He'd hoped Becky would know better than to interfere in his life, but she was so disgustingly happy with Pete, it had, no doubt, been too much to expect.

Of course, he'd never been able to stay mad at his little sister for long, and tonight proved no exception. A hearty meal and a couple of beers went a long way toward mellowing his mood. The laughter and conversation around the kitchen table finished the job.

After supper, Kim and Tina set up a board game. Colin disappeared into Pete's den to play computer games. The four adults settled in the living room.

Sam and Dani occupied opposite ends of the sofa. Pete added a log to the fire, then joined Becky on the love seat. Some kind of sweet, classical music with lots of violins and flutes played softly on the stereo. Sam didn't know much about that kind of music, but he found it pleasant, even soothing.

He rested the back of his head against the sofa, and linked his hands across his belly. Through half-closed eyes, he watched the firelight play over Dani's glossy black hair, his fingers itching to stroke those silky curls. Then Becky's laughter drew his attention in her direction.

A tightness came over his chest as he took in the picture his sister and brother-in-law made. Pete's right arm surrounded Becky's shoulders; his left hand rested protectively on the rounded form of their unborn baby. Her head nestled against the side of his chest, her left hand splayed over his thigh. It was easy to imagine them spending many a peaceful evening in front of the fireplace, talking, loving, exchanging those intimate glances and smiles.

Sam was fiercely glad for his little sister, glad for Pete, a man he'd come to love and respect as a friend, as well as a relative. Their coming together had been painful for both of them at times, and he couldn't think of anyone who deserved to be happy more than these two. And yet, he'd never felt so savagely envious of anyone as he did at that moment.

You can have all of that with Dani, a voice inside his head whispered. *Tenderness, love, children.*

As if she had heard the same voice, Dani turned and gazed at him, her eyes bright, maybe a little misty, with emotion. Sam's throat closed around a hard lump. He couldn't breathe, couldn't move, couldn't look away from her.

All he could do was sit there and want her with a gaping, aching hole in his gut.

The stark anguish in Sam's eyes shocked Dani. She knew he'd been enjoying the evening as much as she had. What on earth could have suddenly caused him such pain?

She reached out instinctively, wanting to comfort him, but dropped her hand in her lap when his expression immediately hardened, masking his emotions. Becky and Peter didn't appear to notice anything amiss, but that didn't surprise Dani. Though they'd been married for over a year, the two of them still acted like honeymooners.

Suddenly Sam lunged to his feet and announced it was time to leave. Dani thanked the Sinclairs for dinner and said goodbye to her children, then accompanied him out to his car. Their breath made wispy plumes in the frigid night air; their boots crunched a fresh layer of snow underfoot.

Neither of them spoke during the trip back to the Circle D. Painfully aware of Sam's brooding presence beside her, Dani watched the star-studded sky through the windshield and wished she knew how to breach the suffocating silence. This wasn't exactly what she'd had in mind when she'd agreed to Becky's plan.

Sam dropped her off at the back door. Dani stood on the steps, half expecting him to turn the car around and head for town, but he drove it into the garage. Assuming he would check on the animals in the barn, she went inside, took off her coat and boots and started setting up the coffee maker.

A moment later, she heard the back door bang shut, then three quick, angry footsteps crossing the wooden floor of the porch.

"I don't want coffee," Sam said.

His deep, gritty tone prompted her to turn and face him. He filled the kitchen doorway, his hat tipped back on his head, face reddened with cold, hands clenched at his sides. His fleece-lined coat and his rigid stance made his chest and shoulders look massive, almost threatening, but it was the intense expression in his dark eyes that caught and held her attention.

"What *do* you want, Sam?" she asked, her quiet voice echoing slightly in the big, otherwise silent room.

He took one step into the kitchen, then another, and another. "You know what I want, Dani." He stopped in front of her and brushed the knuckles of his right hand across her cheek. "And now you've set up the perfect opportunity to make damned sure I'll get it."

"Yes."

"Why? You know I won't marry you."

"I want it, too, Sam," she said, meeting his heated gaze without flinching.

He exhaled a harsh, shuddering breath and closed his eyes for a long moment. When he opened them again, he raised his hands, cupping her face between them. "Well, I hope you can live with that decision, Dani, 'cause I've just run out of nobility."

Then he lowered his head and kissed her with a fierce, hungry passion that drove the air from her lungs. He clamped one arm around her waist, pulling her up onto her tiptoes, pressing their hips together. She clutched at his shoulders for balance, matching him kiss for kiss, and suddenly the world tilted on its axis.

Carrying her high against his chest, he marched into the living room and up the long flight of stairs to the second floor. Dani gazed up at the muscle twitching along his clenched jaw as he strode down the hall to his room, and gulped.

On one hand, it was wonderfully exciting and romantic to be swept up those stairs by a strong, determined, angry man, like Scarlett O'Hara in *Gone With the Wind*. On the other hand, she'd never been completely certain just what Rhett Butler had done to Scarlett after he'd kicked the bedroom door shut. Sam didn't give her much time to worry about that, however.

He shouldered his way into the room and deposited her none too gently in the middle of his king-size bed. He switched on a lamp and tossed his hat like a Frisbee toward the dresser, then peeled off his heavy coat and dropped it onto the floor. The mattress dipped beneath his weight when he sat down and pulled off his boots.

Dani's throat tightened. Acid tears stung the backs of her eyes, but she refused to let them fall. Instead, she leaned back against the headboard and stared at him wide-eyed, not really afraid that he would hurt her, but desperately needing a little tenderness.

The snaps on his shirt gave way with surprisingly loud pops and the bed frame creaked when he stood up, tossed the shirt aside and reached for his belt buckle.

"What's the matter?" he demanded, jerking his belt from its loops in one smooth motion. "Isn't this what you wanted?"

Dani nodded, then changed her mind and shook her head. "Not like this, Sam," she managed to choke past the constriction in her throat. "I didn't mean to make you so angry."

"I don't like being manipulated," he said, letting the belt slide out of his hand.

"I know. And I don't blame you for that, but..." Despite her best efforts, the tears spilled over onto her cheeks, and she quickly ducked her head so he wouldn't see them.

"But what?"

"It was so wonderful between us the last time, and then you acted like..." She paused and swiped at her cheeks with the back of one hand. "And I couldn't get you to talk to me, and—"

"Dammit, Dani, don't cry."

She sniffled and wiped at her eyes, still not looking at him. "I'm not crying. I'm just frustrated. I don't know what I did wrong when we made love before, and..." She sniffled again.

He muttered something under his breath. Then the side of the bed sagged and two long legs stretched out beside hers. One strong arm wrapped around her shoulders and pulled her to his chest, gently urging her cheek against the soft warm cotton of his undershirt. He didn't say a word, but his fingers alternately played with her curls and rubbed her back in slow, soothing strokes.

Dani had no idea how many minutes ticked by, but gradually the regular thump of his heart beneath her ear steadied her emotions. Tentatively, she draped one arm across his abdomen and snuggled closer. His arm tightened around her in response, then he tipped her chin up with his free hand, forcing her to meet his gaze.

"You didn't do anything wrong when we made love before," he murmured. "I enjoyed every blessed minute of it."

"Then why have you been so distant, Sam? Why wouldn't you talk to me?"

"I didn't know what to say," he admitted. "You're not cut out for an affair, Dani. Any fool can see that. And I can't offer you anything more."

"Is there . . . someone else?"

"God, no." He shook his head and sighed. "I wish it was that simple."

"Explain it to me, Sam. Whatever it is, I'll understand."

He rolled onto his side facing her and gently traced the side of her neck with his rough fingertips. "I can't. All I can tell you is that it doesn't have anything to do with you or anything you did. I just don't have any love to give a woman."

Dani didn't believe that for a second, but the hoarse note in his voice prevented her from debating the point. "But you *do* want me."

"Aw, babe." He pulled her tightly against him, showing her exactly how much he did, in fact, want her. "I want you so much it's eatin' me alive from the inside out."

"Then I'll take whatever you have to give, Sam."

He opened his mouth as if he would argue, but Dani didn't give him the opportunity. She pressed her lips against his throat and ran her hands across the hard muscles of his chest, down to the waistband of his jeans and beyond. He groaned and pushed her onto her back, his mouth finding hers instinctively.

Suddenly all hesitancy and inhibition between them evaporated. They rolled over and over on the bed, kissing, touching, caressing. Articles of clothing gave way to hurried, greedy fingers. Soft sighs of pleasure mingled with harsh moans of delight. Hungry mouths nipped and sucked and licked.

Ice covered the windowpanes, but their bodies radiated more than enough heat to dispel any chill in the air. The world narrowed to the rumpled bedspread beneath her back, the strong, sure hands tenderly molding her breasts, the deep, raspy voice murmuring praise and encouragement, telling her what he would do to her next, making her writhe with impatience for each promised act.

His skin was smooth and hot to her touch in places, rough and hot in others. She learned each and every texture of his big, magnificent body, located ticklish spots and erogenous zones with her hands and her tongue, exulted in his willingness to share this part of himself with her.

Then he was above her, surrounding her, deep inside the core of her body, taking her back to that marvelous, shimmering place she'd visited only once before and only with him. She held him close while he shuddered with his own completion, and stroked his back until his ragged breathing returned to normal.

Resting his weight on his elbows, he gazed down at her. The corners of his mustache slowly curved up in a delightfully boyish grin and a chuckle rumbled out of his chest.

"What's so funny?" she asked.

He rolled onto his side and propped his head up with one hand. "I thought I'd imagined how good it was. Who'd ever believe a Mutt and Jeff like us could produce so many fireworks in bed?"

Dani turned to face him, mimicking his posture and his smug grin. "Somebody with a very active imagination."

"I suppose you think you've got one."

"Of course. Don't you?"

He scrunched his mouth into a thoughtful pose and smoothed his mustache with thumb and index finger. "Maybe you'd better show me yours first."

"Are you sure you really want me to?" she asked, toppling him onto his back with a firm push.

The corners of his eyes crinkled with laughter. "I don't know," he drawled. "Mom warned me about you wicked, city gals. Got anything kinky in mind?"

"You can always hope, cowboy," Dani drawled back at him. "You can always hope."

Chapter Twelve

Dani spent the rest of the night in Sam's arms. She would have been more than happy to spend all day Saturday there, as well. Unfortunately a rancher couldn't afford that kind of luxury. Gertie needed to be milked, and Bear Dog, the chickens, the horses and the cattle had to be fed.

After serving Sam his favorite breakfast of sourdough pancakes, sausage and eggs, and sending him out to start the chores with a sizzling kiss, Dani decided it would be fun to tag along. She finished the dishes, then bundled up and hurried outside to find him. A four-inch layer of fresh snow carpeted the land. The sun had risen over the mountaintops, creating a sparkling fairyland that dazzled her eyes.

"C'mon, Cain. Abel, let's go," she heard Sam order from the other side on the barn. "Time to earn your oats."

To Dani's delight, he walked around the corner of the building a moment later, leading two enormous light gray horses. They were heftier than the other horses on the Circle D, built more like the Budweiser Clydesdales she'd seen on television. From discussions she'd overheard at the table, she concluded these must be the Percherons Sam was teaching Colin to handle.

Sam smiled when he saw her. "Wanna go for a ride on the sled?"

"I'd love to," she replied, picking up her pace to join him.

Dani stood back while he settled heavy leather collars over the horses' heads. Then he called her over to acquaint herself with them while he hitched the animals to a broad, flat wagon with wooden runners attached to the bottom. She loved watching him work.

Reddened with cold and covered with calluses and cuts in various stages of healing, his big hands weren't pretty by any stretch of the imagination. But they were strong and competent, and, as she knew from personal experience, they could be surprisingly gentle. Remembering how they had moved over her own naked skin the night before, she shivered.

"Cold already?" he asked, giving her a devilish grin from beneath the brim of his hat. "Maybe you need another pair of long johns."

"I'm fine," she said, returning that grin.

"Well, let's get this show on the road."

He pulled on a pair of gloves, picked her up by the waist and swung her aboard the wagon. Then he climbed up beside her, grasped the reins and set the team in motion. Dani grabbed the wooden rail at the front of the wagon for balance.

"Aren't we going to feed the cattle?" she asked, indicating with a nod the empty wagon bed.

"Yup. But first, we're gonna break down the snow crust. We'll load up with hay from one of the stacks out in the pasture."

"Why don't you just drive a truck out there? Wouldn't that be faster than using the horses?"

"Depends. We usually get three or four feet of snow. When it really starts to stack up, even a four-wheel drive can bog down."

"What about snowmobiles?"

"Damn things break down too often." He tipped his head toward the team. "Cain and Abel may not be fast, but they're dependable. I figure they save me time in the long run. Besides, I like 'em and they aren't noisy."

As the ranch buildings grew smaller in the distance, and Dani asked one question after another, Sam's usual reticence faded. He told her stories about working with his father and grandfather, named the mountain peaks surrounding the Circle D, talked about the trappers and fur traders who had been the first white men to discover the area. Pride echoed in his voice and shone in his eyes, and Dani began to understand that this wild, rugged country was where Sam Dawson's heart truly belonged.

Despite a clear blue sky and a bright sun overhead, a sharp wind cut through her layers of clothing. She moved closer to Sam's side, hoping to share a little of his body heat. As if reading her mind, he held the reins in his left hand and used his right arm to guide her in front of him.

She tipped her head way back and grinned at him. "You make a wonderful windbreak."

He leaned down and dropped a quick, friendly kiss on her lips. "Glad to know I'm good for something."

His right arm settled around her waist, pulling her back against him. Then he took the reins in both hands again, encasing her between his arms. Dani gazed out over the pristine scenery and sighed at the sheer beauty of it.

There wasn't another human being or vehicle in sight. The only sounds she could hear were occasional snorts from the horses, the creak of the harness and a whooshing from the sled runners cutting into the snow. She would have been terrified to be out here alone; with Sam she felt happy, protected, secure.

The rest of the day passed in a golden haze of adventure as Sam shared his world with her in a way he'd never done before. He explained every part of the procedure when they fed the cattle. He told her the history of the ranch. He talked about his mother and pointed out the ridge where his father had built a hideaway cabin for their honeymoon.

It was as if he'd stored thousands of words inside himself over the years and the dam had suddenly burst. Dani loved every second of it. She loved listening to him, loved provoking smiles and laughter from him, loved seeing his dark eyes light up with enthusiasm or soften with fond memories.

When they got back to the barn, she went into the house and started a fresh pot of coffee while Sam took care of Cain and Abel. She was in the bathroom off the kitchen, trying to fluff up the hair mashed flat by her stocking hat, when he came inside and called her name.

"In here, Sam," she said.

He appeared in the doorway a moment later and braced one shoulder against the casing, a smile tugging at his mouth as he watched her struggle with her static-charged curls. "I don't know why you're botherin' with that."

"Most people comb their hair when it gets messed up," she retorted, shooting a laughing glance at his own unruly locks.

He stepped into the room and stood behind her. "Is that so?" he leaned down and kissed the nape of her neck. "Even when they know it's just gonna get messed up again?"

Dani's hand paused in midair, and a delicious shudder ran from the top of her neck to her tailbone at the combination of warm breath and cold lips on such a sensitive place. "Who says it's gonna get messed up again?"

He kissed his way around to the spot just below her right ear, snatched the comb out of her hand and tossed it into the sink. "I do."

Then he put both hands on her hips and turned her to face him. Her arms reached for his neck, his hands plunged into her curls and their mouths came together with hungry urgency. The next thing Dani knew, her legs were clasped around his hips and he was carrying her up the stairs to his bedroom.

But once they returned to his private domain, the need to rush mellowed to a more savoring mood. Peeling away flannel shirts, jeans, long johns and socks became a slow, sensuous game. Rediscovering all the sweet, erogenous places they'd found the night before turned into a delightful exercise in nonverbal communication. They made love over and over again, talking, giggling like a couple of teenagers, their precious hours of privacy ticking away with alarming speed.

Exhausted and replete at last, Sam lay flat on his back. Dani cuddled up to his right side, her head on his shoulder, her arm draped over his chest. She had never felt so fulfilled, so close to another human being in her life. The words tumbled out of her mouth before she could stop to think about them.

"I love you, Sam."

He didn't say a word, but the muscles beneath her head tensed. Smiling, she raised herself up and kissed his whiskery chin. He turned his head away. She cupped the side of his face with her palm and nudged it, demanding that he look at her.

"You don't have to say you love me," she said, meeting his troubled gaze calmly.

"I wish I could, Dani, but—"

"No, don't say anything at all, Sam. I just wanted you to know how I feel about you. What we've shared today is good enough for me."

"It shouldn't be, dammit," he said.

"Well, it is. So just go to sleep and don't worry about it."

With that, she kissed his chin again and snuggled back down into the covers. Gradually his shoulder relaxed, his breathing deepened, and Dani blissfully followed him into sleep.

She awoke hours later in total darkness, uncertain as to what had disturbed her. The wind howling outside the bedroom windows prompted her to pull the blankets more snugly around her neck.

Then Sam moaned softly and thrashed his head back and forth. He mumbled something she couldn't understand, and she suddenly realized his body was dripping with sweat. Concerned, she pulled up on one elbow and stroked her hand across his forehead.

"It's all right, Sam," she murmured. "It's only a dream."

His head jerked away from her touch. "What the hell kind of a . . ." he muttered, his head thrashing harder.

She turned on the bedside lamp and continued her efforts to soothe him. "I'm here, Sam. Everything's okay. Try to wake up, sweetheart."

Every muscle in his body went rigid. His breathing became harsh and ragged.

"No. No, dammit. What the hell kind of a war . . ."

Intending to shake him awake, Dani grasped his shoulders. His right arm lashed out, slamming her head against the headboard. He jackknifed to a sitting position. His eyes flew open, staring at some horror Dani could only imagine.

She sat up, holding the side of her head with one hand. "Sam," she said as firmly as she could manage. "Sam, you're having a nightmare. Please wake up."

His face contorted and his chin quivered, as if he wanted to cry but couldn't. A violent shudder coursed through him and he shook his head in confusion.

"It's all right, Sam," Dani crooned. "Everything's fine."

He turned his head and looked at her, his eyes so filled with torment, she felt tears well up in her own. Certain that he was finally seeing her instead of a phantom, she reached out to touch his shoulder with her free hand. He shook his head again and another shudder racked his body.

"What is it?" she whispered. "What's hurting you?"

Sam pulled away from her and swung his legs over the side of the bed. "Nothing. Just an old dream I have once in a while."

"About Vietnam?"

"Yeah. Did I, uh . . . did I hurt you?"

"Not really." She gave him a rueful grin while she rubbed the knot swelling beneath her hairline.

"What does that mean?" he asked, turning to scowl at her over his shoulder.

"You, um, batted me away and I banged my head." At his harsh intake of breath, she hurried to reassure him. "I'm fine. Really. I've got a hard head."

He cursed under his breath, then got up and yanked on his jeans. "Go back to sleep," he said, shoving his arms into his shirtsleeves.

"I think you should talk about it—"

"I don't." He stalked to the doorway.

"Sam, wait. Where are you going?"

"Downstairs. I'll see you in the morning."

The door snapped shut behind him and he was gone. Dani sighed in frustration, then picked up his pillow and hugged it to her bare breasts.

"Darn you, Sam," she grumbled, "why did you have to close up on me again?"

Of course, she knew the answer to that question. At least she thought she did. A man like Sam could only stand to share a certain amount of himself at one time. During the past twenty-eight hours, he had probably exceeded his limit, and would, no doubt, withdraw from her until he felt comfortable again.

Well, strong, silent cowboys might seem romantic in the movies, but they were a pain in the butt to live with. If he thought she was going to let him go off somewhere and suffer alone, he was wrong. Flinging the pillow aside, she climbed out of bed, grabbed one of Sam's shirts from the closet and a pair of his socks from the dresser and yanked them on. Then she marched down the stairs, rolling up the sleeves as she went.

She found him standing in the kitchen, staring out the window over the sink, every line of his big body rigid with tension. The coffee maker gurgled and hissed on the counter, masking the sound of her footsteps. Not wanting to startle him, she cleared her throat and entered the room. He glanced at her over his shoulder, then turned back to the window.

Dani took two mugs out of the cupboard and set them beside the coffee maker before walking over to stand beside him. He ignored her. She slid her left arm around his waist and rested the side of her head against his arm.

"Dammit, Dani," he said, stepping away from her. "I told you to go back to sleep."

"You think I can sleep after what just happened to you?"

"It's no big deal."

She braced one elbow on the edge of the sink and smiled at him. "Great. Then you can tell me about that nightmare."

"No."

"Why not?"

"Because it's none of your business."

"Oh. Now I get it. I'm okay to sleep with, but I'm not good enough to hear about something that's bothering you."

He raked a hand through his hair. "It doesn't have anything to do with you or being good enough."

"That's how it feels, Sam. I've told you about my marriage and my problems with my kids and my parents, and you've helped me a lot. Why won't you let me return the favor?"

"I don't need any help."

"Well, excuse me if I don't agree." She pointed toward the ceiling. "You were suffering up there. Do you think I can ignore that?"

"I don't talk about the war, Dani. Ever."

She straightened away from the sink and propped her hands on her hips. "Look, at the bar I worked in, we had a lot of Vietnam vets who were customers. I've heard so many war stories, I doubt you could shock me. Do you want a relationship with me or not?

"Is that some kind of a threat?"

"No, dammit, but it hurts when you shut me out. I care about you."

"That doesn't give you the right to grill me."

"Give me a break, Sam." She sighed in frustration, then inhaled a deep, calming breath. "Remember when you asked me what I wanted when I came out here to meet you?"

He nodded but didn't speak.

"Do you remember what I said about wanting someone to share my problems with and let me share his?"

"So? When I've got a problem, you'll be the first to know."

"Yeah, sure. Well, thanks for the great sex, but I don't need your charity."

She turned away from the counter, ready to storm out of the kitchen.

He reached out with his right hand and grabbed her arm. "Charity! What the hell are you talkin' about?"

"That's what you're offering me, Sam. Charity." Glaring at him, she jerked her arm out of his grasp. "What we have here is an unequal relationship. You take care of me and my kids—"

"And you take care of my house and my clothes and my food. Sounds pretty damned equal to me."

"But it's not. I want intimacy, Sam."

His gaze slide up and down her body and a grin tugged at the corners of his mouth. "It doesn't get a whole lot more intimate than we've already been."

"No, you don't understand. I'm talking about emotional intimacy. I don't like being the only one to talk about my feelings. It makes me feel too exposed—"

"You said it doesn't matter if I don't love you."

"I said you didn't have to say it. But for God's sake, I'd at least like to be your friend."

"You are."

She shook her head. "Friends share their problems, Sam. I don't want to be just one more person for you to take care of. As of now, that's what I am."

"That's bull."

"No, it's not. And it's not a sign of weakness to let somebody listen when you're hurting."

"I never said it was. You're making a mountain out of a molehill. You're just like every other damned woman I've ever known."

"I resent that."

"Oh yeah?" His palm smacked the counter with a loud crack, and he lowered his face close to hers. "Well, I resent having you demand to know what I'm feeling. If I want you to know, I'll tell ya, and there are some things I don't tell *anybody*. You can either accept that or leave me the hell alone."

"Then I guess I'll have to leave you the hell alone."

"Fine. I'm goin' out to feed the stock."

Sam stomped out of the room, adrenaline pumping through his system and his heart thundering to beat hell. He slammed the door between the kitchen and the mudroom and leaned back against it, sucking in great gulps of air until his fury abated enough for him to breathe normally again. Then he pulled on his coat and hat and walked outside.

At the barn door, Bear Dog greeted him with a soft woof. Sam leaned down and scratched the dog behind his ears, muttering, "Damn nosy woman," and almost smiled when the animal rewarded him with a canine grin. Unfortunately, a vision of Dani's hurt face danced before his eyes, and a wave of guilt tightened his chest.

Cursing viciously under his breath, he rushed through his chores in the barn and went out to hitch up the team. He finished feeding the cattle in record time, but when he got back to the ranch yard and had taken care of the horses, he knew he wasn't ready to face Dani again yet. He didn't want to see anyone else, either.

Damn. He was tired and hungry and cold, and he couldn't bring himself to go into his own house. Snorting in disgust, he got into his pickup and drove up into the mountains. Without consciously planning it, he arrived at the cabin. Emotions swelled inside him at the sight of the small log building. He didn't come here often because it always reminded him of how much he missed his parents.

Still, it was a perfect place to be alone for a few hours, he decided, climbing out of the truck. Maybe he could think and get his head on straight. He slogged through the snowdrift covering the steps, then slid a loose board in the rafters aside and found the key his family kept hidden there. He unlocked the door and stepped inside.

Nobody had used the cabin in months. It smelled musty, and white sheets covered the furniture in the living room area. The wood box by the back door was full, however. Sam started a fire in the fireplace, then searched the kitchen cabinets for food.

He found a can of stew and a jar of instant coffee, pans and a cup, without much trouble. The can opener turned up in a drawer beside the refrigerator and he found silverware sealed in a plastic bag in another drawer next to the sink. Ten minutes later, he sat on the sofa in front of the fire, eating stew straight from the pot. It wasn't nearly as good as Dani's, but he was too hungry to care.

When he'd finished, he carried the pot back to the kitchen counter, took another one from the cabinet and went outside to fill it with snow. Sam melted the snow by the fire and used the water to make coffee for himself. Then he settled back with his heels propped on the battered coffee table, linked his hands behind his head and finally allowed himself to ponder the situation with Dani. Not that she'd ever been far from his thoughts since he'd left the house. Or since the day he'd met her.

At first he tried to tell himself that a man's nightmares and problems were his own damn business. Unfortunately he'd heard enough other women complain, like Dani, about him shutting them out, that he had to admit Dani might have a point. He hadn't cared about those other women enough to even consider trying to change. But Dani was a different story.

He wouldn't mind sharing his worries about Hank and Tina and personal stuff like that with her. He respected her opinions and she was bound to be a lot more objective about his family than he could ever be, just as he was more objective about her kids than she was. In fact, his nightmare about the war was the only thing he *didn't* want to share with her.

Of course, now that she knew about it, she'd be after it like Bear Dog after a stray calf. If he'd learned anything about Dani Smith, it was that she didn't give up easily. He admired her determination a helluva lot, but in this instance he just couldn't give her what she wanted.

If Dani knew what he'd done, she wouldn't even respect him, much less love him. He'd learned that painful lesson the hard way a week after he'd come home from Nam. If his father, a veteran of the Korean War, hadn't been able to handle it, how the hell could he expect Dani to?

Since he was being so honest with himself, he might as well go ahead and admit that he *did* want Dani to love him. When she'd said that to him last night, his heart had damn near turned a somersault. He still got a warm little glow in his belly every time he thought about it.

This past weekend, he'd felt something with her he'd never felt with anyone else. Dammit, he'd had fun. More fun than he could remember having since he was a kid. It had been wonderful knowing he could touch her or kiss her whenever and wherever he wanted, tell her whatever came to his mind, hold her and make love to her.

If he hadn't had that damned dream, he probably would have proposed to her, because he sure as hell didn't want to let her go when the six months were up. What they needed was a compromise. Could he convince her to let go of this one issue if he promised to share everything else?

The combination of a full stomach, a warm room and two nights with very little sleep began to do their work on him. Stifling a yawn with the back of one hand, Sam slid sideways and stretched out on the sofa. He'd take a nap and then head for home.

Dani was pretty reasonable for a woman. If she really loved him, she'd be willing to give a little. She just had to.

Chapter Thirteen

Dani watched Sam's back disappear into the mudroom, started when the door slammed in her face and blinked back angry tears. She would *not* cry over that pigheaded idiot. She just wouldn't.

Since she knew she wouldn't be able to go back to sleep, she went upstairs, showered, dressed and tidied Sam's bedroom. Then she marched back downstairs, set a kettle of chili on to simmer and mixed up five batches of Christmas cookies. In between shuttling sheets of cookies into and out of the oven, she worked on the parka she was making for Kim.

The baking and sewing soothed her ragged emotions somewhat, but they couldn't completely banish Sam from her thoughts. She doubted an earthquake could have accomplished that, although she might be willing to give it a try at this point. Luckily, Becky and Peter arrived with the kids at two o'clock, providing a welcome distraction.

After telling her all about their trip and after demolishing an entire batch of cookies, Colin dragged Peter into Sam's den to mess with the computer, and Kim and Tina raced upstairs to play. Becky stretched her legs out under the kitchen table and sighed.

"I don't think Junior's gonna wait until Christmas," she said, rubbing her swollen abdomen. "At least I hope he won't."

Dani smiled. "You should have seen me when I was pregnant with Colin. I looked like I'd explode if anyone touched me. I felt like it, too."

"You've got that right," Becky said with a chuckle. "If I get any bigger, Pete's gonna need a crane to get me in and out of bed." She shot Dani a wicked grin. "So tell me. Did you have a nice weekend with Sam?"

To Dani's horror, her throat closed up and her eyes suddenly burned with tears. She clamped her mouth shut against a sob and violently shook her head. Becky reached across the table and patted her hand.

"Oh, nuts. What's that fool brother of mine done now?"

Dani inhaled a shaky breath. "It's just n-not going to w-work," she finally managed to choke out.

Becky lumbered to her feet and retrieved a box of tissues from the counter, then waited patiently for Dani to regain control. "Okay, tell me what happened."

Dani did exactly that, the words pouring out of her as fast as the tears streaming down her face. When she'd finished, Becky nodded her head thoughtfully.

"You're really gettin' to him, Dani."

"No, Becky. If he can still turn on me like that after Saturday, it's time to give up."

"But—"

"No. I really mean that. I can't live with Sam unless he changes a big part of his personality. You know as well as I do that's not going to happen." Dani sniffled and produced a watery smile. "Ann Landers even said so."

"Far be it from me to argue with Ann Landers," Becky replied with a wry grin. "I understand, Dani. I really do. I just wish you'd think it over long and hard before you make any final decisions. What'll you do? Leave Pinedale?"

"I ... no, I don't think so. The kids are doing so well in school, I don't want to uproot them again." She shrugged. "I guess I'll look for another job until I can get my sewing business built up."

"You'd be welcome to move in with us while you're job hunting," Becky offered.

Dani shook her head and smiled. "No way. You don't need that. We'll stay here until I find something else."

"Just remember, if things get too rough for you, the offer's open. Anytime."

"Thanks. I appreciate that."

Becky put both hands on the table and pushed herself to her feet. "We'd better be gettin' home. If I see Sam, I'm liable to whack him over that hard head of his."

"Please, don't feel that way. Sam can't help being the way he is, and I don't want to come between him and his family."

"Aw, don't worry about that," Becky assured her. "I'm madder than hell at Sam, but Dawsons love each other, no matter what."

Tina and Peter came running when Becky called to them, and a few minutes later the three left. Dani cleared away the cups and went back to work.

An hour later, the back door opened and Sam walked into the kitchen, smiling as if nothing unpleasant had passed between them. In fact, for a man who had just smashed her heart into a zillion pieces, he looked disgustingly happy.

Dani turned away and started loading the dishwasher. His boot heels thumped across the floor in her direction. His hand squeezed her shoulder affectionately.

"I'd kiss you, but I probably smell like a goat," he said quietly. "I'm gonna grab a shower and then we'll talk. Okay?"

Without waiting for an answer, he strolled out of the room, grabbing a fistful of cookies on the way. Dani watched him go, her stomach knotted with tension. Of course she would listen to whatever he had to say, but she couldn't take much more of this. She really couldn't.

After his shower, Sam put on the shirt Dani had made for him and a clean pair of jeans. Whistling softly, he combed his hair, splashed on some after-shave and left his room. Dani was furious with him, but he was looking forward to the challenge of sweetening up her disposition. Halfway down the stairs, he heard a familiar voice bellowing from the kitchen.

"Sam Dawson, you old coot! Get that ugly face of yours in here so I can see it!"

"Ginny!" Sam bellowed in return, then raced down the rest of the stairs and barreled into the kitchen.

There she stood, all five feet eleven bone-skinny inches of her, feet braced wide apart, arms outstretched for their traditional bear hug. Happy to oblige, he swept her up in his arms and swung her around in a circle.

"Ginny, you're home!" he crowed.

"Put me down, shorty!" she demanded, laughing and pounding him on the back.

He set her back on her feet and held her out at arm's length while he checked her out from the tips of her long, golden hair to the pointed toes of her cowboy boots. "My Lord, Gin, you're fatter than ever."

"Yeah, and you're still as homely as the north end of a southbound mule."

"Thanks. You always were good for my ego."

Ginny brushed her bangs out of her eyes, then tipped her head toward the stove. "Uh, Sam? Maybe you'd better introduce us."

Sam turned to find Dani staring at the two of them as if she thought they belonged in a maximum-security institution. Sam couldn't blame her for that, but he figured that, before long, she'd like Ginny as much as he did. Feeling more than a little sheepish, he led Ginny across the room.

"Sorry, Dani. I didn't see you standing there. This is Ginny Bradford, an old friend of mine from high school. Ginny, this is Dani Smith, my, uh, housekeeper."

The women shook hands and made the appropriate, polite remarks. Then an awkward silence fell over the room. Sam cleared his throat and turned to the refrigerator.

"Want a beer, Gin?"

"Have I ever said no to an offer like that?" she asked with a broad grin.

"Not that I remember. Grab a seat."

Tugging the hem of her sweater down over her hips, Ginny pulled out a chair, flipped it around and straddled it, her gaze darting from Sam to Dani and back to Sam. He took the chair at a right angle to Ginny's and plunked both bottles on the table.

"Want one, Dani?" he asked.

"Oh, no thanks," she answered. "I need to get a few things ready for dinner."

Sam turned to his old friend and smiled. Damn, but it was good to see her again. "You'll stay, won't you?"

"Course I will." She patted his hand before turning toward Dani. "That is, if you don't mind. I didn't mean to barge in at supper time, but it smells terrific in here."

"I don't mind at all," Dani replied. "Wouldn't you rather visit in the living room? You'll have more...privacy."

"Shoot, we don't need privacy," Ginny said with a chuckle, "although we may bore you to tears. Let me know when it's time to set the table and I'll be glad to do it for you."

"So how did your finals go?" Sam asked, watching Dani from the corner of his eye. She didn't appear to be paying any attention to them, but her cheeks looked unusually flushed.

"Piece of cake," Ginny answered. "One more semester of student teaching and I'll be done. With any luck at all, I should be able to get a job in either Pinedale or Big Piney."

"I'm proud of you, Gin. Real proud."

"Hey, I couldn't have done it without you." Ginny reached over and clasped his right hand between both of hers. "Once I've got a job, I'm gonna pay back every single cent."

"No you're not. I promised Charlie I'd get you through school, and I've been damn glad to do it. He'd have done the same thing for me. That's what friends are for, Gin."

"It's been too much, Sam."

Sam scowled at her. "I don't want to hear another word about it."

Ginny threw back her head and roared with laughter. "Are you still tryin' to pull that I-don't-wanna-talk-about-it bull, Dawson? Good Lord, does anybody let you get away with it?"

"Everybody but you."

Wiping at her eyes, Ginny turned toward Dani. "You don't take that from him, do you?"

"Not anymore," Dani replied, sending Sam a smile sweet enough to rot his teeth.

Oh, man, was that a glint of jealousy in Dani's eyes? Sam wondered. Yeah, it sure was. Her cheeks were even redder now, and she was kneading that bread dough like she wanted to strangle somebody. The idea tickled him no end. If Dani was jealous, that meant she still loved him despite the hostile looks she'd been sending him when she thought he wasn't looking.

"Thanks a whole helluva lot, Ginny," he grumbled, struggling to keep a sour expression on his face.

Ginny burst into another fit of laughter. When she regained control, they moved on to a discussion of their families and other old friends and neighbors. Sam couldn't resist flirting with Ginny, just to see what Dani would do.

His smiles for Ginny took on a new warmth, and he touched her hand or her arm or shoulder as frequently as he could. After a few minutes, Ginny leaned back and shot him a what-the-hell-do-you-think-you're-doing? kind of look. Sam glanced pointedly in Dani's direction and winked. Raising one eyebrow, Ginny studied him for a moment, then grinned, shrugged and played along with him all through supper.

To Sam's gratification, Dani fell for the act. She banged dishes onto the table like an overworked waitress who wasn't expecting a tip. She didn't respond to one of Ginny's attempts to draw her into the conversation. And her face was so rigidly controlled, it could have been carved from a pine tree.

When the meal was over and Dani started clearing the table, Sam felt a pang of guilt. He'd suffered enough jealousy over Dani to enjoy watching her squirm, but it looked as if she was going from angry to hurt. Ginny was a good friend and he didn't want Dani to hate her.

Before he could figure out what to do about the situation, however, Dani finished her work and left the room uttering a stiff "Nice meeting you, Ginny."

"I hope you know what you're doin', Sam," Ginny said when Dani was out of earshot.

"Aw, I was just havin' a little fun with her. She'll get over it."

"I wouldn't bet on it. That little gal wanted to slice out my liver and feed it to your dog."

"No, I think it was mine she wanted," Sam said with an uneasy laugh.

Ginny leaned forward and crossed her arms on the table. "So tell me what the hell's goin' on, will ya? How'd she ever wind up workin' here?"

Sam sighed and rubbed the back of his neck. Then he fortified himself with a long drink of beer and related the outline of the story. Ginny hooted at Hank's initial involvement, but by the time Sam finished, her expression was more concerned than amused.

"You shouldn't have teased her like that, Sam."

"Maybe I shouldn't have, but—"

"But nothing. You love her, don'tcha?"

"Yeah."

"Good." Ginny grinned wickedly. "I like her a lot. Have you slept with her?"

He nodded.

"Have you *told* her you love her?"

"Not yet. It's...complicated, Gin."

Ginny rolled her eyes in disgust. "Well, hell, Sam, no wonder she hates me. I couldn't have come at a worse time."

"That's the dumbest thing you've ever said," Sam grumbled. "You're welcome anytime. That'll never change."

"I know that's how *you* feel, but you've gotta look at this from Dani's point of view. She's pretty much risked everything for you, and—"

"Well it's not like I've made her any promises, Ginny. Hell, I never wanted to get involved with her. It just sorta...happened."

"Knock off that defensive bull," Ginny ordered. "The fact is, you *are* involved with her. What's more, I don't believe that it-just-sorta-happened stuff, either. That's not your style, pal."

"Aw, what do *you* know about it?"

"I know plenty. I went to kindergarten with you, Dawson. Shoot, you're a mighty big boy, especially compared to Dani. What'd she do, shove a gun in your face and force you to sleep with her?''

"She might as well have." Sam sighed and rubbed his eyes with his fingertips. "You don't know how that woman pursued me, Gin."

"Why, that hussy! And you just couldn't fight her off, could you? Oh, you poor, sweet baby."

"Listen, Ginny—"

"No, Samuel James, *you* listen. You wanted her one helluva lot, or nothing would have happened. You still do, or you wouldn't be acting like the biggest damned idiot I've seen since Charlie died."

Truly shocked by her outburst, Sam gaped at her. "You loved Charlie, Ginny," he said quietly.

She banged her beer bottle on the table so hard, some of the liquid foamed out of the top. "You're damn right I did. But that doesn't mean I'm not still madder than hell at him for dyin' the way he did."

"He had cancer, hon. He couldn't help it."

"Bull! The kind of cancer he had has a seventy-percent survival rate, but he didn't even try to fight it. You know what? I think he was glad when the doctors told him what was wrong with him."

"I don't believe that."

"Believe it. And I know why he did it."

"Why?"

"He couldn't let go of the war, Sam. It'd been over for twenty years, but he still had nightmares, he hated himself...he couldn't even talk to me about what happened to him over there."

"But I thought—"

"Yeah, I know what you thought," Ginny said with a bitter laugh. "Everybody thought we had a terrific marriage. Sometimes we did. But that damn war was always there in the background, just waitin' to sneak out when I'd least expect it. He let it destroy our chance for happiness, Sam. For God's sake, don't let it destroy yours, too."

He took both of her hands in his, his heart wrenching at the tears in Ginny's eyes. Ginny never cried. "I'm fine, Gin. Honest."

"No. You're not," she whispered, squeezing his hands with a desperate strength. "You've got a real nice woman livin' right here and she loves you. I can see you love her and those kids, so what the hell are you doin' playin' games with her? Are you tryin' to screw up the relationship before it even gets off the ground?"

"Of course not. At least I don't think so," Sam answered. "Why didn't you tell me any of this before?"

"Pride. Guilt." She shrugged, as if to say, "What difference does it make?"

"You don't have anything to feel guilty about. That's... irrational."

"Who said guilt was a rational emotion? It's like a worm gets into your brain, Sam. And no matter what you do, you can't get away from it. You know what I'm talkin' about, don't you?"

Sam looked away, then nodded. "What did you feel guilty about?"

"Oh, you know...." She gulped, then pulled a tissue out of her pocket and blew her nose. "I kept thinkin' that if I'd just loved Charlie a little more, been more patient with him, more understanding, insisted that he get counseling, maybe things would have been different."

"That's ridiculous."

"I know it. Charlie was almost as stubborn as you are." She gave him a misty smile. "Nobody could have changed his mind about... well, about much of anything. But it's not too late for you, Sam. Don't wreck your life and Dani's the way Charlie did ours."

"I'm not doin' that."

Sadly shaking her head, Ginny stood and walked around the table to Sam's chair. She laid one hand on the back of his neck and pressed his head against her midriff. He closed his eyes and put his arms around her waist.

"Yes you are, pal." She gently stroked his hair with her other hand. "Now listen, and listen good. I'm your friend and I won't lie to you. I've been worried about you because every time I come home to visit, you've isolated yourself a little more. You stay here and you take care of this ranch and you take care of your family, but who takes care of you? You're a good man. You deserve a woman like Dani and you deserve to be happy. Do you hear me?"

His throat too tight to speak, Sam nodded.

"All right, then." After planting a maternal kiss on top of his head, Ginny released him and stepped back. "Walk me to my car before we get all sloppy and sentimental."

Sam cleared his throat, then pushed himself to his feet and accompanied her outside. It had started to snow again, but his mind was still reeling so hard from everything she'd said to him, he barely noticed. When they reached her car, he pulled her into his arms for one last hug.

"Thanks, Gin," he whispered.

"You're welcome." She leaned back and gave him a wiseacre grin. "You'd better get inside and tell Dani you love her. And don't forget to tell her that sleeping with me would be worse than sleeping with Becky, will ya?"

"Will you come to the wedding?"

Ginny opened her car door, paused and rolled her eyes at the fat snowflakes pelting her from above. "Do mosquitoes suck blood? Do rabbits have babies? Does a bear you-know-what in the woods? Shoot, Dawson, I never knew you were this dumb."

Sam threw back his head and laughed. Ginny climbed into her car and slammed the door. He watched her until her car was out of sight, then turned back toward the house, suddenly eager to find Dani. To his surprise and disappointment, she wasn't in the living room, or in his den messing with the computer or anywhere else on the main floor.

He climbed the stairs and walked down the hall, noting the empty bathroom on his way. Surely she hadn't gone to bed this early, he thought, glancing at his watch. Damn. It was already ten-fifteen.

She ought to be damn tuckered after the past two nights, he reminded himself, and she hadn't had a nap like he had. Smiling at the memories of why she hadn't had much sleep, he silently opened her bedroom door and stuck his head inside the darkened room. The light pouring in from the hallway revealed a lump in the middle of the bed.

"Dani?" he whispered, just in case she wasn't asleep yet.

No response. Nuts. He wanted to crawl in there with her, but with the kids home . . . Nah, better not. Biting back a sigh of disappointment, Sam closed her door and headed down the hall to his own room. He'd talk to her tomorrow.

Through sheer force of will, Dani remained absolutely still when Sam opened her bedroom door. She suspected she knew what he wanted to say to her, but she couldn't bear to hear it—not yet, anyway. During the endless, gut-wrenching hour she'd spent in her room tonight, she had finally faced facts and made some decisions, but she wasn't ready to talk to anyone. Especially not Sam.

There were no tears. She still hurt too much for that. One thought pounded through her brain over and over again.

Sam Dawson had lied to her.

He'd told her there was no one else, but he'd lied, and the sense of betrayal cut Dani clear to her bone marrow.

Perhaps he hadn't meant to lie. Perhaps he wasn't even consciously aware of his feelings for Ginny. But the bond of affection and respect between the two of them was real and strong, and it had a history of shared experiences dating back to childhood. Dani couldn't fight that if she wanted to.

She had felt better after having talked with Becky. Though Dani had been angry with Sam when he'd first come home, she'd regarded his request to talk a positive sign, and she'd let herself hope they could still work things out. But seeing Sam with Ginny Bradford had nailed the coffin shut.

After that dinner from hell, Dani had put Kim to bed, said good-night to Colin and escaped to the privacy of her own room. Then she'd slipped on a warm flannel night-gown, curled up on the bed like a wounded child and admitted something else. She had lied to Sam, too.

What she'd shared with him during this weekend *wasn't* enough. Dammit, she *did* want him to love her, and she thought he did, in a way. But she wanted him to say it out loud and mean it. And she wanted him to look at her the way he looked at Ginny—as if she were his dearest friend on earth. She'd bet a month's salary he'd shared his troubles with Ginny and hadn't even stopped to think about it.

Though she'd never had a psychic experience in her life, Dani could see Sam's future as clearly as if it were being played out on a movie screen. Ginny would complete her education and come back to Pinedale to teach. Sam would stop in to visit her occasionally, under the guise of checking up on his best friend's widow.

Their good-buddy camaraderie would continue to grow and deepen as they spent more time together. Then one day their hands would brush unexpectedly, and their eyes would meet, and a spark of sexual attraction would ignite between them. Since Charlie had been dead for two years now, it wouldn't take long for Sam and Ginny to dispense with any guilt they might feel about him, and they'd walk blissfully down the aisle and live happily ever after.

However much she wanted it to be different, one truth remained—Dani Smith wasn't the only woman who could make Sam Dawson happy. In fact, she had every reason to believe that Ginny would be better for Sam than Dani could ever hope to be.

Ginny had more in common with him. She had ties to the community he lived in. She was tall enough that nobody would snicker and nudge someone else in the ribs when seeing Sam and Ginny together. She knew all about ranching. Sam was more comfortable with her.

The list had gone on and on in Dani's mind until she'd jumped from the bed and marched to the window. Resting her hot face against the cold glass, she'd looked out into the night. The light above the back porch suddenly had turned on below her window.

Dani had wanted to turn away, but her feet had refused to budge. Her heart had contracted when she'd seen Ginny turn into Sam's arms for an embrace. It had cracked when he'd held her to him for an achingly tender moment. It had shattered when Ginny had driven away and he'd stood out there with snow drifting down on his dark hair, gazing wistfully in the direction she had taken, long after she'd disappeared from sight. He'd looked so... lonely.

Feeling ancient and drained, Dani rolled onto her back, tears finally dribbling down her cheeks and into her ears. She let them come, knowing they were the first step toward healing. She would grieve for Sam as she had grieved for Ray, but somehow her life would continue.

She would even do her best to make their parting easy for him. No embarrassing scenes. No recriminations. No sad goodbyes. Tomorrow morning she would put an ad for her sewing business in the newspaper and start looking for another job. Then she would quietly fade out of his life.

Chapter Fourteen

Sam hurried out of his bedroom the next morning, intending to catch Dani alone for a few minutes before the usual get-the-kids-off-to-school craziness set in. He paused at the top of the stairs, surprised to see the living room empty and the television screen blank. A door opened behind him in the hallway.

"Good morning, Sam," Colin said.

So much for plan A. Sam greeted the boy with a resigned smile and told himself plan B would be better, anyway. If he waited until Dani came back from driving the kids to the bus stop, they wouldn't be interrupted. Maybe they'd even go back to bed....

The minute he entered the kitchen, however, Dani blew that idea all to hell. Wearing a full-length apron to protect her rose-colored skirt and blouse, she stood at the stove, flipping slices of French toast. She looked up and smiled when Sam and Colin entered the room.

"Oh, good, you're early," she said.

"What's up, Mom?" Colin asked. "Why aren't you flapping your flab with Jane Fonda?"

"I have some things to do in town this morning, so I'm driving you and Kim to school. The radio announcer said the roads are bad, and I want to have plenty of time."

That explained the skirt, Sam thought, pouring himself a mug of coffee. He took his usual chair and sipped the steaming brew, then sat back and admired Dani's legs while she carried a platter of bacon and French toast to the table. Her high heels clicked on the tile floor as she walked back to the stove, the sound so unusual to Sam's ears, it made him look at her again.

Her hair was neatly combed; the artfully arranged curls didn't bounce around the way they generally did, so he figured she must have used hairspray or something. He wasn't used to seeing her wear that much makeup, either, although what she had on looked natural enough. Small gold studs decorated her earlobes and a gold pendant nestled in the hollow of her throat. A matching bracelet dangled from her right wrist, and . . . good Lord, she'd polished her nails to match her skirt.

She carried the coffeepot back to the table. "Is there something wrong with your breakfast, Sam?"

"Oh, uh, no," he answered, buttering his French toast. "Just thinking."

Just thinking she really was a pretty woman. That he wished she would meet his gaze and give him one of those special pixie smiles. That she must have some awfully important business in town to get that gussied up. Pinedale wasn't exactly a dressy place; a clean pair of jeans would take her just about anywhere she wanted to go.

Why the sudden change? Was she still jealous of Ginny? Maybe trying to show him how good she could look? The idea touched him and tickled him at the same time. Shoot, he'd grown damn fond of those stretchy, clingy little pants she wore around the house. He'd have to set her straight about Ginny first chance he got.

"I'll be glad to drive you to town if you can wait until I feed the stock, Dani," he offered.

She shot a quick, polite smile in his direction, but didn't really look at him. "No thanks, Sam. I'll be busy all morning. In fact, don't expect me until one-thirty or two."

Before he could ask what would keep her tied up that long, she rushed out of the room, yelling at Kim to hurry and come down for breakfast. Sam helped himself to another cup of coffee, stalling in hopes of grabbing her attention long enough to at least tell her he wanted to talk with her. Unfortunately, every time he moved closer to her, she'd remember something one of the kids might need for school and flitted off after it.

Though her expression remained amiable, there was a subtle tension about her that told Sam she was still angry with him. Damn. It wasn't like Dani to hold a grudge, but he knew he wasn't imagining the sudden distance she was creating between them.

Uneasy, he bundled up and went out to take care of the stock. He trudged back into the house at noon, disappointed because Dani's car wasn't in the driveway, even though she'd told him she wouldn't be home until later. He fixed himself a sandwich, then decided it wouldn't hurt to have a little peace offering for when she arrived.

He raced into town, bought a bouquet of pink roses at the flower shop and stopped at the Stockmen's liquor store drive-up window for a bottle of champagne. Wanting to beat Dani back to the ranch, he didn't take the time to cruise around town and see where her car was parked, though the thought did occur to him. Back at home, he put the champagne in the fridge and set the flowers in the middle of the kitchen table.

The waiting made him too restless to concentrate on paperwork. He went out to the barn and worked on the tack, practicing on Bear Dog what he wanted to say to Dani, until he heard her tires crunch the gravel in the driveway. Smiling in anticipation, he cleaned up his mess and hurried into the house. When he got there, Dani stood in the middle of the kitchen, still wearing her coat and gaping at the bouquet.

"They're for you," he said quietly, leaning one shoulder against the door casing.

Sam wasn't sure what he'd expected—a kiss maybe, at least a hug or a smile. Unfortunately Dani just glanced at him, then calmly unbuttoned her coat, took it off and folded it over her arm.

"Don't you like roses?" he asked.

"They're very nice, Sam," she said slowly. She turned and looked directly at him before adding, "But I think you should give them to Ginny."

Chuckling, Sam straightened up and walked toward her. "You've got the wrong idea about Ginny and me, Dani. We're just buddies."

"It looked like a lot more than that to me."

"Yeah, I know, and it's my fault. I could see you were a little jealous last night, and—"

The phone chose that particular moment to ring. He glared at it until it rang again, then sighed and went to answer. "Hang on a minute, Dani," he said when she turned toward the living room.

"I'm just going to hang up my coat," she replied.

Sam picked up the receiver, and his brother-in-law's voice boomed cheerfully from the other end of the line. "Where the hell have you been, Sam? I've been trying to reach you for hours!"

Wedging the receiver between his ear and shoulder, Sam lowered himself onto a chair. "Out in the barn. What's up, Pete?"

"You're an uncle again. Becky produced a whopping big boy at eleven o'clock this morning. I'll bet he's close to nine pounds."

"She all right?"

"Oh, she's wonderful, Sam." Peter's voice grew thick with emotion. Sam smiled when he heard his brother-in-law clear his throat before he continued. "She didn't need any drugs at all during the delivery, but she's higher than a kite now. I'm having a helluva time keeping her in bed."

"Where are you? At the hospital in Jackson?"

"Don't I wish. Your crazy sister decided she didn't want to go to the hospital and sent me off to work this morning knowing she was in labor. By the time she finally called me and I got home, it was too late to go anywhere. Can you imagine that? As soon as she's back on her feet, I'm going to wring her neck."

Sam chuckled. "Hey, you knew she was a stubborn brat when you married her. Good thing you're a doctor."

"True on both counts," Peter admitted with a laugh. "But I hadn't planned on delivering my own kid. Scared the daylights out of me until I was sure there weren't going to be any complications."

"Does my nephew have a name?"

"Yeah. How does Jonathan Samuel Sinclair strike you?"

Sam's breath caught in his chest and it was his turn to clear his throat. "That's a ... that sounds like ... aw, hell, Pete, I'm real flattered."

"Becky wants to talk to you."

"Hi there, Uncle Sam," she said an instant later.

"Congratulations, sis. How do you feel?"

"Well, they don't call it labor for nothing, but I'm fine. Wait'll you see Jonathan. He's absolutely gorgeous."

"You mean he's not all red and wrinkled up like a little prune?"

"Not *my* baby," Becky retorted with a chuckle.

"Well, then, I'd better get over there and take a look, seein' as how you saddled the poor kid with my name."

"You don't mind, do you, Sam?"

"Course not. I'm just glad you're both okay. Sounds like you took a few years off Pete's life, though."

"I knew he could handle it." Sam heard Peter snort in the background. Becky said something to her husband, then came back on the line. "Much as I hate to get practical, we could use a little help."

"Name it," Sam said. "Want me to pick Tina up after school and bring her here?"

"Maybe later. The biggest problem is getting Grandma D at the airport in Jackson. Her plane lands around four."

"I'll pick her up. Bet she's madder than a wet hen she missed all the excitement."

"That's an understatement, but I'm sure you can charm her into a better mood."

"Right. How about if I go get her, and I'll bring Tina home with me when I drop Grandma off at your place?"

"Sounds like a plan to me. That way Tina can have some time with Jonathan. I hope she won't be too upset."

"She's been lookin' forward to the baby as much as the rest of us, Beck. Why would she be upset?"

"I'm just afraid she'll feel a little displaced, is all. You know, like sibling rivalry? Be sure you spend as much time with her as you can, Sam."

"No problem. Dani and the kids'll help. I'd better get goin'. See ya later."

Sam hung up, glanced at the clock and swore under his breath as he rushed upstairs. Grandma D would nail his hide to the barn door if he wasn't there to meet her plane the second it landed. Dani followed him and waited outside his bedroom door while he filled her in on the news and changed into clean clothes.

They walked back downstairs together and into the kitchen. Sam hesitated at the back door, wanting to clear the air with Dani before he left for Jackson Hole.

"Do you want to come with me?" he asked.

She smiled and shook her head. "Somebody's got to be here to meet the kids. You'd better get going or you'll be late. I'll take some dinner over to Peter after the bus comes."

"All right, but you and I have to talk later."

"Okay."

The plane was an hour late because of fog in Missoula. Grandma D bombarded Sam with questions about the baby all the way home, sniffing in disgust that he hadn't taken the time to get all the details she wanted to know. When he finally managed to sidetrack her from that topic, the nosy old bat started grilling him about Dani. Of course Sam refused to tell her anything, and they finished the last forty miles of the drive in a mutually disgruntled silence.

The half hour he spent with the Sinclairs brightened his mood. Feeling awkward as the proverbial bull in a china shop, he held his new nephew, who, in Sam's unspoken opinion, did look pretty red and pruney. Despite that, little Jonathan tugged at Sam's heart with his tiny, randomly groping fingers, and made him ache to straighten things out with Dani. When the baby turned his face toward his uncle's chest and started rooting around for a nipple, Sam gratefully climbed to his feet.

"Here's the lady with the equipment you need, kid," he said softly, handing Jonathan to his radiant mother.

Since Dani had already taken Tina back to the ranch, Sam said a quick goodbye to everyone and headed home. His foot rode heavily on the gas pedal, weighted by his eagerness to see Dani. The minute he walked in the door, however, he knew he wouldn't get the opportunity for a discussion anytime soon.

Colin and Kim sat at the kitchen table amid the remains of a half-eaten supper, their foreheads creased with worried frowns. They both smiled in relief at his arrival.

"What's goin' on?" Sam asked.

"Tina locked herself in the upstairs bathroom and Mom can't get her to come out," Kim replied. "She's crying really hard."

"What happened?"

"Who knows?" Colin answered with a shrug. "We were just talking about the new baby, and the kid totally flipped out. I took care of the stock for you."

"Thanks."

Sam hurried through the living room and took the stairs three at a stride. Turning into the hallway, he saw Dani kneeling in front of the bathroom door, squinting through the keyhole.

"Tina, please," she begged, "come out and let me help you, honey. Everything's going to be okay. I promise."

"I w-want my d-dad," the little girl replied between sobs that ripped Sam's heart into confetti.

Dani looked up and saw him. "Sam, thank God you're home."

Sam hunkered down beside her and called through the door. "Tina? Come out and talk to me, sweetheart."

"I'm not c-comin' out until m-my dad g-gets here."

"That's not fair, babe. His last postcard said he'll be here next week. You'll starve before then and I'll wind up feelin' all sad and guilty."

"Go away, Uncle S-Sam. L-leave m-me alone."

"No way, Tina. You're my best gal. I can't leave you in there cryin' all by yourself. Let me in and I'll cry with ya."

"You don't never cry."

"Sure I do. You've just never seen me do it."

"Oh yeah?"

"Yeah. C'mon, babe, open up. If you don't, I'll have to get some tools and take the door off the hinges."

There was a long moment of silence. When Tina spoke again, her voice sounded closer to the door. "You gonna be mad at me, Uncle Sam?"

"Nah. Like I said, you're my best gal. A fella can't be mad at his best gal, now, can he?"

Another silence stretched out, but at last Sam heard the quiet grating sound of the bolt sliding back, and the door slowly swung open. He held out his arms, catching the little girl close when she launched herself at him. Sobbing, she clung to his shoulders and buried her face against his neck.

Stroking her back, he straightened up and carried her into her bedroom. He sat on the bed, rearranged her gangly little legs across his lap and gently rocked her back and forth while she wept. Dani came in a few minutes later and handed him a cool wet washrag.

"Have you eaten, Sam?" she whispered.

"No, but I'm not hungry."

"I'll leave you a sandwich in the fridge."

Before he could thank her, she left the room. He wiped Tina's face with the cloth and helped her stretch out on the bedspread.

"Wanna tell me what brought this on?" he asked quietly.

Tina gulped, then nodded. "I'm bad, Uncle Sam."

"Oh, really? Why do ya say that?"

"I don't like Jonathan. I think he's a pain in the butt."

Sam considered that statement carefully. "Well, if that makes a person bad, I guess I'm bad, too."

"How come?"

"I felt the same way when your Aunt Becky was born. It was bad enough havin' Hank horn in on my action, but Becky was even worse."

"Really?"

"Shoot, yeah. She looked like a squallin' little rat, and I couldn't figure out why everybody thought she was so dang

special just because she was a girl. I don't think I really
liked her until she was about six or seven.''

''What happened then?''

''She figured out she was a tomboy and started gettin' in
trouble, same as me and your dad.''

Tina giggled at that. Then she exhaled a heart-wrenching
sigh and looked at Sam with sad, tear-swollen eyes. ''I miss
Dad, Uncle Sam.''

He smoothed her bangs out of her eyes before answering. ''I know you do, hon.''

''Do you really think he'll come home next week?''

''If he doesn't, I'll go find him for ya.''

''Promise?''

''Cross my heart and hope to die.''

Stubborn as any other Dawson, Tina kept Sam nailed to
her side for another hour and a half before she surren-
dered to exhaustion. Afraid of waking her if he moved, he
sat beside the sleeping child for another ten minutes, silently promising to make her world happy again. Then he
marched down to his office and started dialing the list of
phone numbers Hank had left in case of an emergency.

Two hours later, after talking to what felt like half the
population of Oklahoma, Sam finally gave up trying to lo-
cate his brother. Hank had been everywhere on the list, but
nobody had seen him for three days.

As he wandered through the quiet house, shutting off
lights, he realized he still hadn't talked to Dani. He went
upstairs and hesitated outside her room before deciding to
wait until morning. What he had to say to her was too important to tackle when he felt so emotionally drained.

Unfortunately, due to a cold front that swooped down
out of Canada, the temperature plummeted the next day.
Sam couldn't afford to hang around the house waiting for
a chance to talk with Dani. He dragged the hay for the herd
into a sheltering line of trees and spent a frustrating hour
trying to get a malfunctioning heater for one of the water

tanks to work. He ended up having to chop through the ice with an ax and drive into town for a new heater.

When he returned to the ranch, he found a shiny black pickup with out-of-town plates parked in his usual spot. A moment later, the back door banged open, and Hank hurried down the steps, a gleaming ebony cane in his left hand. Heaving a sigh of relief that his brother was all right, Sam turned off the ignition and stepped out of his truck.

"Heard you had a little excitement yesterday," Hank said, approaching Sam with a broad grin.

"Might say that," Sam answered.

"Dani says Becky's baby's a cute little dude."

"Yeah. He is. Dani tell you about Tina?"

Hank's grin faded. "Yeah. Don't worry, I'll make it up to her. Brought her a new saddle from Oklahoma City for Christmas."

"I don't think you can buy your way out of this one, Hank. You've got one ticked-off little gal on your hands."

"Aw, don't lecture me, Sam. She'll forgive me. I'm home early, aren't I?"

"Plannin' to stay?"

"For now. Till I figure out what I'm gonna do, anyway."

"What about the deal in Oklahoma?"

Hank shook his head and gazed off toward the mountains to the west. "I'm not goin' back. If I can't compete, I don't want to be around rodeos. Nothin' like seein' those young bucks raisin' hell out there to make a guy feel like an old has-been."

Sam smiled and clapped his brother on the back. "I think you've got a few good years left."

"Yeah, right. Just not for rodeo." Hank sighed, then gave Sam a wry smile. "But I'll think of somethin'."

"Of course you will." Sam nodded toward Hank's cane. "Good to see you on your feet again."

"Thanks." A frigid gust of wind made Hank shiver. "Let's get in the house before I freeze my butt off. Dani's got coffee and fresh cinnamon rolls in the kitchen."

"Go on ahead," Sam told him. "I've gotta get the new tank heater I just bought, workin'. Be in in twenty minutes."

While Hank walked away, Sam reached into his pickup for the tank heater. Dammit, he wished Hank would've stayed away just one more day. The longer he had to wait to talk to Dani, the more distant she seemed and the colder his feet got. They were close to being frostbitten now, but he just couldn't bring himself to make his move in front of ol' smooth-talkin' Hank.

As the days rolled by, life at the Circle D became more and more chaotic. Convinced that Becky needed help taking care of Jonathan, Grandma D stayed at the Sinclairs' house. She demanded that everyone follow the Dawson Christmas traditions all the same, and kept everyone hopping with preparations for the holidays.

Kim and Colin exhibited the manic giddiness kids tended to get when school was dismissed for two weeks and the stack of presents grew beneath the Christmas tree. Tina stayed at the Circle D, clinging to Sam and tormenting her father at every opportunity.

Hank frequently went off on mysterious errands, and though he always invited Tina to go with him, she always refused. When he walked in the door, the little girl would either vanish or silently glare at him, her eyes cold enough to give an Eskimo hypothermia. Hank teased, coaxed and ignored her worst behavior, but the kid hadn't softened toward him one whit.

Sam figured that kind of uproar came with the territory called family living. On the other hand, Dani really had him worried. Oh, she was as bubbly and energetic as ever. And she still did her job and made it look easy, even though there were two more people living in the house now and even though Grandma D popped in and out all the time to make sure her orders were carried out.

But it had gradually become as clear as a mountain lake that Dani's attitude toward him had changed. At first, he'd hoped she was just trying to be discreet about their relationship. With the house so full, privacy was at a premium, and he'd understood and was even grateful that she'd kept her distance from him when his grandmother or brother were around.

It hadn't taken long to realize, however, that there was more going on under that mop of curls than discretion. Dani was just plain avoiding him.

Instead of bringing in a pot of coffee and a plate of cookies herself when he was working in the den, she sent them with Colin or Kim or Hank. She never touched him unless it was unavoidable, and stayed away from the barn as if it were a death trap or something. She went to bed early and didn't turn up in the kitchen in the mornings until she was sure Hank or one of the kids would be there.

Worst of all, while Sam hadn't been able to finagle a private conversation with her yet, she spent plenty of time with Hank and appeared to be enjoying his company immensely. Jealousy ate at Sam's gut like buzzards on a deer carcass whenever he saw the two of them together, and he sincerely regretted his little game with Ginny.

Still, his pride wouldn't allow him to say anything. If Dani preferred Hank to him, well, Sam wasn't about to force himself on her. He felt hurt and confused, angry with her for withdrawing from him, and twice as angry with himself for blowing the golden opportunity he'd had to get his brand on her.

The fact was, he missed her—in his bed at night, and every other hour of the day, as well. He tolerated the situation until the day after Christmas. But when he overheard Dani telling Hank that his cane made him look dashing and debonair, Sam finally lost his patience.

He stomped into the kitchen and propped his fists on his hips. "Dani, I want to talk to you in the den."

She looked up from the assembly line of bread she'd laid out for turkey sandwiches, obviously startled. Mug in hand, Hank turned away from the coffee maker, his eyebrows raised in surprise. Dani gestured toward the counter.

"The kids are hungry, Sam. Can't it wait until after lunch?"

"No, it can't," Sam snapped. "Hank can feed the kids. I want to talk to you *now*."

"Go ahead, Dani," Hank said quietly.

"All right."

She wiped her hands on a dish towel and walked into the hallway ahead of Sam, cheeks flushed, head held high. She started toward the chair at the front side of the desk, but settled into a corner of the sofa when he indicated that was where he wanted her to sit. Then she trained a steady, indifferent gaze on Sam that darn near curdled his blood.

"What did you want to talk about?" she asked.

"Us," Sam answered, sitting as close to her as he dared. Her expression didn't change, and he mentally stomped on his rising temper. If ever there was a time for a cool head and a soft tone of voice, this was it. "I've missed being with you, Dani."

She looked down at her hands. "You said you wanted me to leave you the hell alone."

"Well, I'm sorry I did, 'cause I sure don't like it when you do. I've been tryin' to apologize ever since, but you've been damn good at avoiding me."

"I haven't . . . well, yes, I have."

"I told you Ginny and I are just buddies. And I bought you flowers. Wasn't it clear I wanted to set things right between us?"

Dani propped her elbow on the sofa's armrest and looked into his eyes. "Yes, it was clear. But I decided there wasn't any point in doing that."

"Why not? Don't you believe me about Ginny? Jeez, Dani, I was just tryin' to get your goat a little by flirtin' with her. I've been jealous over you since...well, it seems like forever. She's a real good friend, but that's all."

"All right, I believe you."

"Do you really?"

"Yes, but it doesn't matter."

Despite his good intentions about his keeping his temper, Sam leapt to his feet and glared down at her. "Well, it sure as hell does to me. I'm sorry I hurt your feelings, but—"

"Listen to me, Sam, please," she said. "You were right all along. We're just too different to make things work. I've submitted job applications all over town. As soon as I find something, we'll be moving out."

Flabbergasted, Sam dropped back onto the sofa and gaped at her for a long moment. "That's why you got all dressed up that day," he whispered. He cleared his throat, then said, "Dammit, Dani, you can't do that. I love you."

"Oh, Sam." She sighed and shook her head. "I wish I could believe that, but don't you see? It's awfully convenient for you to say it now, when I've told you I'm leaving."

"I've been tryin' to tell you that for days," he protested. "But you wouldn't let me. Every time I came near you, you'd skitter off like a damned field mouse."

"And I was wrong to do that," she admitted, "but I still don't think we can make a relationship work."

"You said you loved me."

"I do. But I need more than you're willing to give. I hope that we can be...friends."

Sam snorted in disgust, then raked one hand through his hair. "I don't want to be *friends* with you. I want to marry you. Doesn't that mean anything?"

Tears glistened in her eyes. "It means more than you'll ever know," she whispered, blinking rapidly. "But I can't do it, Sam."

The sadness in her eyes and the finality in her voice convinced him she wasn't going to change her mind. Silence fraught with pain and tension filled the room.

"Is it Hank?" Sam finally asked. "Have you fallen for him instead of me?"

"It doesn't have anything to do with Hank or anyone else," she said, climbing to her feet. "My first marriage wasn't a very close one, Sam. I've told you that. If I ever get married again, it'll be to a man who needs me as much as I need him. One who wants to share every part of his life with me."

With that, Dani quietly walked out of the den, leaving Sam staring after her in misery and disbelief. He was still sitting there a moment later when Hank stormed into the room.

"What the hell did you do to Dani?" he demanded.

"Not a damn thing," Sam retorted.

"Then why did she run upstairs bawlin'?"

"Danged if I know." Sam shrugged, then cleared his throat. "She's movin' out soon as she can find another job."

"For God's sake, don't just sit there, ya big ox. Get up there and tell her you love her."

"I did that not five minutes ago. Asked her to marry me, too."

Hank's eyes bugged out in surprise. "You did?"

"Yup. She turned me down flat."

"Did she say why?"

"Guess she didn't believe me when I said I loved her."

"Damn." Hank sat on the cushion Dani had recently vacated and bit his lower lip thoughtfully. Eventually he said, "Well, talk's pretty damn cheap. You're gonna have to *show* her you love her."

"Oh, right," Sam said with a bitter laugh. "You know me, Hank. I oughtta be *real* good at that."

"Aw, it won't be that hard. Even a lunkhead like you can do it, if you want to bad enough."

"How? Write her love poems?"

Hank studied him for a moment, then laughed and shook his head. "Nah! She'd *never* believe that. Ya just gotta romance her. Women go for little stuff, like helpin' 'em with the dishes and holdin' hands. Ya know... affection. They wanna know you've been thinkin' about 'em."

"Yeah, and then they wanna know *what* you've been thinkin'," Sam said glumly.

"So? Tell her. It won't cost you a penny to say she looks nice or smells good, Sam."

"If I try that, she's just gonna freeze me out, Hank."

"So? Keep doin' it anyway. You're gonna have to wear her down."

"What if she gets another job before I can do that?"

"Anybody thinkin' about hiring her is gonna want a reference. You're the man they'll call."

"I can't give her a bad reference, Hank."

"Of course not. But you could explain the situation and ask 'em to wait a little while, now, couldn't you?"

"Maybe." Sam considered the idea for a moment, then nodded slowly. "Yeah, I could do that. But she's been hidin' behind you, Hank. You're gonna have to stay outta my way."

"No problem. I'll keep the kids occupied, too."

"All right. I'll try it," Sam said with a grimace. "But cripes, Hank, everybody in town's gonna know about this, first time I get a call about her."

Hank chuckled and clapped him on the shoulder. "Well, that's a risk you're gonna have to take. Don'tcha think Dani's worth it?"

"Yeah," Sam answered. "She sure is."

Chapter Fifteen

By the last week of January, Dani hadn't received a single request to come in for a job interview, and she was starting to feel desperate. She'd picked up a lot of sewing business from her newspaper ad, but she wasn't making enough money from it to live on yet. If she didn't get away from Sam Dawson soon, however, she was going to lose what little was left of her mind.

She could have handled it if he'd been unpleasant after their confrontation in his den. She'd expected him to be moody, cold and distant at best. But now she was seriously considering the idea of calling the *National Enquirer* to report a man whose body had been invaded by an alien life form.

Suddenly Sam was always cheerful, unusually talkative and so helpful, he practically did her job for her. Suddenly he loved casseroles, enjoyed drying dishes. Laundry baskets and grocery sacks were far too heavy for her to carry. Suddenly he didn't have anything better to do than scrape the ice from her windshield, change the oil in her car and give it a tune-up, and buy her top-of-the-line studded snow tires, which he charged to the ranch because she used her own car for grocery shopping.

Gifts began to appear, as if by magic. A new package of bobbins next to her sewing machine. On her dresser, a pair of purple slipper socks with rubber treads on the bottoms so she wouldn't slip on the kitchen floor. A single red rose on her pillow.

A new, four-slice toaster replaced the old one that only worked when it felt like it. A state-of-the-art food processor, a shiny set of measuring cups, a big wooden key ring cut in the shape of her initial and painted hot pink that wouldn't get lost in the bottom of her purse.

Of course Sam denied all knowledge of how any of those things could have found their way into the house, and calmly suggested that as long as they were there, she might as well use them. When Dani retorted that she couldn't be bought with presents, he changed tactics.

Overnight, the man who had shunned physical displays of affection unless they were completely alone, couldn't seem to keep his hands off her no matter where they were or who was around. Her hands, shoulders, knees and the nape of her neck were his favorite targets. He also perfected the art of hit-and-run kisses that lingered just long enough to start her hormones raging. When she invariably protested, he'd laugh and walk away.

The way he looked at her was equally unsettling. Sometimes he would sit at the kitchen table with his chin propped on the heel of his hand and gaze at her with a silly grin, as if he were Colin's age and she were a little blond cheerleader.

At other times he would lounge back with his legs stretched out in front of him, one hand on his hip, the other on the table, the better to show off his broad shoulders. Then he would study her through half-closed eyelids, a slight, but oh-so-sexy smile on his lips, and she just knew he was remembering what she looked like naked. His voice would take on a husky note that brought images of making love with him to her mind, and she would flush and have to leave the room. Otherwise she'd jump his bones on the spot.

And the compliments that popped out of his mouth! According to him, she smelled better than wild honeysuckle, she was prettier than the first butterfly in spring, her hair was shinier than Hank's new pickup and softer than dandelion fluff, her eyes bluer than Fremont Lake in July. Granted, it wasn't exactly deathless poetry, but coming from a man like Sam, it was close enough to suit Dani.

How in the world was she supposed to fall out of love with a man like that?

With every day that passed, the thought of leaving the Circle D became more and more repugnant, and she constantly found herself trying to justify giving their relationship another chance. She had plenty of encouragement to do that from everyone else in the house, too.

Her children thought Sam's new behavior was hilarious, and were obviously eager for their present living arrangement to be made permanent. Hank came up with all kinds of bizarre excuses to leave her alone with Sam, including hay rides for the kids, last-minute trips to the movies in Big Piney and suddenly remembered promises to take them to see little Jonathan.

And yet, much as she wanted to, Dani couldn't quite bring herself to trust the "new and improved" Sam Dawson. No matter how sweet or touching his latest gesture, a little voice inside her head said, *This can't last, Dani. One of these days, you'll hit on one of those topics he doesn't discuss with anyone, and he'll shut you out so fast, your head will spin.*

Sam's unrelenting pursuit continued until Valentine's Day. By three o'clock that day, Dani's nerves were shot.

She hadn't seen Sam or Hank since lunch. All day long, she had waited for some grandiose, romantic stunt to unfold, but she hadn't received so much as a card.

Refusing to admit she was the least bit disappointed, she turned off the sewing machine, made a meat loaf and wrapped some potatoes in tin foil for dinner. The house seemed so quiet, she put a disc in the CD player, cranked it up full blast and sang along with Reba McEntire while she mixed up a cake for dessert. She slid it into the oven, set the timer and turned to find Sam standing in the doorway to the mudroom, watching her with tenderness, amusement and an oddly expectant expression in his eyes.

His Stetson sat at a jaunty angle on his head. His ears and cheeks were red from the cold and his coat was buttoned up to his chin. He held her parka in his left hand. Before she could say anything, he crossed the room, untied her apron and tossed it onto the counter.

"What do you think you're doing?" she demanded when he grabbed her right hand and poked it into the sleeve of her coat.

"Abducting you."

"I can't go anywhere. It's almost time to pick up the kids."

Sam smiled and repeated the procedure with her other hand. "Hank's gonna do that."

"But I just put a cake in the oven."

"Hank'll take care of it when the timer buzzes."

He turned her around and zipped her coat as if she were a kindergartner, then scooped her up in his arms and headed for the back door. Dani wiggled and squirmed, but he only tightened his grip on her legs.

"Put me down. I don't even have any shoes on," she wailed, sticking one foot up in his face when he reached the back door.

Sam stopped walking, glanced at her slipper sock and smiled. "Don't worry about it, darlin'," he said in that husky tone that made her nerve endings tingle. "Where we're goin', you won't need any shoes."

Then he lowered his head and kissed her, long and hard and deep. She knew she should fight, at least argue with him, but his lips were so warm and firm against hers and his arms were so strong and she'd missed this so much, the last of her will to resist vanished. By the time he broke away, her arms were wrapped around his neck, and she laid her head on his shoulder with a weary sigh.

"It'll be all right, Dani," he murmured, gently kissing the top of her head. "I promise."

A blast of arctic air hit her face when he opened the door. He hurried down the back steps and deposited her in the passenger seat of his pickup, which was already running, the heater going strong. After fastening her seat belt and closing her door, he raced around to the driver's side and hopped in. As he drove away, Dani glanced back at the house, which was shrouded in a mist of vapor from the exhaust.

"Still worryin' about the kids?" Sam asked. "Hank'll take good care of 'em."

"I know he will," she replied, a smile forcing its way onto her mouth. "I've just never been abducted before. Tell me, what's the proper etiquette in this situation?"

"Well, I've never abducted anyone before, so I guess we'll have to make up our own rules as we go along. First one is, you sit back and let me do all the work."

Dani chuckled. "I can live with that. What's the second one?"

"No arguments and no sulking. This is supposed to be fun and romantic."

"I don't sulk."

"Now quit that," he ordered, softening his words with a grin. "You sound like you're fixin' to break rule number two already. We won't do anything you don't want to do."

"Am I allowed to know where we're going?"

"Nope. That's a surprise. We'll be there in a few minutes."

"All right. Whatever you say, boss."

She drew her feet up onto the seat and sat cross-legged to keep her toes warm, then settled back to enjoy the ride. Despite the frigid temperature, the sky was a clear, solid blue overhead. The fence posts and pine trees on either side of the road wore white, pointed caps, and the land in the open spaces wore a thick, deep carpet of snow.

At the junction with the gravel road that led to the highway, he turned left instead of right, and headed up into the mountains. The pickup bounced along on the snow-packed road, making conversation difficult. Dani didn't mind. At the moment it was enough to be out in this natural wonderland with Sam.

She was tired of fighting her attraction to him. Tired of holding him at arm's length. Tired of worrying about the future. After all he'd done for her, the least she could do for him was relax and enjoy his surprise.

Five minutes later, they topped a rise, and Sam turned off into a steep, rutted path. The pickup fishtailed in the deep snow as they rounded a sharp curve, but thanks to four-wheel drive and Sam's skill, it stayed on the road. Dani smiled at him in admiration, then gasped with delight at the sight before her.

A small log cabin was nestled in front of a half circle of tall, straight pines. At least a foot of snow covered the roof and the porch. Golden light shone from the big windows on either side of the door, and white smoke rose in a lazy spiral from the rock chimney.

"It looks like a Christmas card," Dani whispered. "This is your parents' cabin, isn't it?" she asked, turning to Sam.

But he was already out of the truck, plowing through a drift to get to her. She put her arms around his neck when he reached for her, and marveled at the quiet of the surrounding forest as he carried her to the front door.

"I could get used to traveling like this," she teased him, resting her head on his shoulder.

He tossed her up in the air a few inches and caught her again, laughing when she squealed in surprise. "Be all right with me. Shoot, you don't weigh much more than a bale of hay."

Sam kicked the snow from his boots, opened the door and set her on her feet inside. Dani was so busy taking in the interior of the one-room building, she didn't even hear him shut the door. A fireplace, complete with a roaring blaze, dominated the wall to her left. A sofa, two overstuffed chairs and a somewhat battered coffee table huddled in front of it.

A broad bunk, covered with what looked like a stack of homemade quilts, was built into the far wall. Bookcases stuffed with paperbacks filled the rest of the space. A kitchen area, containing a stove, refrigerator and a small, round table sat off to her right.

A white linen cloth covered the table. A bouquet of red roses, flanked by tall, slender red candles in silver candlesticks, graced the spot between two place settings complete with china, crystal and silver. The hardwood floor gleamed in the soft light from the gas lantern suspended over the table. The lemon scent of furniture polish mingled with a mouth-watering aroma coming from the kitchen.

Sam hung his coat and hat on a peg beside the door, then turned Dani around and unzipped her parka. "Do you like it?"

"Oh, Sam, who wouldn't?" she asked. "It's beautiful, it's cozy, it's—"

"Private," he finished for her, bending down to steal a kiss. "Very, very private," he added, stealing another, and then another, each kiss longer than the last.

Dani's knees trembled with the strain of holding herself upright by the time he raised his head and exhaled a deep sigh. Then, to her disappointment, he set her away from him.

"Go on and curl up on the sofa, honey. I'll be right back."

She obeyed his order, feeling incredibly humbled that he'd gone to so much work to please her. She heard the oven door open and close, then the back door, followed by a loud pop and a clink of glassware. A moment later he joined her, carrying a champagne bottle with melting snow dripping off the sides and two long-stemmed crystal flutes.

He poured them each a glass, handed her one and raised his own in a toast. "To you, Dani. Happy Valentine's Day."

"Thank you, Sam." She clicked her glass against his, her eyes threatening to mist with tears until she sipped and the exploding bubbles tickled her nose.

He sat beside her, stretching his arm along the sofa back behind her head. "Your feet warm enough?"

"They're fine."

"Hungry yet?"

Now *there* was a loaded question. "No, but whatever you're cooking smells delicious."

"Beef Stroganoff," he informed her. "Becky made it."

"It sounds wonderful."

They watched the flames in silence, sipping champagne and stealing sidelong glances at each other. Then Sam fished a small, square box wrapped in bright red foil and sporting a lace-edged white bow from his shirt pocket and set it on Dani's left knee.

"Happy Valentine's Day again," he said.

Dani eyed the package as if it might contain a bomb. Her fingers itched to open it, but the shape and size were right for something she knew she couldn't accept. And, Lord, she didn't want to fight with Sam now.

He picked it up, placed it in her palm and curled her fingers around it. "It won't bite."

She shot him a crooked smile, then carefully peeled away
the tape holding the paper together. Sam gently took the
wrapping from her. She let it go without looking at him,
reluctantly studying the velvet-covered jeweler's box in her
hand.

Exhaling an impatient, yet amused sigh, he flipped open
the hinged lid, revealing a gold, heart-shaped locket on a
delicate chain. As she stared at the necklace in openmouthed delight, Sam removed it from the inner wrapping, released the catch and spread the two halves open for
her examination. Kim smiled at her from the left side, Colin
from the right.

Before she could look her fill at the beautiful photos
she'd never seen before of her children, he snapped the
locket shut and turned it over, showing her an inscription
engraved in tiny intricate letters. Taking it from him, she
held it up to the light and read silently, "To Dani. All my
love, SJD."

Slowly she raised her gaze to meet his and whispered,
"You don't fight fair, Sam."

"Does that mean you like it?" he whispered back.

Her throat too tight to speak, she nodded. He took the
necklace from her trembling fingers and fastened it around
her neck. With an index finger, he traced the chain to the
bottom, settling the golden heart between her breasts. Then
he cupped her face between his big hands and softly kissed
her eyelids closed. Murmuring all the while, he saluted the
tip of her nose, her eyebrows, her cheekbones, temples and
chin with his lips.

"You've made me a desperate man, Dani Smith. You've
turned my life upside down and inside out. I don't want to
lose you."

"Oh, Sam—"

"Shh," he commanded, continuing his tender on-
slaught. "Just let me love you, babe."

With a moan of surrender, she wrapped her arms around his neck and gave herself up to the magic of his mouth on hers, his tongue tasting hers, his hands moving gently over her body. His woodsy cologne filled her head, opening a deep, aching need inside her. She plunged her fingers into his thick, glossy hair and kissed him desperately, silently urging him to hurry.

"Easy there, Little Bit," he crooned, scooping her onto his lap. "We have all the time in the world."

"I'm not a horse," she muttered.

A chuckle rumbled out of his chest and he teased the side of her neck with his mustache. "No, you're not. You're a beautiful, warm, funny, talented, wonderful, luscious, desirable, exciting—"

Each syllable enhanced the tickling sensation on her sensitive skin. She hunched her shoulder to her ear. He switched to the other side of her neck and continued as if she hadn't interrupted his litany.

"—loving, cuddly, soft, sweet, sensitive, sexy—"

Giggling helplessly, she managed to get one hand beneath his chin and push it back. "Stop that, you crazy man."

His head jerked up. "You don't like my sweet nothings?"

The mournful, wounded-puppy expression in his eyes made her laugh. She reached up and tweaked the left side of his mustache. "I would if you'd quit tickling me with that paintbrush."

"Want me to shave it off?" he asked, his muscles tensing as if he would leap to his feet immediately and find a razor if she told him to.

"No, Sam." Smiling into his eyes, she curved her hand around the back of his neck and applied pressure until she felt his warm breath on her lips. "I want you to shut up and kiss me again."

"My pleasure, ma'am."

But it seemed that the pleasure was all hers. He applied himself to the task with the dedicated enthusiasm of a man who loves his work. He nibbled at her lips, uttering greedy little groans of delight. He slid his tongue over the edges of her teeth, then plundered her mouth again and again, as if he needed the taste of her more than he needed oxygen.

At last he pulled back, his breathing ragged. "Was that better?"

"Magnificent." She reached for him again, but he lifted her from his lap and set her firmly on the cushion beside him.

"That was the appetizer," he said when she opened her mouth to protest. "I didn't bring you up here just to jump your bones."

He climbed to his feet, refilled her champagne glass and handed it to her before striding off to the kitchen. Dani sighed, then rested her head against the sofa and sipped the wine, her free hand coming up to stroke the locket he'd given her. It was, without a doubt, the most thoughtful gift anyone had ever given her. How had he gotten those pictures of the kids taken without her knowing about it?

A loud clatter of pots and pans and a muttered curse from the other side of the room made her smile. For a man who could do so many things competently, Sam was awfully awkward in the kitchen. Hearing him fumble around made what he was trying to do for her that much more special.

He approached her a moment later, one hand outstretched to help her up. He escorted her to the table and held a chair out for her. Dani spread her linen napkin across her lap and marveled at the elegant place settings in such a rustic setting.

"This looks lovely, Sam."

"I wanted everything to be just right," he said with an abashed grin.

He tipped his head to one side and studied the table, as if running through a mental checklist. Then he snapped his fingers, hurried over to the window and switched on the portable CD player Colin had received from her parents for Christmas. Soft classical music filled the cabin, and Dani chuckled.

"And you said you weren't a very romantic kind of a guy," she teased him.

Sam grabbed her plate and dropped a warm, sweet kiss on her smiling lips. "I'm learnin'."

He picked up his own plate and walked to the stove, an expression of intense concentration on his face as he dished up the rice and covered it with the fragrant meat and gravy mixture. When he came back to the table, Dani didn't have the heart to tell him he'd given her enough for three people. He filled their water glasses and wineglasses and brought a basket of dinner rolls to the table before finally joining her.

Conversation was sparse at first, and what there was of it, was stilted. Sam gradually relaxed, however, and began telling her about his hopes and plans for the ranch. Dani was sure the food must have been delicious, but she was so entranced with him, she barely tasted anything.

It amazed her that even after living with him all this time, she could become so aroused just by looking at him and listening to his voice. Halfway through the meal, her feelings must have started to show on her face. Sam stopped talking in midsentence and gazed at her for a moment. Then he reached for his wineglass and took a long gulp.

"You'd better stop lookin' at me like that if you want dessert," he said, his voice low and gravelly.

"How am I looking at you?"

The corners of his mustache twitched. "You know."

"I can't help it, Sam. Nobody's ever done anything this wonderful for me before. I think *you're* wonderful."

His neck and ears turned red. "I just wanted to make you happy."

"You have," she assured him, reaching across the table and covering his hand with hers. "But I don't need all this to make me happy."

"What do you need?"

"You."

She wasn't sure who moved first, but suddenly she was in his arms and he was raining kisses all over her face with a desperate hunger. Then he slid one arm behind her knees, straightened and carried her to the bunk. He set her on her feet in the middle of the mattress and crushed her against him, his cheek resting against her hair, his hands splayed over her back.

"God, it feels good to hold you like this. I've thought about it, dreamed about it night after night."

"I have, too," she murmured, hugging him as hard as she could.

When he released her, she reached for the hem of her sweater, but he trapped her hands against her hips.

"No, sweetheart, please. Let me undress you."

He slid his thumbs under the fabric and slowly, slowly lifted it, his lips trailing a burning path up the center of her body. She raised her arms to help him, her head falling back as he nuzzled her cleavage and moved on to the indentations above her collar bones. By the time he peeled the sweater the rest of the way off and tossed it at the foot of the bed, she had to clutch at his shirt for balance.

His dark eyes gleaming, he lowered the straps of her bra, then kissed each bare shoulder before reaching behind her to unfasten the clasp. The lacy garment dropped to the quilt, and he sighed as if her naked breasts were the most beautiful sight he'd ever seen. His palms brushed over her nipples, coaxing them into prominence.

Bending to take one between his lips, he whispered, "Lord, this is killin' me."

It was killing her, too. The sensation of his warm, wet mouth at her breast sent her heartbeat galloping out of control. Her lungs couldn't draw enough air. Impatience gnawed at her insides.

She sank her fingernails into his shoulders and called his name, her voice breathless with urgency. But he would not be hurried. While his mouth moved to her other breast and lingered, his rough fingertips roamed her back and torso in feathery caresses, sending bolts of excitement along her nerve endings.

He brought his lips back to hers, his kisses hot and deep and tasting of wine. When her knees buckled, he wrapped a muscled arm around her waist and eased her stretch pants and panties down over her hips and thighs with his other hand, then lowered her to the bed. His gaze burned over her as he shed his clothes in a few, quick motions.

Looking up at his big, strong body outlined by the firelight, she shivered with anticipation and need. He stretched out beside her, gathering her close, telling her in a hoarse murmur all the deliciously wicked, erotic things he intended to do with her. His caresses became more intimate, more insistent, and yet there was a reverence in his touch that made her want to weep.

When he finally joined their bodies together and moved within her, there was power and pleasure and tenderness.

When their voices mingled in cries of completion, his arms were there to shelter her and bear her safely back to reality.

When he rested his weight on his elbows and gazed down at her, his chest heaved with exertion. Joy and satisfaction were etched into his features. And she felt as if he had opened his heart and soul to her the way she had opened her body to him.

Entranced by the love shining in his eyes, she raised a trembling hand and traced the edges of his mustache. He captured one finger between his teeth and bathed it with his tongue. Then he rolled onto his side, bringing her with him, their heads lying close together on the same pillow.

"You *do* love me, Dani," he said quietly.

"Yes, I do."

"Then marry me."

"Oh, Sam, I ca—"

"The sooner the better," he went on in a rush. "There's no waiting period in Idaho. We could drive over there next weekend with the kids and—"

She laid two fingers across his lips. "Whoa, boy."

He kissed her fingertips, then pulled them away from his mouth. "If I do, you'll say no."

"I don't want to say no, Sam, but I have to."

"Because I haven't said I love you? I do, you know."

"I know." Suddenly feeling chilled, she sat up, grabbed her sweater from the foot of the bed and yanked it over her head. "Unfortunately, sometimes love isn't enough."

Sam raked one hand through his hair and swung his legs over the side of the mattress. "Dammit, Dani, that doesn't make any sense. I've done everything I can think of to show you how much I love you and your kids. We get along fine and enjoy living together, and I'll be happy to support all of you. What more do you want from me?"

"I've already told you. Emotional intimacy. That means no barriers and no secrets."

"What you mean is, you want to know about that damn nightmare I had. Don't you think you're carryin' that tune a little too far?"

"I need to know you really trust me."

He pulled on his jeans, then scowled at her over his shoulder. "It's not that I don't trust you, Dani. I just dream about the war sometimes. Believe me, it's not something you should hear about."

"But that's just it, Sam." She sat on her heels and held up both hands in a plea for understanding. "I want to share everything with you. The good and the bad."

"It's not that important."

"Then tell me about it. Whatever happened to you, I'll understand."

Sam picked up his shirt and shoved his arms into the sleeves. "I know you'd try to. But it's too damn ugly and it really doesn't have anything to do with you and me. It never did."

"I don't agree," she replied, pulling on her own pants and standing to face him. "It's haunted you for over twenty years. It's affected your whole life, and what affects you, will affect me and my kids. If you'll hide this . . . whatever it is from me, how do I know you won't hide other things, too? Things that I really *do* need to know."

He sighed and rested his hands on her shoulders. "I promise I won't do that. Maybe someday I'll be able to sort out that time in Nam, enough to tell you about it, but I can't do it just yet."

"Then I can't marry you just yet, either," Dani said, her voice breaking along with her heart at the pain in his eyes. "And if you haven't sorted it out in twenty years, I'm not going to put my life on hold, waiting for you to do it, Sam."

"Dani, please. We have so much going for us. Don't be so stubborn about this one little thing."

"I'm not doing this out of stubbornness," she wailed. "Why can't you understand that? If I ever get married again, I want it all, Sam. I can't settle for less."

His fingers tightened, as if he wanted to shake her. Then he released her, dropping his hands to his sides in a gesture that reeked of defeat. "Boy, I must have really scared the whey out of you that night. Truth is, you don't trust *me*. You think I'm one of those wacko Vietnam vets, liable to flip out some night and shoot all of you in your sleep. That's what this is all about."

"That's ridiculous."

A bitter smile twisted his lips as he shook his head and slowly sank down onto the side of the bunk. Clasping his hands together, he propped his elbows on his knees and stared into the dying flames in the fireplace. His lips clamped into a hard, straight line. A muscle ticked at the side of his jaw.

Dani knelt in front of him, frightened by the bleak, lost expression in his eyes. "Sam, listen to me. I'm not worried about you hurting me or the kids. I'd have left a long time ago if I thought there was any possibility of that happening."

He glanced at her, gulped, then looked back at the fire. "It's all right. When I got home, nobody really wanted to know what happened over there. Lots of folks looked at me like they expected me to go berserk any minute. I learned real fast to keep my mouth shut and pretend I'd never been in the army."

"You don't have to do that with me," she argued, tears streaming down her face.

Sam turned his head and gazed at her, his eyes glistening with moisture, though no tears fell. "I have to do it with you most of all, Dani," he whispered. "I couldn't stand to see you turn away from me in disgust. I've kept it locked inside me for so long, I wouldn't even know how to start letting it out. Maybe I *would* go nuts. It's too late for me to change."

"I don't believe that."

He shrugged, then looked back at the fire, his tone flat with finality. "Believe whatever you want. At this point, I don't even want to try."

Anger roared through Dani with the force of a tornado racing at full speed. She swiped her tears away, wanting to scream at him, hit him—beat the self-pity out of him and knock some sense into him. But it wouldn't do any good. She knew that as well as she knew her life would never be the same.

She pushed herself to her feet and finished dressing. Sam continued to sit there like a rock, staring at the flames, so lost in thought, he didn't appear to be aware of her presence. She went to the kitchen, blew out the candles and cleared away the remains of their dinner. When she'd finished washing the dishes, she put on her coat and stood at the door.

"Take me back to the ranch, Sam."

He started, and looked at her as if he barely recognized her.

"I'm ready to leave now," she said. "I'll wait for you in the pickup."

Then she slipped outside and ran to the pickup, with only her purple slipper socks to protect her feet from the ice and snow. But she was beyond caring about frostbite. It couldn't hurt any worse than her shattered hopes did.

Chapter Sixteen

During the silent drive back to the ranch, an odd, but welcome numbness settled over Sam. Dani bolted from the pickup the instant it stopped rolling. He wasn't surprised by her action, but he *was* surprised to see lights blazing all over the house.

Opening his door to turn on the truck's dome light, he looked at his watch. Eight o'clock. They'd left the house at three-thirty. Funny, a lifetime should have passed since he'd abducted Dani. Four and a half hours didn't seem like nearly enough time for a man's dreams to die.

Needing a few minutes of solitude before facing anyone, he shut the door and shoved his hands into his coat pockets. The fingers of his left hand curled around the other gift he'd bought for Dani, crushing the satin bow on top of the small box. He'd had the ring made especially for her—a diamond surrounded by sapphires as blue as her eyes. Would she have liked it if she'd seen it? He would never know.

A lump formed in his throat. Fearing his thoughts would cut through the blessed numbness, he forced his mind to go blank and stared out the windshield at the stars until the light over the back door turned on. A moment later, Hank limped down the steps with the aid of his cane. Sam stepped out of the truck and walked toward him.

"What the hell happened?" Hank demanded.

"It didn't work."

Hank grabbed Sam's arm when he would have brushed past him. "Whaddaya mean, it didn't work? One look at that set-up and Dani should have been fallin' all over you. The plan was foolproof."

Sam jerked his arm away and headed for the house. "Not quite."

"Dammit, what happened?" Hank shouted, hurrying after him.

Sam turned on the top step and snarled at his brother. "None of your damned business. Now drop it, Hank."

"Or else what? I'm not afraid of you, Sam."

"Well, you damned sure oughtta be."

Hank opened his mouth as if he would argue further, but something in Sam's soft, deadly tone or his icy glare must have convinced him to wait. He closed his mouth with an audible snap and followed Sam into the mudroom. Sam hung up his coat, then wiped his boots and entered the kitchen.

Raised voices came from the living room. Before Sam could try to make sense of what anyone was saying, Kim raced through the doorway and hurled herself against him. Her arms wrapped around his hips in a death grip. Her body heaved with sobs. "M-Mom and Colin are f-fighting again. P-please stop them."

Sam picked her up. "Shhh, honey," he crooned, stroking her dark hair. "It's all right, baby. Everything'll work out sooner or later."

She buried her face against his neck, wetting his collar with her tears. He carried her into the living room, and discovered Dani and Colin standing nose to nose.

"Look," Dani said, her face pale with strain, "I know you like it here, and I know you're disappointed it didn't work out. I'm sorry for that, but I can't do anything about it. We're moving out tomorrow."

Colin loomed over her, the tendons in his neck standing out in sharp relief. "You always wreck everything!" he shouted.

"Colin, please. . . ." Dani rubbed the bridge of her nose with her thumb and forefinger. "Just go upstairs and pack."

"No! I hate you! And I won't go with you. I'd rather stay with Sam, and he'll let me. You'll see."

"Do as your mother says, Colin," Sam said quietly.

Mother and son whirled to face him. Colin's eyes widened with pleasure for an instant, then flashed with anger as the content of Sam's order registered. His chin rose in a gesture of hurt defiance.

"You want me to go?"

"It's not a question of what I want. You're the man of the family. Try acting like one for a change and help your mother out instead of giving her so much guff."

Colin recoiled from the sharp rebuke as if he'd been backhanded. Sam set Kim on her feet and reached one hand toward the boy. "I'm sorry, Colin," he said.

But it was too late. Colin was already halfway up the stairs to his room. Sam sighed, then turned to find Dani glaring at him.

"Don't you *ever* take your anger at me out on my kids again," she said, pulling Kim away from him and into her arms, as if she feared he might contaminate the little girl.

"I wasn't," Sam protested. "He shouldn't talk to you that way."

"He shouldn't do a lot of things. But he's not your problem. He's mine."

"You're right. I . . . I'm sorry."

Feeling as low as something that had crawled out from under a flat rock, Sam went into his den and quietly shut the door. He sat behind his desk, propped his feet up, ignoring the stack of bills that toppled over the side and onto the floor, and leaned his head against the high back of the swivel chair. A few moments later, he heard footsteps going back and forth, back and forth overhead. Dani was packing.

He closed his eyes, waiting for the pain to start, knowing that it *should* start. But it didn't. After that last flash of shame for hurting Colin, it seemed as though all of his emotions had frozen. Or died.

Sam was gone when Dani came downstairs the next morning. She told herself that was just fine with her, that she wouldn't mind never seeing him again, but she didn't believe it. Not really.

A stubborn, incredibly stupid part of herself still hoped that somehow she and Sam could heal the awful rift between them. But she didn't believe that, either. Not really.

She went through the motions of cooking breakfast and tried to act normally for the children's sake, but it wasn't easy. Colin and Kim pushed the food around on their plates and shot her enough resentful glances to last her a lifetime. Hank didn't fare much better with Tina.

To Hank's credit, however, he kept up a steady stream of chatter with the three sullen monsters and herded them outside to drive them to the bus stop without a single cross word. Dani bustled around the kitchen, loading the dishwasher and wiping down the counters for the last time. She was sweeping under the table when Hank returned.

He poured himself a mug of coffee, then rested one hip against the counter. "You're really determined to move out today?"

Blinking back tears brought on by his compassionate tone, Dani nodded. "I have to, Hank. It'll be too... awkward if I don't."

"Wanna stay with Becky and Pete for a while? I know they wouldn't mind."

Dani shook her head. "Not if I can help it. They've got so much going on with the new baby, they don't need house guests."

"All right. Let me see what I can do to help."

He set down his mug, walked into the living room and came back a moment later with the latest issue of the local newspaper. After locating the want ads, he laid the page on the table and ran his finger down the list of properties for rent.

"Here's one you might be interested in," he said, beckoning to Dani. "It's a little house with three bedrooms, two blocks from the grade school. I know the guy who owns it, and I'll bet it's in pretty good shape."

"Is it furnished?"

"Yup. Rent's reasonable, too. Want me to call him?"

She studied the ad for a moment. The rent *was* reasonable, especially by Chicago standards, but she wished she'd at least found a part-time job. Still, she'd been able to save a fair amount of her salary from the Circle D, and she really didn't have much choice in the matter. "Thanks, I'd appreciate it."

While Hank dialed the number, Dani went into the bathroom and splashed cold water on her face. Her eyes were red from the gallons of tears she'd shed during the night, and Hank's kindness was about to start another deluge. Somehow, she had to pull herself together.

"You're in luck," he announced when she returned. "The last tenants moved out day before yesterday, and

Jack's gonna have the meters read this morning. He'll meet us at the house in a couple of hours, so we'd better get crackin'."

To Dani's surprise, Hank exhibited an extremely practical streak, insisting that she take from the ranch whatever linens, dishes and kitchen implements she would need to set up housekeeping.

"You can give it all back when you get your own, but there's no sense in going broke tryin' to buy everything new right off the bat. We won't even miss this stuff," he said to silence her protests.

He helped her organize everything into boxes and carried them out to his pickup while she went through the house, searching for misplaced possessions. She left Sam's den for last, knowing that particular room would hurt the most. Taking a deep breath for courage, she opened the door and slipped inside.

She found one of Colin's books on the computer table, a pair of Kim's shoes beside the sofa. She picked them up and turned to leave before memories of all the wonderful times she'd spent here with Sam could overwhelm her. Despite her efforts to hurry, however, a wave of emotion welled up inside her, nearly choking off her oxygen supply.

As if compelled by an unseen force, she paused, then walked over to Sam's big desk, running her hand over the smooth surface, remembering the first time they'd made love. She touched the indentation on the headrest of the swivel chair, imagining it was still warm from his body. Gulping, she set down the book and the shoes, and with trembling fingers, undid the locket he'd given her.

She held it up to the sunshine coming through the window, admiring the way the light made the golden heart gleam. After a moment, she refastened the chain's clasp and gently laid the necklace in the middle of the desk where

Sam would be sure to find it. Then she grabbed her chil dren's things and fled.

With Hank's support, she managed to get through the rest of the morning with her composure intact. Her new home turned out to be a twenty-year-old yellow ranche with white trim. Though the furnishings were plain and somewhat sparse, everything looked clean. The landlord was a pleasant man in his late fifties, who stayed to help them unload the pickup and offered to buy the paint if Dani wanted to spruce the place up.

While Dani unpacked, Hank bought a load of groceries and made a late lunch of tuna sandwiches, potato chips and Ding Dongs. When they'd finished eating, Dani reached across the small Formica table and patted his hand.

"You're a fraud, Hank Dawson," she said, softening the accusation with a smile.

"Oh yeah?" he asked, raising an eyebrow at her in mock scowl. "What makes you think so?"

"The way you took charge today. You've cultivated this devil-may-care image, but you know how to get things done when you want to. I appreciate all your help."

"Aw, heck, Dani. It seemed like the least I could do was help you get settled. I'm sorry I got you into this mess."

"You've done more than enough to make up for any part you had in it." She gave him a crooked grin. "Your scheme came awfully close to working."

"You wanna talk about what happened between you and Sam?" he asked quietly.

"No. Not yet, anyway."

"Well, then," he said, pushing back his chair and reaching for his cane, "I'd best be headin' home."

She walked him to the door and gratefully accepted the brotherly hug he offered.

He pulled away and lifted her chin with his forefinger. "If you ever need a shoulder to cry on, I've got two o 'em."

"Thanks. I'll be all right."

"I know you will. But I want you to call me if you need anything. Promise?"

Her eyes filled with more tears and her throat wouldn't work. Sniffing, she nodded. Hank studied her face, then pulled her back into another hug.

"Don't give up on Sam, Dani," he said. "He's gonna miss you like hell. It won't be long at all before he comes after you, beggin' to make things right."

"I don't know why, but I wish I could believe that."

"You can. Your movin' out'll shake him up good. You'll see."

Dani stepped away, wiping her eyes with the backs of her hands. "Stop being so nice and get out of here, before I flood this place," she said with a shaky laugh.

"All right. See ya later."

She stood in the doorway, watched him climb into his truck and returned his final wave. As he drove away, she whispered, "Take care of Sam for me."

During the next two weeks, Sam stayed away from the house as much as possible. For one thing, there were too many painful memories of Dani and the kids waiting there to ambush him. For another, he was afraid he might break down and ask Hank how Dani was getting along. Though Hank never mentioned her name, Sam knew his brother was staying in touch with her.

He was even more afraid that if he did ask, Hank would say something like: "Oh, she's just fine. Happy as hell without you," or, "She's dating Andy Johnson." Sam figured either response would make him crazy.

Luckily, in an experiment designed to get a head start on the calf crop this year, Sam had turned the bulls in with the cows earlier than usual the previous May. As a result, the calving season started two days after Dani moved out, giv-

ing him the perfect excuse to work long, grueling hours
The constant activity kept him sane, but just barely.

When he had to pull a calf, he found himself wishin
Colin was there, so he could share his knowledge with th
boy the way his own father had done with him. Tina race
out to the pasture after school each day to check out th
new babies, and her squeals of delight made him thin
about how much Kim would have loved to see the frisk
little devils.

And always, no matter how busy he was, there was a
ache the size of the Tetons in the middle of his chest wit
Dani's name on it. The pain had started when he'd foun
her locket on his desk. It didn't show any signs of easing i
the near or distant future, either.

The only thing that had improved since she'd left wa
Hank. Sam wasn't sure what had gotten into him. For lac
of a better description, Sam would have said that hi
younger brother was finally settling down.

Though Tina still gave him the proverbial raspberry a
every opportunity, Hank had refused to let Grandma I
move the kid back to Becky's house. While he couldn
match Dani's homemaking skills by a long shot, this tim
he was working a helluva lot harder at keeping the hous
orderly than he'd done before. Sam had actually caugl
him reading Grandma's cookbooks last week.

Even more surprising, Hank enrolled in a correspor
dence course in accounting from the University of Wyon
ing, and worked diligently on his assignments at the kitche
table every night after he tucked Tina in bed. Sam knev
several retired teachers in town who'd probably drop dea
of shock if they ever saw that phenomenon.

All things considered, Sam thought he'd survived th
breakup with Dani fairly well, until one afternoon in th
middle of March. When he went out to check the calves, I
found three of them bawling with hunger, and their motl
ers kicking them away every time they tried to nurs

hading his eyes with one hand, Sam looked at the nearly
linding glare coming off the snow from the weak sun
hining overhead.

The problem wasn't serious or even unusual; the cows
imply had sunburned bags, which made their teats sore.
Vhen their babies tried to nurse, the cows naturally ob-
cted. Unfortunately, the solution—herding them all into
ie barn, hobbling the cows with gunny sacks, greasing
own their bags and reintroducing the calves—required
iore patience than Sam thought he possessed at the mo-
ient.

Of course he'd have to do it anyway. The calves would
arve if he didn't. Cursing under his breath, he re-
iounted Smokey, whistled a signal to Bear Dog and started
ie animals moving.

The first two cows didn't give him much trouble, but the
iird one was a hellion from the get-go. She fought the
alter and rammed him against the wall of the stall before
e could tie her up. She kicked him and stomped on his
and when he hobbled her. As a final insult, she splattered
is boots and legs with manure.

Sam whacked her on the rump with his hat and bel-
wed at her. "Knock it off, you damn, mangy, walkin' pile
' hamburgers!"

"Need some help?" Hank asked from the other side of
ie barn, his voice laced with laughter.

"Aw, shut up, Hank," Sam replied, shooting his brother
sheepish grin.

Hank strolled the length of the building, his limp barely
erceptible. It suddenly struck Sam that Hank wasn't us-
ig his cane. The realization made Sam smile sincerely for
ie first time in weeks.

"Hey, you're really movin' good. When did you give up
ie cane?"

"A week ago," Hank replied.

"Well, I'll be damned. I can't believe I didn't notice."

"You've had other things on your mind."

"A few," Sam admitted. Then he clapped his brother o[n] the shoulder. "I'm real glad for you, Hank."

"Yeah, me, too." Hank looked over the side of the sta[ll] and watched the calf nursing enthusiastically. "Hungr[y] little critter, isn't he?"

Sam nodded in agreement. "Did you need me for some thin'?"

Hank's expression sobered. "Not exactly, but we'v[e] gotta talk. I'd rather do it before Tina gets home fro[m] school. Got a few minutes?"

"Sure." Sam gestured toward a stack of bales at the en[d] of the row of stalls. "Let's sit down over there." When the[y] were settled, he asked, "What's on your mind?"

"I've finally figured out what I want to do," Hank be gan. "You're probably gonna think I'm crazy, but I kno[w] I can make it work."

"What is it?"

"I'm gonna buy a dude ranch."

"A *dude* ranch?"

"Yeah. The old Gunderson place is for sale, and I'[m] thinkin' about makin' an offer on it."

Sam sighed and shook his head. "You're right. I thin[k] you're crazy. One good windstorm, and every building o[n] the place'll collapse. I don't even want to think about wh[at] kind of shape the fences'll be in."

"That's all fixable, Sam," Hank argued. "It's got a s[u] per view, plenty of water and some great places for pac[k] trips."

"It'll take most of your capital to get it runnin'. As I r[e] call, the Gundersons never did make much of a profit."

"Dude ranches weren't that popular then, and the[y] didn't know anything about advertising."

"And you do?" Sam asked.

"Not yet. But I will. I'm not askin' for advice, Sam. [I] need to try it."

Sighing, Sam leaned his head against the rough board all. "Dad always wanted us to work this ranch together, ank."

"Dad's not here anymore." Hank hesitated, then unged on in a rush. "You were the one he really wanted have the Circle D."

"That's not true. I know you didn't get along with him ry well, but—"

"That doesn't matter anymore," Hank interrupted. You were the one he counted on, and you can't deny that. ou've run this place for so long, I'll always feel like a sec- d banana. Think about it. A dude ranch is perfect for e. I'll have lots of folks around from all over the coun- y, so I won't get bored. And it's time I accomplished mething on my own."

"What about Tina?"

"She'll come with me."

"She's not gonna like that."

"She doesn't have to." Hank sighed and rubbed the back his neck. "Look, I know I haven't been a very good dad r the kid, but that's gonna change. I love her, Sam."

"I know you do. But she's so damn mad at you, I don't e how you're gonna get through to her."

"That's another reason we need to leave. We've gotta arn how to be a family together, just Tina and me. If 're livin' by ourselves, she won't be able to run to you or ecky or Grandma D when she needs something. She's nna have to come to me."

"That makes sense," Sam said, nodding thoughtfully. When will you go?"

"It'll take a while. I'm still tryin' to get 'em to come wn on their price."

Sam sighed, then held out a hand to his brother. "I'm nna miss you guys."

Hank shook it and grinned. "Aw, I'll be back so often, rrowin' all your tools, you won't even know I'm gone."

"You're welcome to 'em, as long as you put 'em bac where they belong," Sam replied. "If you ever need ar help, I'll be here."

"You've always been here for me and everybody else the family. But it works both ways, Big Brother. I'm gonr be so responsible from here on out, you won't hardly re ognize me."

Sam laughed and shook his head. "I'll believe that whe I see it."

"Just you wait. You *will* see it," Hank retorted, pusl ing himself to his feet. "Becky's invited us all over for su; per tonight. Be ready by six."

"Aw, I'm not gonna go," Sam replied. "I've got a heif that might need some help tonight. Tell Beck I said thanl for the invite."

"Will do."

Hank started to walk away, but Sam stood and called hi back. "Hank? What about the Circle D? You still own third of it. Becky's happy to get her slice of the profits even year, but do you want me to buy you out?"

"No. Put my share in a college fund for Tina. Then if tl dude ranch goes belly-up, she'll still have something."

"My God, you *are* turnin' responsible."

Chuckling, Hank left the barn.

Later that evening, Sam sat at the kitchen table with beer and a roast-beef sandwich that had about as mu appeal as sawdust. The house was utterly quiet, the silen pounding with the rhythm of his chewing. One thought r verberated through his mind with every bite.

This is what it's gonna be like for the rest of my life.

Becky and Pete were so content together, Sam knew sl wouldn't be back. After seeing the determination in Hank eyes that afternoon, he believed his brother would make success of his dude ranch, and Tina would stay with hir Grandma D was so crazy over little Jonathan, Sam doubt she would ever return to the Circle D for more than an occasional visit.

Sam couldn't blame any of them for their decisions to leave, and he wanted them to be happy. But where the hell did that leave *him?* He shoved his plate away so hard, it slid off the other side of the table and shattered on the floor.

Ever since he'd come home from college and his dad had died, he'd dedicated his life to one thing—protecting. Protecting the ranch, his family and his miserable secret from the war. What did he have to show for it?

His family didn't need him anymore. His damned secret had cost him the only woman he'd ever loved. And the Circle D didn't mean a whole helluva lot if he had to live on it all by himself. Would Tina or Jonathan or any other nieces or nephews who might be born in the future ever want it? God only knew.

Agitation drove him to the windows. He looked out toward the barn and saw Bear Dog curled up at his usual post. Sam watched the animal for a moment, wondering if he would eventually get lonely enough to bring Bear into the house for company. Would he turn into one of those crusty old bachelors who started acting odd because he'd lived out in the boondocks by himself for too long? Did he have any choice?

Of course, you have a choice, a voice inside his head insisted. *All you've got to do is tell Dani the truth.*

It seemed so simple. And yet, so damned hard. What if she wouldn't even talk to him? What if she listened, but turned her back on him? On the other hand, what if she listened, and loved him anyway?

He turned away from the window and gazed around the room. Her sewing machine had filled that empty corner. The food processor she'd enjoyed so much still sat on the counter. If he closed his eyes, he could see her flitting from the stove to the table, filling the room with energy and happy chatter.

And the kids. God, how he missed those kids, with their messes and their bickering and their funny, uncensored remarks. Did they miss him even half as much as he missed them?

Ginny would tell him to spill his guts and be damn quick about it. The question was, did he have the nerve to risk Danii's rejection, once she knew what he'd done? Sam gulped, then sucked in a harsh breath as a new thought occurred to him. Maybe that wasn't the question at all. Maybe the real question was, what the hell did he have to lose by trying?

"Not one damn thing," he muttered, rocking back and forth from his heels to his toes. Then he said it again, with more volume and conviction. "Not one damn stinkin' thing."

Chapter Seventeen

Unable to concentrate, Dani switched off the sewing machine and roamed through the unusually quiet house. Kim was spending the night with the little girl next door. Colin had gone to Jackson Hole with Jimmy Simpson and his parents for a weekend of skiing.

A rational single parent would enjoy an opportunity for some uninterrupted private time. Unfortunately, Dani hadn't felt rational since she'd left the Circle D. Was this...loneliness all she had to look forward to when her kids were grown? Yuck!

When the phone rang, she lunged for it, and barely bit back a disappointed sigh at the sound of her sister's voice.

"Hi, Dani, it's me. How are you?"

"Fine, Micky."

"You don't sound fine. What's going on?"

"You want to know the truth?" Dani demanded, her temper flaring as it did so often and so quickly these days. "I'm miserable! I'm so damn miserable, if I were a horse, somebody would do the kind thing and take me out and shoot me."

"It's still Sam, isn't it."

"Of course it's still Sam. I've made a terrible mistake, Micky, and I don't know how to fix it."

"You might try talking to him."

"I'm too chicken."

"Well, then, I guess you'll have to stay miserable. Won't you?"

"Thanks for the sympathy."

"Hey, you don't need me to feel sorry for you. You're doing just fine in that department all by yourself."

Dani sighed, then rubbed the back of her neck. "I'm sorry, sis. And I know you're right. I just can't seem to make myself do anything constructive."

"The longer you wait, the harder it's going to get."

"I know that, too. If he'd just give me some little sign that he still cares, it would make it so much easier."

"From what you've told me, I don't think he's going to do that."

"I don't, either," Dani grumbled. A heavy pounding started on her front door. "Hang on a minute."

Stretching the phone cord to its limit, she peeked through the living room window and saw Sam's pickup parked in her driveway.

Suddenly breathless, she said, "I've gotta go, Mick. Sam's here."

"Oh my God," Micky muttered. "Call me back the minute he leaves, Dani, or you're dead meat."

"Yeah. Sure. Talk to you later."

Dani banged down the receiver, wiped damp palms on the seat of her stretch pants, then inhaled a deep breath and went to answer the door. Oh, Lord. He looked tired and ten pounds thinner, but just as wonderful and handsome and dear as ever.

"Hello, Dani," he said quietly. "Mind if I come in?"

Unable to speak, she shook her head and moved back, opening the door wider. He stepped inside and took his hat off, then gazed around the room with obvious interest.

"Are the kids here?"

She shook her head again, then cleared her throat and told him they were both out for the night. He sighed. In relief, she thought. She hoped. God, what if he'd only come to see the kids?

"Would you, um, like a cup of coffee?" she asked.

"That'd be real nice," he answered.

She led the way to the kitchen, painfully conscious of his eyes boring into her back as he followed her. Since she hadn't bought a coffee maker yet, she set a pan of water on the stove to heat and grabbed the jar of instant crystals from the cupboard. Sam stood awkwardly in the middle of the room until she gestured toward the dinette table.

Then he lowered himself onto one of the chairs, stretched out his long legs and silently studied her until she carried two mugs across the room and took the seat opposite him. While he blew on the steaming liquid and sipped slowly from his cup, Dani's nerves stretched tighter and tighter. There were so many things she wanted to say to him, but since he'd come to her, she felt obligated to let him speak first. At last he did, quietly, sincerely, holding her gaze with his.

"I've missed you, Dani."

His blunt statement released the worst of her tension. "Oh, Sam," she whispered, smiling at him with misty eyes, "I've missed you, too."

He gulped audibly and shut his eyes for an instant. Then he reached across the table and took her right hand between both of his. "All right. If you're still willing to listen, I'm ready to tell you about that nightmare. It's pretty ugly, but—"

"No. You don't have to, Sam," she interrupted, adding her free hand to the stack between them. "I've thought about it a lot, and if it's too painful for you to talk about then I don't need to know. It was selfish of me to try to force you.''

"It wasn't selfish, hon," he said, slowly shaking his head. "I think you *do* need to know what happened. Remember when Ginny was here?"

Dani rolled her eyes at the ceiling. "How could I forget?"

He grinned at that and gently squeezed her fingers. "Well, she told me that Charlie wouldn't tell her about what happened to him in Nam, and it always stood between 'em. I don't want that to happen to us. But I need you to promise me one thing."

"What's that?"

"After I've told you, I want you to be honest. Don't be kind or try to spare my feelings, okay?"

"Okay."

He disentangled his hands from hers and withdrew to his own side of the table, wrapping his fingers around his mug so tightly, the bones of his knuckles nearly poked through his skin. He cleared his throat, started to speak, hesitated, then sighed in frustration. He looked at her with a bleak, helpless expression in his eyes.

"It's hard, Dani," he said, choking out the words. "God, I didn't know how hard it would be."

"It's all right, Sam. Take your time."

He nodded, inhaled several deep breaths and finally started to speak in a low, emotionless monotone. His sentences came slowly and a bit disjointed at first, describing his unit and the goal of their mission—to find and destroy a cache of weapons hidden by the Vietcong. In the same flat voice, he told her about the mosquitoes and the constant fear, about Bubba Jackson's being wounded by a sniper and about his carrying the man for miles through the jungle.

When he told her about coming to a village, sweat popped out on his forehead and his eyes focused on some point, half a world away. His words came faster, choppier.

"I saw him sneaking from one hut to the next, and I knew he was up to something. I warned the other guys and picked up my rifle," he said, breathing hard now. "He ran into the open then, right for us, holding something up in his hand. I didn't even stop to think. I just drew a bead on him and fired like I was out hunting deer or elk."

A single tear slid down his cheek and splashed into his coffee mug. "He jerked, but he kept coming and I fired again. I think some of the other guys fired, too. I'm not sure. He dropped the grenade and it exploded. And then he fell onto his back and just lay there. The villagers came running to see what was goin' on. I ordered them to stay back while I went to check the body. Make sure he wasn't booby-trapped, you know?"

He looked at Dani, but she wasn't at all certain he was actually seeing her. She nodded anyway, then asked, "Was he the first man you'd ever killed?"

"No," he whispered, his head snapping back and forth in a violent motion of denial. "I wish to God he had been. I could have lived with that, but he wasn't. Not by a long shot."

"What was different about this time, Sam? Why has this man bothered you all this time?"

"Because..." Another tear rolled down his cheek and his throat worked repeatedly before he could go on. "Because, when I got up to the body? I found out it wasn't a man. Sh-she looked so damn young, I don't th-think she was even a w-woman yet."

Dani couldn't bear his suffering for another second. She flew around the table and gathered him into her arms, stroking his hair and murmuring soft syllables of comfort.

Raising his tortured gaze to meet hers, he choked, 'Goddammit to hell, Dani, she couldn't have been more

than twelve or thirteen. What kind of people send kids lik
that to war?''

She rained tears and kisses over his upturned face. ''Cry
Sam. Let it all out. You didn't know. It wasn't your faul
darling. Oh, I love you so much, Sam.''

He stared at her for an endless, aching moment. Then hi
face suddenly crumpled and a harsh, gut-wrenching so
ripped through him, followed by another and another. H
buried his head between her breasts and clung to her, hi
body convulsing with the force of his grief.

Giddy with relief that he'd finally been able to release th
storm of emotion, she wept with him, rocked him, poure
out her love for him. It could have been hours later—per
haps only minutes—she would never know for certain—bu
at last, he pulled away from her and desperately searche
her face.

''You don't hate me,'' he said, his voice hushed wit
wonder.

''Of course I don't,'' she said softly. ''You didn't d
anything wrong. It was a horrible tragedy, but you were i
a kill-or-be-killed situation in the middle of a war.''

''But—''

''There aren't any buts, Sam. You did what you wer
trained to do, and I happen to be awfully glad you did. Yo
haven't told anyone about this, have you?''

''Just my dad. He fought in Korea. I tried to tell hir
about it when I came home.''

''What did he say?''

Sam's gaze darted away, as if he felt ashamed all ove
again. Dani clasped his head between her hands and force
him to look at her again. ''What did he say, Sam?''

''He told me never to tell Mom or Grandma D or Beck
about it. Because it would upset them too much.''

Dani muttered a word that made Sam's eyebrows shoo
up in surprise. If the truth were told, she was a littl
shocked at herself, but honestly! Sometimes men were s

tupid, a woman had to wonder how they'd ever gotten
emselves out of living in caves.

"And you got the message that no woman could ever
ove you if she knew about this. Right?"

"Yeah," he admitted with a shrug, "I guess that about
overs it."

"Well, your dad was wrong, Sam. Dead wrong. My
od, wasn't he glad you survived?"

"Of course he was, but killing a woman, a young
irl—"

"Who tried to throw a grenade at you! I didn't know
our mother, but I *do* know your grandmother and your
ster, and they both adore you. It would hurt them to hear
bout what happened, but they'd be hurt because it hurt
ou. They wouldn't be disgusted with you any more than I
m."

"Then all these years..."

"All these years, you've tormented and punished your-
elf by locking all this inside. How do you feel now?"

He tipped his head to one side and thought about that for
moment. "Better, I think."

She held her hand out to him and tugged him to his feet
hen he accepted it. "C'mon, cowboy," she drawled,
ading him to the refrigerator. She handed him a bottle of
eer she kept on hand for Hank's visits, grabbed one for
erself and continued on into the living room. "What you
eed is a good stiff drink and a cuddle."

"You're startin' to sound like a gal from Wyoming,
ani," he said, lowering himself onto the sofa.

She wrinkled her nose at him, then snuggled up beside
im. "Yup. Amazing, isn't it?"

Chuckling, he curved his arm around her shoulders and
an his hand up and down her arm, as if reassuring himself
e was really there. They drank in silence, giving them-
lves time to reestablish their emotional equilibrium.
hen Sam set the bottles on an end table, Dani crawled

into his lap and rested her head on his chest as if there wa
no other place on earth she wanted to be, which, in fac
there was not.

He wrapped his arms around her with a contented sig
His lips brushed the top of her head. She smiled and looke
up at him, then drew him down for a deep, hungry kiss.

"I love you, Dani," he said.

"I love you, Sam." Smiling, she traced the edges of b
mustache with her finger. "Whaddaya think we should d
about it?"

"Well, I reckon we could get hitched."

"Yeah, we could."

"And we could raise a herd of little Dawsons and fill u
that big old house."

She raised an eyebrow at that. "How many did you ha
in mind?"

"Oh, ten or twelve oughtta do it."

She drove her elbow into his ribs. "How many?"

"I'd settle for one or two."

"I could be talked into that."

"Oh yeah?"

"Yeah. If you'll take your turn at two o'clock feedin;
and changing diapers."

He put his hands at her waist and lifted her off his la
Then he kissed her and ordered, "Don't move. I'll be rig
back."

Without bothering to get his coat, he ran out the fro
door, leaving Dani staring after him in consternation. I
returned a moment later, however, a self-conscious grin c
his face and one hand behind his back.

"What in the world are you up to?" Dani asked.

He knelt on one knee in front of her and set a sma
somewhat mangled box in her lap. Dani recognized the to
and dirty foil paper and the smashed bow immediately, a
raised questioning eyes to Sam's. "You had this up at t
cabin."

"Yup. I carried it around in my coat pocket for weeks ter you left and finally threw it in the glove compart- ent. Go on and open it, honey."

She obeyed him eagerly, tossing the wrapping on the oor. She pried the hinged lid of the jeweler's box open th trembling fingers, then gasped in admiration at the rgeous diamond-and-sapphire ring inside.

"Do you like it, Dani?"

"It's the most beautiful thing I've ever seen," she an- ered, scarcely able to breathe.

Sam cleared his throat, covered both of her hands with s and gazed deeply into her eyes. "Dani Smith, will you ase be my wife?" he said in a tone solemn enough for y church.

Dani threw her arms around his neck and hugged him statically. "Yes," she answered, laughing and crying at e same time. "Yes, yes, yes!"

He scooped her into his arms and climbed to his feet. en he kissed her soundly and demanded that she put the g on the appropriate finger. When that was accom- ished, he carried her into her bedroom and reaffirmed eir love for each other in an earthy and extremely satis- ing manner.

Afterward, Dani propped herself up on one elbow and ew circles in his chest hair with her other hand. "Sam?"

"What, honey?" he mumbled around a sleepy smile.

"We probably ought to get married pretty soon."

"Why's that?"

"I quit taking the Pill when I left the ranch." She fal- ed at the stunned look in his eyes, then rushed on before could say a word. "I didn't see any reason to keep tak- g it after I moved out. If you want a big wedding, we're obably okay, but I'd hate to be a pregnant bride again. y mother would never let me hear the end of it, and—"

Sam's shout of laughter cut her off midbabble.

"It's not funny, Sam," she scolded, tweaking his che
hair hard enough to make him yelp. "I know it sounds st
pid to worry about what my mother's going to say, and
know you probably didn't want a baby quite this soo
but—"

He shut her up with a long, lusty kiss. When he finally l
her up for air, he said, "Honey, I'd love to have a baby t
morrow if we could pull it off, and I'm gonna spend the re
of the night tryin' like hell to start that little herd of Dav
sons. That is, if you don't mind."

He paused long enough for her to shake her head, the
continued. "I'd be delighted to pass on a big wedding, b
lieve me. We'll round up what family we can and get ma
ried in Idaho Falls on Monday, and then we'll honeymoo
at the cabin. Hank'll stay with the kids for us."

Dani heaved a dramatic sigh, batted her eyelashes ar
simpered at him. "I just *love* it when you get all masterfu
Sam."

Chuckling, he gently swatted her fanny. "Smart aleck
He slid his fingers into her hair, absently playing with h
curls. "Would you rather go someplace else? I'm a tak
charge kind of a guy, but I won't run roughshod over you

"The cabin sounds wonderful. I hope we can use it a l
the way your parents did."

"Count on it," he said with a smile. "You know, aft
tonight, I'm convinced there's nothin' in this world we ca
handle. We've just gotta remember to compromise a
keep lovin' each other."

"Um, Sam? I have another confession to make."

He kissed the tip of her nose. "Well, let's hear it."

"The honeymoon will have to wait a little while. You se
I just agreed to help make new uniforms for the high scho
band. It's a great job."

"How long will it take?"

"Only three or four months."

He shot up off the mattress and stared at her in dismay. Three or four months! I want some time alone with you. ank's gonna leave pretty soon. If we don't go now—"

"I've already promised to do it, Sam."

"Uh-uh. No way, woman. A man's got to put his foot own some—"

"Sam! What happened to compromising?"

His mouth dropped open. His neck and ears turned red. It's not always gonna be easy for you and me, is it?"

"Nope," Dani agreed, running one heel up the back of s leg. "We'll probably argue a lot, but that's okay."

He shot her a skeptical look. "Oh yeah?"

"Yeah. Whenever we start getting out of hand, I've got e perfect solution."

"Mind lettin' me in on it?"

"I'll just say, 'Sam, will you *please* shut up and kiss me?' d then you'll do it, and we won't feel like arguing any- ore. Whaddaya think of that idea?"

His eyes sparkling with laughter, he aligned his lips with rs. "I think it has potential. Maybe we oughtta test it t."

The kiss naturally led to another, and then another.

Much, much later, Sam snuggled an exhausted, but ppy and oh-so-satisfied Dani against his side. "There's little problem with your solution, hon."

"What's that?" she asked, opening one eye.

"It'll work just fine at home, but we'd sure as hell better arn not to argue in public. Now, about that honey- oon..."

* * * * *

Silhouette Special Edition

COMING NEXT MONTH

AVAILABLE THIS MONTH:

"GET AWAY FROM IT ALL" SWEEPSTAKES

IERE'S HOW THE SWEEPSTAKES WORKS

NO PURCHASE NECESSARY

enter each drawing, complete the appropriate Official Entry Form or a 3" by index card by hand-printing your name, address and phone number and e trip destination that the entry is being submitted for (i.e., Caneel Bay, anyon Ranch or London and the English Countryside) and mailing it to: Get way From It All Sweepstakes, P.O. Box 1397, Buffalo, New York 14269-1397.

responsibility is assumed for lost, late or misdirected mail. Entries must be nt separately with first class postage affixed, and be received by: 4/15/92 the Caneel Bay Vacation Drawing, 5/15/92 for the Canyon Ranch Vacation awing and 6/15/92 for the London and the English Countryside Vacation awing. Sweepstakes is open to residents of the U.S. (except Puerto Rico) d Canada, 21 years of age or older as of 5/31/92.

r complete rules send a self-addressed, stamped (WA residents need not fix return postage) envelope to: Get Away From It All Sweepstakes, P.O. Box 92, Blair, NE 68009.

1992 HARLEQUIN ENTERPRISES LTD.   SWP-RLS

- -

"GET AWAY FROM IT ALL" SWEEPSTAKES

IERE'S HOW THE SWEEPSTAKES WORKS

NO PURCHASE NECESSARY

enter each drawing, complete the appropriate Official Entry Form or a 3" by index card by hand-printing your name, address and phone number and e trip destination that the entry is being submitted for (i.e., Caneel Bay, anyon Ranch or London and the English Countryside) and mailing it to: Get way From It All Sweepstakes, P.O. Box 1397, Buffalo, New York 14269-1397.

responsibility is assumed for lost, late or misdirected mail. Entries must be nt separately with first class postage affixed, and be received by: 4/15/92 the Caneel Bay Vacation Drawing, 5/15/92 for the Canyon Ranch Vacation awing and 6/15/92 for the London and the English Countryside Vacation awing. Sweepstakes is open to residents of the U.S. (except Puerto Rico) d Canada, 21 years of age or older as of 5/31/92.

r complete rules send a self-addressed, stamped (WA residents need not fix return postage) envelope to: Get Away From It All Sweepstakes, P.O. Box 92, Blair, NE 68009.

1992 HARLEQUIN ENTERPRISES LTD.   SWP-RLS

"GET AWAY FROM IT ALL"

Brand-new Subscribers-Only Sweepstakes

OFFICIAL ENTRY FORM

This entry must be received by: June 15, 1992
This month's winner will be notified by: June 30, 1992
Trip must be taken between: July 31, 1992—July 31, 1993

YES, I want to win the vacation for two to England. I understand the prize includes round-trip airfare and the two additional prizes revealed in the BONUS PRIZES insert.

Name _____

Address _____

City _____

State/Prov._____ Zip/Postal Code_____

Daytime phone number _____
(Area Code)

Return entries with invoice in envelope provided. Each book in this shipment has two entry coupons — and the more coupons you enter, the better your chances of winning!
© 1992 HARLEQUIN ENTERPRISES LTD.   3M-CPN

"GET AWAY FROM IT ALL"

Brand-new Subscribers-Only Sweepstakes

OFFICIAL ENTRY FORM

This entry must be received by: June 15, 1992
This month's winner will be notified by: June 30, 1992
Trip must be taken between: July 31, 1992—July 31, 1993

YES, I want to win the vacation for two to England. I understand the prize includes round-trip airfare and the two additional prizes revealed in the BONUS PRIZES insert.

Name _____

Address _____

City _____

State/Prov._____ Zip/Postal Code_____

Daytime phone number _____
(Area Code)

Return entries with invoice in envelope provided. Each book in this shipment has two entry coupons — and the more coupons you enter, the better your chances of winning!
© 1992 HARLEQUIN ENTERPRISES LTD.   3M-CPN